STRONGHOLD

STRONGHOLD

Stanley Ellin

Random House
New York

Copyright © 1974 by Stanley Ellin
All rights reserved under International and Pan-American
Copyright Conventions. Published in the United States by
Random House, Inc., New York, and simultaneously in Canada
by Random House of Canada Limited, Toronto.

Library of Congress Cataloging in Publication Data
Ellin, Stanley.
    Stronghold.
    I. Title.
PZ3.E4558St [PS3555.L56]   813'.5'4   74–9064
ISBN 0–394–49129–7

Manufactured in the United States of America
9 8 7 6 5 4 3 2
First Edition

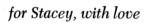

for Stacey, with love

Articles of Agreement

The Company's project will be carried out in three phases.

Phase one:

To reconnoiter the target area at Scammons Landing, Lake George, New York.

To obtain in the Miami, Florida, area sufficient small arms to seize the target area.

To obtain in the Miami area sufficient automatic weapons and ammunition to maintain a defense of the target area should it be put under assault. Also to obtain gas masks, since tear gas may be used by an assaulting force.

To obtain in the Miami area a car for transport of the Company and its weapons to the target area.

Phase two:

To seize and occupy the target area in Scammons Landing, and to take the necessary hostages.

To arrange for the delivery to the Company of four million dollars in cash.

To negotiate for the transport of the Company and its hostages by bus to the airport at Glens Falls, New York, then by turboprop to Logan Airport, Boston, then by jet to St. Hilary, Windward Islands, West Indies.

Phase three:

To make the necessary payment to those officials of St. Hilary who will act as intermediaries for the Company and will arrange for air transport of the Company and its hostages to whatever area in South America or Africa will receive them and offer them refuge.

Read and agreed to by all members of the Company. Raiford Prison, Florida, December 25th, 1972

James Flood

Hubert Digby

Harvey Shanplin

Lester Shanklin

James Flood

Came April, I was the first of the Company to wind up my time at Raiford Prison, then a month later the Shanklin brothers were let out, and two months and three weeks after them Coco got his papers. He went direct from Florida to St. Hilary out in the Islands to set up phase three of the Company project and came back to Miami from there. The day he finally showed up in Miami was the first time the Company held a meeting outside those Raiford walls.

Which, despite poetic license, do a very effective prison make.

So here we are in this Cuban restaurant in Miami— James Flood, manslaughter; brothers Harvey and Lester Shanklin, conspiracy to commit grand theft; Hubert (Coco) Digby, assault with a deadly weapon—all with our sins against the state of Florida redeemed, all waiting itchy-assed for somebody named Santiago. At least, says Harvey Shanklin, who had made the contact with Santiago, that is his name this week. It is Santiago This Week who is going to redeem us from the greatest sin of all. No money.

For me, the hardest part of that time waiting for Coco to finish off his Raiford count had been the no money. The Shanklins had gone back to their mamma and daddy in South Miami, helped try to keep the family gas station out of bankruptcy—not likely, the way the little independents were getting a classical reaming from the big boys—mowed the lawn, made it to church Sundays, where everybody looked at them slant-eyed the first Sunday, then next Sunday welcomed them joyously as lost lambs returned to the fold. There is much to be said for the Pentecostal pissworks, as Harvey pointed out. Four times the elders rattled the contribution plates that first Sunday, and at each rattle daddy, tears streaming from his eyes at the return of his prodigals, shelled out five dollars per prodigal. And with the last handout, a flock of angels, their wondrous tits plumping out their diaphanous gowns, descended from heaven right into the church and kissed Harvey and Lester on the brow. Kissed them tenderly and whispered: "Play it cool, boys. No tapping the till at the gas station, no humping thy neighbor's lusty wife, because help is on the way. It is getting close to big money time."

Since they had the oxlike patience of all dedicated weight lifters, it wasn't too bad for them, marking the days until Coco showed up. Before Raiford, they had worked the beachboy line, dazzling Gold Coast hotel guests with their musclebound charms, servicing mink-coated and mink-spirited matrons and occasionally handling blow jobs for carpetbagging patrons, all the while in those high-priced hotel beds sizing up the available cash, jewelry, and furs, calculating the safest time and means of entry, and then turning over the job to the Mob for the heist itself. If Harvey and Lester had any resentments, it was because they had to take the Mob's word about what the goods brought on the market, and there was always a large discrepancy between the Mob's word and the newspaper account of the merchandise's valuation. It was different with me. I told them in Raiford that we were setting up our Company with four equal shareholders, each getting an equal cut of the profits. And if they doubted it, they would be the ones to make the division when the time came. Half their size, I was Big Daddy after that. I have my own form of genius. The ability to turn on sincerity when it is needed is not the smallest part of it.

Meanwhile, marking my own calendar until Coco showed up, I landed a job on a charter fishing boat run by a beery bastard named Sharpless who was happy to put me on as live-in crew, no questions asked, as long as I was ready to work for just tips. This gave me stake enough after a month to take off on Company business and make my reconnaissance of the old home territory up in Warren County, New York, after which I headed right back to Dade County, Florida, only nickels and dimes left in my pocket. So it was Cap'n Sharpless and the bait buckets again, but I had bed and board this way, and that was the name of the game until Coco showed up.

For a while Sharpless itched with curiosity about this man of mystery scrubbing down his decks, and I gathered from his unsubtle questions that he had me figured either as a fugitive from the law or a reformed lush. But when I didn't turn a hair if the law showed up on the dock sometimes, he finally settled on me as someone on the cure, some laddie of good family and good breeding— what the hell, I actually read books; he could see them all around my bunk—who was sparing his high-toned folks the shame of his downfall, and he let it go at that. He never asked my last name, glad enough not to have to tend to employment papers and social security red tape, and after a while even stopped checking the level penciled off on the liquor bottles stowed in his locker. In the end I was as much a natural, inobtrusive part of the boat to him as a can of bait. If he didn't see me around, he probably noted my absence. When I was around he took no notice. I became the invisible man, neutral in

9

size, shape, and coloring, blank of face, characterless as a glass of tap water.

For the superior man, the controlling agent, who, whatever his reason, takes orders from his inferior, there is a perverse sense of power in such a relationship. The dog, tugging at its leash, thinks he is leading the master. The master, going along with the joke, is amused by his own forbearance in not slitting the hound's throat and ending the comedy right there. Do you know, doggie, that you are always only one breath away from having that hairy throat slit?

For three months I scrubbed down the deck of the good ship Ballbreaker and considered Captain Sharpless' hairy throat. Even on that day when Harvey Shanklin strolled along the dock as the signal Coco was finally in town, I did nothing memorable in saying goodbye to doggie. Now my captain took surprised and unhappy notice. There would be a large empty space on the boat tomorrow. "If it's a matter of money, Jimmy boy," he said hopefully, "since you worked out all right, I been kind of thinking—"

"No," I said, "I have to be moving on."

And move on I did, along Biscayne Boulevard by bus and into the Cuban restaurant for my class reunion.

Raiford, 1973.

Coco.

Hubert Digby, out of St. Hilary, the Windward Islands. Blacksnake beautiful, Watusi graceful, making even a walk around the Raiford yard a slow dance, as if the yard were Port St. Hilary on carnival day and he was leading the steel-drum parade. Talked the Island talk, a turkey gobble when he turned it on fast, a sad, sweet Windward music when he slowed it down. *Oh, mon, when I ahm oat it is bock to thee Eye-londs foh me.*

He comes floating toward us where we sit at our table in a corner, and while the restaurant manager leading the way squeezes between the tables where overstuffed Latins are further stuffing themselves with black beans, chicken stew, and fried plantains, Coco, following along, oozes his way through the tight spaces, dances that slow dance of his, the King of Spades stepping up to the throne. He takes the chair beside me, and the first thing he says to us after three months and three weeks is, "Who picked this place?"

"Santiago," says Harvey Shanklin. Harvey is the older brother and does most of the talking for the Shanklins. "I didn't like it, but he said this was it and no place else."

"That manager knows him," Coco says. "When I came in the door he was very lofty. But when I said I was a

11

guest of Mr. Santiago he did everything but kiss my shiny ass." Coco looks around. "There is a good chance others here know him too. This is not good."

"It's a seller's market," I point out.

"True," Coco says. "But there are people to be disposed of. Afterward, when the authorities say, 'Well now, what company has this Mr. Santiago been keeping lately?' his friends will not have taken notice of you, man, because you are not noticeable. But I cut an outstanding figure, man. And Harvey and Lester are conspicuous in any company."

Harvey says, "Yeah, but the only other contact I could make wants cash in advance. Fifty percent of the payment in his hand before delivery."

"That one is a good businessman," says Coco.

I say to him, "Talk straight. Do you want to call it off right now?"

"I am considering a postponement. After phase one, we will be on the road several days. Each day we will be more vulnerable. This is a three-phase operation. I would dislike to see it exploded before we even arrive at phase two."

"Forget it," I say. "No delays, Coco. God did not intend me to spend my life hosing the fish stink off a Miami charter boat."

That is it. The master's voice. They have equal shares in the Company, but not equal voice. The Shanklins are in charge of phase one, I am responsible for phase two, phase three will be all Coco's—but the whole conception is mine, the fitting together of the parts is mine. I was the one in Raiford who realized that if you fit together these particular parts—Harvey and Lester Shanklin of South Miami; Hubert Digby of St. Hilary, the West Indies; and James Flood of Scammons Landing, New York—you have, so to speak, compounded nitroglycerin. And as head chemist, I am *Numero Uno*, the policy-making echelon.

It has worked well so far, it will continue to work because the other shareholders understand that I am the necessary balance to their opposing extremes. The Shanklins, strong as oxen, are as stolidly patient as oxen. Coco, on the other hand, is an exposed nerve, a born worrier. He wants guarantees. At any given moment he likes to know where he will be a week from now and why he will be there. Blacks, of course, are not generally of this disposition. For sure, the blacks I knew in the Movement and then at Raiford weren't. Animal-indifferent to the next moment, they threw a rock or wielded sharpened steel with a sense of explosive release, and the whole future as far as they could see it would be only that instant when the rock smashed through the window or the steel drove into the flesh of the victim. Coco despised them for this. The one Island man in our cellblock, he called the conglomerate of dark skins around him the A.A.A., the Afro-American Apes. And survived it, because pressed to the wall, he could wield sharpened steel even more efficiently and much more guilefully than they could. The pig-poker, the prettily tooled, needlepointed piece of bedspring, was his baby. Twice he used it there, and each time he was away so smoothly after the sudden, perfectly camouflaged thrust that by the time the crowd gathered around the victim, Coco was on its outskirts, peering over heads to see what had happened, shocked at what he was seeing, a halo twinkling over his head. They smelled him out, all right, which was what he wanted. Blacksnake, they called him, Snakey, baffled by his independence, not only of them, but of the turnkeys, of everyone, in fact, but of the little whitey, James Flood.

Emotional balance. The Shanklins, too stolid, and Coco, too volatile, needed an agent to weld them together and extract the best from them, and that was James Flood. That was the founding of the Company.

Assets? Almost zero.

Anticipated profits? Four million dollars.

Divided four ways, one million dollars each.

Correction.

Assets in cash almost zero.

Assets in human resources unlimited.

A million dollars per partner had been an arbitrary figure. It had become an obsessive figure with the Shanklins. Out of the family's broken-down gas station on a back road in South Miami, they had never seen more than pocket money. The most profitable hotel heist they had set up paid them together four thousand dollars. The most urgent strong-arm job they had performed for the Mob—a rib-breaking, stomping instructional session with a grudging debtor—was for two thousand dollars. These and other thousands spaced far apart were enough to give them a passionate taste for the good life, and more important, a passionate conviction that they were entitled to it. They were bigger, stronger, better-looking, and even meaner than the Miami Beach big spenders they catered to, so what the hell law of nature or Congress said they had to be the ones sullenly grubbing for tips while they were beachboying it instead of being the ones handing out the tips?

Coco bought this. He understood the power generated by a proper, soul-consuming motivation. The Crown Colony of St. Hilary had gone for independence. Hubert

Digby, prize-winning scholarship boy, tossed out of London University in England for taking his Negritude too violently, had come back to his Eye-lond home to help extract it from the maw of the British Empire. Independence had come. It was coming anyhow, the British only too happy to dump this Caribbean sand spit—population fifty very rich whites, five hundred medium-rich browns, and fifty thousand very poor blacks—and at last it did come. And what happened to Hubert, who had expected a slice of the action for his noisy part in the great event? Expected, at least, a piece of the gambling casino when it was built and licensed; possibly a piece of the hotel construction getting under way? Nothing happened. At least, nothing more than a chance to be a stickman in the casino or a clerk in one of the new hotels, because all the action went to the medium-rich browns, who didn't quite see Coco as one of them. They liked him, they admired him as one of their loudest Freedom Fighters, they would have been pleased to offer him that job as stickman or clerk, but all the gaudy new institutions in St. Hilary which would win it its place in the sun were the products of their own cash investment, along with what money came from anonymous investors in Miami and Las Vegas. All cashless Coco would do was stand outside the kitchen window and look at the pie on the table inside. Look hard, drooling from the mouth, but hung up outside that window.

He kissed off St. Hilary, but the drool still dripped, the hunger was there more than ever.

For myself, out of Scammons Landing on Lake George, New York, I had toiled in the vineyards of the rich as a youth, had lived on crumbs from the tables of the rich, and so determined very young what my portion would have to be some day, although it was not until the Company was founded in Raiford that I knew how I would hit the jackpot.

I made mistakes along the way, the SDS and Weather-man ventures among the most instructive of them. The ventures may have paid off in headlines, but—except for some brilliant opportunists among us, not to mention our collection of FBI informers—never in cash. It was my childish impression at the outset that you could fire-bomb the rich out of their fortress and occupy it in their place. I was also under the mistaken impression that my companions were led to the struggle by high ideals. It took me a while to understand that every human being on earth is out for a slice of the action, and that born losers are only rationalizing their failures by playing up idealism. Unable to make it, they point out that battling for a slice of the action is a defiling way of life and crawl off the battlefield claiming to have won the war.

It took me almost too long to comprehend the point of the whole joke. We are hauled out of mamma's belly, given a whack on the butt, and set to crawling through a maze for the rest of our lives, trying to reach the jackpot planted in the middle of it. A few lucky crawlers make it. A few, smarter and tougher but not so lucky, begin to wonder after a while why they are crawling. So they get up on their feet and smash down the impeding walls and march straight to the goal.

A million dollars? To that extent I agree with the Shanklins. One million is a magic number.

Santiago, who should come on like a Latin Humphrey Bogart, turns out to be a Latin Porky Pig, about my middling height but padded with a hundred pounds of excess blubber. He stands there at our table in a corner of the restaurant, taking us in, and then he says to nobody in particular, "Santiago."

"Harvey," Harvey says to him. "I'm the one was on the phone with you," and Santiago sits down and pulls his chair up to the table until his belly presses into it, which still leaves the rest of him a long distance from his cutlery. He tucks a napkin into his collar. "Flan," he says to the waiter. "The large portion. And coffee."

"Flan," Lester, the body-builder, says disapprovingly. He eyes Santiago's blubber. "Sugar pudding. *Hay moros en la costa.*"

"*Caballo grande ande o no ande,*" says Santiago.

"Speak English," I tell him, "and stick to business."

The piggy eyes examine me, trying to make out what instrument I play in this quartet. "Yes. Sure. Business. Well, I have the goods. That's half the business. The other half is, do you have the money?"

I gesture at Harvey. He pulls a manila envelope from his pocket, opens the flap to flash a subliminal view of a sheaf of bills. The sheaf is play money, each banknote nicely imprinted *One Happyland Dollar*. Santiago reaches for the envelope, but Harvey tucks it back into his pocket.

"It's three thousand," I say. One way to make a suspicious man less suspicious is to drive a hard bargain with him.

"Oh?" says Santiago.

"On delivery," I say.

Santiago swivels his head toward Harvey. "The last thing I said was four thousand."

Harvey shrugs. "The last thing I said was three."

Santiago says amiably, "The price is four thousand. You said you had three and could get up the rest before delivery. I can wait. My merchandise won't spoil."

The waiter sets a cup of coffee and a plate of flan before Santiago. Nobody says anything until the waiter takes off, then I say, "Your merchandise won't improve with age, either."

"Unless," Coco points out, "one has a notion to sell it off as antiques some day. I have been told there is a considerable profit in antiques."

Santiago spoons a large helping of pudding into his mouth. Savoring it, eyes half closed, he looks like Porky Pig working up to a hard-on. "Four thousand," he says.

"Thirty-five hundred," I say.

"Yes," says Santiago, "I thought we'd get around to that." He goes through that process again of studying us one after the other. "We're talking business, right? Suppose we talk some good sound business. Some interesting possibilities."

"Interesting to you, man?" Coco says. "Or us?"

"Let's explore that. The project you're working on—"

"You don't know anything about any project," Coco says.

"Look, the merchandise you ordered—well, it means something big is in the making. Now let's turn off the shit machine and get down to cases. I'm an investor, maybe a little bit of a gambler. If your project is political, count me out. But if it isn't, well, you can't go wrong with a partner who'd be willing to extend some credit to you."

"Who says we can't?" Coco asks.

"Everybody has to have faith in people. Look at it from my angle. How do I know you're not the law just setting me up for the kill? But I have faith in you. Extending credit is an act of faith."

"Beautiful," Coco says. "What is your church, man? The First National Bank of Miami?"

I say to Santiago, "What have you got against political projects?"

"They're all investment and no return. And look what comes out of them. Look at this Watergate mess. Who was at the bottom of the pile? My people. Simple Cuban patriots. Visionaries. Pigeons for the plucking." Santiago sucks in another huge mouthful of flan, then waves his spoon back and forth before us like a metronome. "But not me, my friends. No, thank you."

"Forget about the project," I say. "All you have to do is supply the merchandise and collect your money. When and where do you deliver?"

"Do you know the Everglades?"

"Yeah, some," Harvey says.

"You know Ninety-four where it cuts off from the Trail?"

"I know it."

"Watch your mileage after the cutoff. Just about three miles, and there is this burned-out shanty. Drive around it, and you'll see a track going south. That will take you to a canal. Wait there."

"You bringing the stuff by boat?" Lester asks.

"Maybe yes, maybe no. That's my business. Your business is to be there tomorrow morning. Ten o'clock sharp. With the money."

"Thirty-five hundred," I say.

"Four thousand. Make up your minds about it now. The whole four thousand on delivery."

All of us in the Company look at each other. Coco shakes his head. He solemnly says to me, "It won't leave us much. We'll be down to bedrock, man."

"We're not being offered any choice," I say just as solemnly.

"Bedrock or no deal, that's how it looks," Harvey says. Coco heaves his shoulders. "Well, it's only money. Filthy lucre, right?" He says warningly to Santiago, "But no pig in a poke, man. I want to look over everything in the inventory before we make payment."

"Naturally," says Santiago. "After all, my friend, faith can be extended just so far."

After he waddles away, leaving us to pay his check, I say to Harvey, "You ought to tell baby brother not to ask questions at the wrong time."

"That's a fact," Harvey says.

Lester opens his big blue eyes wide. "What questions?" he says innocently. I mean innocently. He is not putting us on.

Harvey says to him, "Like if Santiago's coming by boat."

"One if by land," I say. "Two if by sea."

"Ain't no sea," Lester says. "Just swamp canal. And I was only trying to do some figuring. Makes a difference if we have got to lay for him two different ways. Up to now I was just thinking of one way."

Harvey says patiently, "You can't do such thinking out loud, Les. You put that man's back up, and he didn't trust us that much to start with."

"Oh. Ah," Lester says, catching on. "Well, it don't make that much difference as long as he does show up." He mentally shifts into high. "And he'll show up. Once he got a look at the money, that's all he needed. You did that fine, Harve. I would have thought that money was for real myself, if I didn't know about it."

"We all did fine," I say. "But it still leaves us not

knowing if he'll show up by road or by canal. He won't be coming alone, either."

Coco says to Harvey, "Do you know that area off Ninety-four?"

"Some. I know that burned-out shack. South of it is deep swamp. Anyhow, we'll be looking it over before Santiago shows up."

"Any cover there?" Coco says.

"Maybe not. We can make cover."

"Do not underestimate that fellow," Coco warns. "There is fat everywhere on him except between those cute little ears. He knows there is the chance of an ambush. He could be at the area before ten o'clock, waiting for us."

"Sure," Harvey says. "But don't you worry, we'll be there before him."

"Tonight?" I ask. "Right from here?"

"Can't do that."

"We don't have to set up the stakeout in the dark. We can wait until morning. But this way we'll know for sure we're there ahead of him."

"Can't stay away from the house all night," Harvey says apologetically. "Daddy'll raise hell. No sense having him look Les and me over, wondering what's up. Better to tell him we'll be going fishing in the morning, let it go at that. No questions that way. No fuss."

"Sweet and loving Jesus," Coco says. "I hear this man but I refuse to believe what I hear. Daddy does not want his little lads up all night. Daddy says that if they intend to go out in the morning to knock over some Cubano game, they must get a good night's sleep and make sure to drink their milk before they leave the house."

"You motherfucking black clown," Harvey says without heat, "nothing is changed. We pick up the cash and the car from the old man before he knows it, and if we tell him it's fishing tomorrow, we got almost all tomorrow head start. If we take off tonight and he makes bed check, first thing he'll do is look-see what happened to his cash. We'll be hot even before we meet with Santiago."

"That's the truth," Lester says.

"What do you think?" Coco asks me.

"It looks like daddy is too smart for us." Then I say to Harvey, "What about the license plates on the car? We'll be on the road between Florida and upstate New York about three days, but we'll have only one day's head start on daddy. The next two days those plates can make trouble. Or is there a good chance daddy won't turn the cops loose on you, once he wises up?"

"No, he'll turn them loose on us," Lester says. "Won't be the money as much as the car."

I could believe it. Harvey had said there was never more than a couple of hundred dollars stashed away in the brick wall of the gas station against emergencies, but that the car was only a few-years-old LeSabre, tuned to sweet perfection.

"I've got other plates for the car," Harvey says. "Old-time customer of daddy's left his heap up on blocks in the garage. I'm switching plates with him."

"And," says Lester, "nobody'll take notice of what plates that heap is wearing. Not right away, anyhow."

I say to Coco, "It looks like phase one is in good hands."

"Perhaps," Coco says.

"It goddam well is," Harvey says. "Another thing, I figure we can't take a chance on shorting out of gas on the road, so I'm taking along sixty gallons in reserve cans."

"Sure enough," Lester puts in. "Ought to get us right past New York City. If that kind of load in the trunk don't bust us an axle."

"We're not out of Florida yet," Coco says. "What about tomorrow morning right here in the swamp?"

Harvey says, "We get everything together sunrise, then pick up you and Jimmy. Then we get out to the area and set up to cover the road and the canal. You got a place to sleep tonight?"

"A lady of my acquaintance is expecting my company tonight," Coco says. He looks at me. "And you?"

"My bag's in a locker over at the Greyhound depot. Any room around there will do, if we can raise the money for it."

We lay out our money on the table. Eighteen dollars from the Shanklins, eight from Coco, two from me. Twenty-eight dollars minus fifteen for the Company dinner. Thirteen dollars net.

I take five, give Coco five and the Shanklins three.

For the waiter's tip under a plate, One Happyland Dollar.

Marcus Hayworth

Perhaps there is something about flawless July mornings in the pine-scented Lake George country which brings out the randy in a man more than usual. So this day starts off in fine style, myself at fifty-five waking pleasingly robust, Emily at fifty-one pleasingly compliant, and after we have ended a rousingly youthful bed-clattering session, Emily lies back in smiling relaxation and says, "You see? Nothing ventured, nothing gained."

I say, "Seems so, doesn't it?" Then I can't keep myself from saying, "You know, the *Times* had something in it yesterday about that estrogen stuff you take. About how women who take it run the risk—"

"I read it too, dear. And it's birth-control pills that make the problem, not estrogen. And I am well past the birth-control stage."

"Deborah isn't," I remind her. "She does take those pills, doesn't she?"

"Yes, she does. But she happens to be twenty years old and very much married now. She and David can work out their own medical problems, I'm sure."

"Doesn't she want children?"

"I haven't asked her. And, Marcus dear, you are not to ask her, either."

"Emily, I am not really the bull in the family china shop you make me out to be."

"Sometimes you are. After two years you still can't accept the fact that your daughter is a married woman. It makes for some broken china now and then."

Poor Emily, the peacemaker. I say, "Well, whatever's broken, I'm sure David can mend it. After all, that's his trade, isn't it?" And it is. My son-in-law, God help us, after surveying all the prospects I could open to him, had decided to become a handyman, no less. Anyone who doubted that need only drop in at the Fix-It-All Shop on Front Street in the township of Scammons Landing. The shabby gent behind the counter is the son-in-law. The pretty girl, usually barefoot and raggle-taggle, sweeping the floor while she listens to his words of wisdom is my daughter Deborah, whose marriage to this paragon I am supposed to rejoice in.

Emily is determined to press the issue. She says teasingly, "Thee must open your heart to David, Friend. He is a good man, and you know it."

"A thirty-five-year-old man who'd marry a child of eighteen with her head full of feathers?"

"Marcus dear, Deborah and David were visited by the meeting's Committee on Clearness and the marriage fully approved."

"Committee on Clearness. The Marcy sisters are a couple of eighty-year-old spinsters who get starry-eyed when anyone mentions young love to them. And Ethel Quimby thinks she has to be matchmaker for everybody in sight, whether they're Quakers or not."

Emily seems to find this funny. "Of course, the proper committee would have been you all alone, holding the fort."

I resent this. And the resentment leads me to come out with the thought which had nagged me during the wedding in the meeting house, but which I had never expressed before. "Damn it, if it had only been Janet he wanted to marry. She was twenty-five, then, that much closer to his age. All right, she may not have Debbie's looks, but I've seen the men she works with at the bank take plenty of notice of her."

"Oh?"

"Well, they do. So it can't be that she feels insecure about her looks. Certainly not about her brains. Yet she's a very unhappy girl, Emily."

"If she is, your watching her with that worried, fatherly expression won't make her any happier."

"Talk about unfair. I never let my feelings about her show."

"Dear, you are the most totally transparent human being I know. But I'm not complaining. After all, that's why I married you."

So now I'm supposed to feel guilty for my concern about my older daughter. And I do. That sense of guilt, of course, is part of the Calvinism the colonial Hayworths of Marblehead in Massachusetts lived by. That, like the incongruous design of this old sea-front house with its widow's walk on the roof, not overlooking returning ships but virgin forests, is something that their emigration here and entrance into Quaker meeting could not eradicate.

More and more, in recent years, I seem to suffer pangs of guilt whatever direction I turn my eyes, inwardly or outwardly. I am burdened with the feeling that along the two-mile length of Ridge Road—that enclave made up of my house and outbuildings, the house Emily inherited and we now rent to a youthful commune, the Friends meeting house, the old Marcy place where Anna and Elizabeth, who only a little while ago had been brisk, middle-aged women, are now sharing their peppery but timeworn eighties, the Friends cemetery itself—this whole peaceable kingdom of my childhood is under assault from subtly destructive forces, all strange faces,

31

strange manners, strange thoughts, trying to penetrate, confuse, and confound it. And my abiding guilt is that where I should perceive the Light in these strangers, I often cannot, but instead find myself closing my heart to them in resentment.

Guilt, too, that in a world of oppression and deprivation I am so comfortably shielded from suffering. And trying to assuage that guilt by heavy contributions to every good cause that comes by only makes it that much worse. Gives me the embarrassed sense as I make out the check that I am buying my way into grace.

A missionary *manqué*?

Hardly. In fact, the word missionary itself has been anathema to such as the Hayworths and the Oates, Emily's family, for some hundred and fifty years and more, since the time Friend Elias Hicks came out of Long Island and opened the split between his breed of Quaker and the evangelicals with his message that the Light in Jesus was no more meaningful than in any man since time began, that the guidance we may find for ourselves in the communion of silent meeting for worship is as sound as the guidance once found by those who wrote the Bible. So spake old Elias, and put Scammons Landing Monthly Meeting in the hands of the Hicksites, after a loud and un-Quakerly separation. Since reunion only a generation ago—a reunion I myself had labored toward for many years, in more committee meetings than I care to remember—we have often been in happy cooperation with the orthodox, but there is still in me a compulsive shying away from the concept of pastoral meetings with their hired ministers and altars and hymn books, a Hicksite wariness of, especially, the evangelical outlook, the peculiarly arrogant sense of religious mission, as if any Friend is bestowed with a Light which all humanity in this diverse world must accept as the one unchallengeable truth.

So there is no sense of mission in me, but that guilty feeling that I have it too easy in my life, and unable to bring comfort to that vast population on earth which has it so hard, that I might be better off if I myself had it less easy. On the other hand, I am, as my son-in-law David once remarked, as much a birthright banker as I am a birthright Quaker. He did not, I was irritably grateful to observe, go as far as some Quakers by convincement and suggest that birthright Quakers are not quite up to snuff, but about the banking he was only telling the truth. I inherited a prosperous bank and made it into several prosperous banks, and what the devil would I designate as my talent if I made application to join such as the Peace Corps? A skill at calculating mortgage rates?

And whose money made from banking patched and repaired and finally rebuilt the meeting house? And whose money largely supports what activities the meeting engages in?

And yet, and yet, is that all Marcus Hayworth amounts to? Financial mainstay of an antique meeting where un-Quakerly dissidence so often prevails? Kindly landlord of a so-called commune where a group of fuzzy-minded young people are trying to demonstrate a way of life which Friend Hayworth finds sticking in his craw? Amiable delegate to Yearly Meeting, where he draws strength from morning meetings for worship-sharing with unfamiliar Friends from afar, and then finds the strength ebbing in bewildering evening sessions where youth comes not to seek guidance, but to hurl challenges?

And to return home and find that my son-in-law can offer a certain degree of clarity and reason and balance. That is the most awkward part of it. The guilty knowledge that if he were not my younger daughter's husband, I might respect and admire him much more than I do.

33

This way it is like living intimately with a perpetual irritant, an outwardly kindly but inwardly disapproving superior.

A perpetual toothache.

Emily and I are last down to the breakfast table, the whole clan already gathered around it, including Ray McGrath, one of the commune's elders, which is how I think of the somewhat middle-aged founders of the curious institution down the road. He and Lou Erlanger, the other founder, and some of their junior communards —the juniors all seem to have the ability to grow full beards at puberty and so remain largely undistinguishable from each other—have a way of dropping in on us for breakfast without notice, taking our hospitality for granted, and making it plain that we are free to trespass on theirs just as casually, although after my first visit to the commune once it was in operation, the mere thought of eating at their table can turn me queasy.

And of course, Sarah Frisch, our housekeeper, is already at her place at the table, so now has to hop back and forth between dining room and kitchen, serving Emily and me. God knows when the Hayworths established the convention that household help must dine with the family, no matter the illogic or discomfort of it, but it may well have been when the early Hayworths, giving up their Massachusetts Puritanism for New York Quakerism, discovered they had to wrestle with their Quaker consciences about being masters over hired help. But I

35

remember my grandfather when he ruled the roost, and he was a firm ruler for all his mild manner, complicating the lives of newly hired backwoods help when he insisted on their company at the dinner table, and I remember my father's dilemma when housekeeper Wilhelmina Snyder, who came to us too well trained by some rich summer people on Lake George, flatly refused to ever take her place at the table, the final compromise being that, willy-nilly, she had to set that place for herself at every meal, and there she and the rest of us would face the reproach of an empty chair and untouched setting.

Intransigence on my part and Emily's? A wistful clinging to a dead past? Well, whatever the inconvenience, our housekeeper dines with us, and, in the old style, is always addressed by her full name.

So Sarah Frisch bustles back and forth between kitchen and dining room, her own eggs cooling as she sees to ours—add a touch of guilt to the reserve already measured for me before breakfast—and Emily talks to Deborah about something to do with shopping, and Ray McGrath discusses with my son-in-law David some commune problem, and Janet sits silent and brooding over her usual breakfast of a cigarette and black coffee.

I study Janet surreptitiously. For all she has lately managed to work herself down to skin and bone, and persists in wearing her hair in a straight, lank style like drapes on each side of her face, she is, in fact, a good-looking woman. All right, it was Deborah who brought David into the house, but why then couldn't he have seen how much more suitable Janet would be for him? On the other hand, if he had, what would this have done to Deborah, who so openly and childishly adored him?

Considering this, I am slow to get the point of his discussion with McGrath. It seems that some of the children of the commune people are past the age when they should have been registered in school, and the school board is taking a hard line about the failure to ship them down to Scammons Landing Elementary.

"It's a good school," I cut in. "Why not send them there?"

"It's not our kind of school," McGrath says.

Since the school does impose a certain discipline on its students, I can understand that. "Well," I remark, "I don't see you have any choice, unless you're looking for trouble with the law. And even the Amish defer to local regulations until their children are out of grade school."

"We're not deferring to anybody," McGrath says. "We are not going to have our children programmed by the other world."

"The other world?"

"The world we've rejected," McGrath says. "What we'll do, as I've been explaining to David, is set up our own school. We've got one boy, Mike Roos, who could qualify for that if he completed his ed courses at college. Only he doesn't have the money for it. I understand the meeting's Community Services Committee does have some money in reserve, though."

McGrath and Lou Erlanger are occasional attenders at our meetings for business as well as meetings for worship and probably know as much about our affairs as any member.

Janet abruptly presses her cigarette out and looks hard at McGrath. "Last week some of your pixies tore up half the Marcy sisters' rose garden, and when Elizabeth Marcy caught them at it, they put her down in language she hasn't heard in all her eighty years. Now just how much part of the community does that make you, McGrath?"

"I'm sorry," McGrath says. "I really am. But these are

37

kids. And they haven't been brainwashed to the importance of property rights over human rights. But I am sorry they stepped on your feet."

Janet's lip curls. "How very kind of you."

With the atmosphere growing sticky, Emily says pleasantly to McGrath, "I'm afraid the idea of a scholarship fund for an outsider might be a bit traumatic around here. The last time we tried to fund a boy through college, it didn't work out at all."

"Who was that?" David asks.

"Jimmy Flood, wasn't it?" Deborah says. "That must have been about ten years ago."

"An outsider?" David says. "What does that mean exactly?"

Emily says, "A town boy. His father was a clerk at the bank for many years. The mother wasn't too stable, really. When she ran off with some man, the father took to drink, so the meeting took Jimmy under its care. A brilliant boy. We used to give him odd jobs and a school allowance, and eventually we saw him right into college. He was very much scholarship material. Enormously intelligent and introspective."

"Now I remember," Deborah says. "He shot a garbage collector in town when he was a kid, didn't he?"

Emily doesn't like the way this is put. "It was an accident, dear. Entirely an accident."

"Well, we don't have guns at the commune," says McGrath. "For that matter, we don't have garbage collectors. And I don't think you folks should hold Jimmy Flood's sins against us."

"If you're talking about crazy Jimmy Flood," Sarah Frisch remarks, coming in with a pot of fresh coffee, "I can tell you something I didn't like to bring up before, considering everything. But he was in town again, about a month back."

This surprises me. "Are you sure? What reason would he have to be here now that his father's dead?"

"Don't know," Sarah Frisch says, "but he was. My nephew told me. Didn't even know it was Jimmy at first, what with them dark glasses and beard and all, but it was. Told my nephew he was just passing through."

"At least he could have stopped up here to say hello," Emily says.

"He could have," Sarah Frisch says, "and just as well he didn't. Anyhow, he asked all about you, my nephew says. But he must have been glad enough not to run into you close up after what he got himself into, shooting and bombing people in college when he was supposed to be studying from his books. And on you folks' money at that."

"Well, well," David says, and Janet says pointedly to him, "Oh, yes. He joined the rip-off crowd in college and did some extensive bombing and burning before he dropped out. Not much of a recommendation for scholarship funding, is he?"

"Look," McGrath says to Janet, "you know damn well we're trying to build a community of love and sharing down the road here. You people should be the ones to most appreciate and support that."

Janet says, "I appreciate you've got about two dozen healthy people in your commune who are only copping out. I don't approve of copping out. I don't see why we should support it."

"That's something to think about," David says. Janet glances at him sharply and McGrath looks surprised. After all, it was David and Deborah who had made the case for renting the property to the commune, much against my better judgment.

McGrath says to David, "Hey, I thought you were on our side," and David says, "I am. But I can see it from

Janet's angle too. You and your people have let that place get run-down as hell, Ray. And so far, all the talk about truck gardening there hasn't turned up one radish."

"Well, once we get a little more structured—" McGrath says, and Janet wickedly cuts in, "But you keep pointing out you're against any structuring."

"We want it to be voluntary, that's the idea," McGrath says. "We don't take your line. We don't want to impose demands on anyone."

David says, "If you're suggesting that the meeting imposes demands on any Friend, Ray, forget it. I wouldn't be a member if that were the case."

A mystic, my son-in-law. A man too much fascinated by Zen and ashrams and the like, and too easily won over by arguments of the half-baked in favor of any weird social experiment.

But, I must admit, a practical sort of mystic, and what else is a good Quaker supposed to be?

James Flood

All night in my bargain-rate hotel bed I dream of swamps.

No.

Not swamps. Bogs, quicksand, nothing green growing in or around them. An endless oozy morass, and myself, James Flood, solo in the world, caught in the middle of it, knee-deep in the warm ooze, slowly going down, down, down. Bog sand tickles my thigh, my hip, my belly. I wake gasping and sweating, understand I am in my creaking bed in a three-dollar-a-night Miami hotel room, but the tickling continues. It moves steadily up my chest, a piece of my nightmare crawling right into waking reality, and I look down at it and see a monstrous cockroach—one of those Florida roaches that come the size of the midget turtles you buy for souvenirs—which is steadily ascending my naked chest as if aiming at the jugular.

I come out of bed with a yell, slapping away the animal from my chest, dancing around to keep it from starting a fresh ascent of me from the floor. I pull the cord of the overhead light—a dim bulb which doesn't offer much more light than the predawn gray already filtering into the room—and I see other roaches, a pride of them, scurrying away to corners of the room, miraculously

43

dragging their fat, glossy-brown bodies out of sight through spaces too small to even be visible from where I stand.

Five o'clock.

Still an hour to go before the Shanklins pick me up at the Greyhound terminal, but I can't kill any of that time in this zoo. Anyhow, sweltering hot outside, it is even worse in here.

Much as I want to get out of the room fast, I force myself to dress slowly. I need the time to pull my finger away from The Button. I started thinking of it as The Button maybe ten years ago, when I was sixteen. The Button that made fantasy into reality. The fantasy is the violent response to the infuriating event. Someone steps on your toe in a crowd. The fantasy has you stealthily draw the razor blade from the pocket, slice it across his thigh and slip away before he even feels the sting of it, feels the ooze of blood through the trouser leg.

Fantasy, so far.

But push The Button without realizing it, and suddenly there is a real blade between your fingers, the real yelp of pain as it slices across the thigh—in the reality after The Button is pushed things always happen faster and more unpredictably than they should—and so there must be a hard intellectual awareness of the existence of The Button, and an awareness, too, that if you press it, you may be springing a trap on yourself.

The treading on the toe; the contempt of the big male for the smaller male in this generation of hulking, oversized males; the viciousness of the castrating female; the treachery of self-declared friends; the bullying of those who are invested with any authority over you—I won't even lay stress on the police, who go around, gun and manacles on hip, always rooting for trouble like hogs in a truffle patch, always so righteously pleased when they manage to come up with yet another truffle—but

44

needn't go further than the humble garbage collector (in India without caste, in Scammons Landing without humility), who, overpaid to allegedly dump your garbage into his truck, manages to dump part of it over your sidewalk.

How easy, watching this slob foul up the walk outside your home, so that you, age fifteen, will be commanded by your snarling papa to go out and scrape up the leavings, and how natural to fantasize the new Remington rifle, a .22 single shot, strictly hardware-store stuff, into your hands. Fantasize further, and you can feel the cartridge shoved into the chamber, feel the stock against your shoulder, see the garbage man in your sights. Oh, heart-hammering fantasy, a squeeze of the trigger and a .22 bullet goes slamming through that brimming pail he is preparing to heave up into his truck.

Unconsciously you have pushed The Button. Somehow there is a .22 short, not slamming into that pail, but drilling into that brawny, hairy, garbage-scented forearm. The garbage slob has dropped the pail. He has grabbed the damaged arm with his hand, is staring at it in stupefaction. He is bellowing, "God damn it! God damn it!" staring around now, looking up at you in the window where you are frozen, rifle on display, not in Fantasyville, but right there in Scammons Landing, the old hometown.

Without knowing it, you have pushed The Button, you have made the dream real. What then? Officer Duffy, a heavy-handed cop on the rise. Do you know what attempted murder is, kid? Now talk, you little son of a bitch. And, oh yes, Mr. Dillingworth, the probation officer. Two hundred and fifty pounds of false sympathy. A back-patter and hair-tussler. Mr. Dillingworth, sir, didn't anyone ever tell you that a back-patter and hair-tussler is a groper who doesn't have the guts to grope?

So, no matter the sweaty agony, one must take care not

to push The Button unknowingly. Consider that over-packed New York subway car when its doors opened at Fourteenth Street, and this hulk, along with a thousand others, shoved his way in, bearing down on my shoe with his, then kicking at my shoe for daring to be in his way. The razor blade in its wrapping was in my pocket, not meant for a smoother, smoother, smoother shave, but for scraping paint from a bathroom mirror. The fantasy was of a slash across that fat thigh wedged against mine, a flawlessly timed slash that would, as soon as I was through the door at the next station, suddenly gout blood in a fountain, jetting it over the other hulks who held me pinned against this foot-trampler and kicker. He would look down in disbelief and see his life spurting out of him, would glance through the closing door and catch a glimpse of me smiling at him—

Reality rushed in. The hulk yelped, savagely thrust me back, and looked down at the slit in his trouser leg above the knee. He looked at the razor blade between my fingers. "Son of a bitch! You crazy son of a bitch!"

He grabbed for the collar of my jacket, and this time I slashed with full awareness, slicing open the extended palm, then hurled myself like a battering ram at the mobs surging through the door as it opened on Thirty-fourth Street. The shock of that second assault on him held him back just long enough to give me a fair start. Then he followed roaring, the grizzly bear pursuing the fox, but too late.

Maleness. The Shanklin brothers are not male merely because of a superabundance of muscle, but because when the Mob's price was right, they willingly exercised that muscle on the chosen victim. Coco, doe-eyed artist with the sharpened blade, did not dull the needle point and honed edge carving loving messages on tree trunks. This is for the boys, but a man knows better uses for them.

As for myself, J. Flood, it was The Button which earned me my credentials. The danger is that where sometimes I am in charge of the happening, sometimes I am not, and so run the risk of being overwhelmed by it, by winding up with howling pursuers hot after me.

Now, in this roach-ridden three-dollar-a-night chamber of horrors, the stink of mildew in it so strong it almost gags me, I find a fantasy taking uncontrollable and dangerous shape. That scrawny night clerk at his desk downstairs, a junkie in full itch if I ever saw one, and his contemptuous reassurance to my query, "You're sure this place is clean? No bedbugs?" "Sure, I'm sure. What the hell you think this is, a flophouse?"—that clerk, itching and scratching and eye-watering and nose-dripping, will be politely asked to refund my three dollars. He will be contemptuous in his refusal, that clerk, and then suddenly there will be the menace of a weapon in my hand, and he will eagerly thrust my money on me. All the man-in-charge pretensions will leave him like air from a pricked balloon. He will whine, moan, slobber gratitude that his windpipe is still intact, unaware that in another instant it will be pouring out whatever watery blood is stored in that scabby body. The body, blood clotting on it, will lie behind the desk, the roaches coming from all sides to sample the remains. There will be no body in a little while. Just a pullulating mass of roaches in the shape of a defunct desk clerk.

So I dress slowly, allowing myself time to wipe away the fantasy before it swells into dangerous reality, before I press The Button without knowing it and actually find myself in that lobby downstairs standing over a nonentity I have butchered just three days before I am intended to come into my first million.

Ironic to have abstained from women, alcohol, grass, pills, and every other encourager of the loose tongue for

47

an endless three months and then to trigger myself into useless murder.

I dress, and bag in hand, go full tilt down the stairs and out into the street, not allowing myself even a glimpse of the clerk, my hand a safe distance from The Button.

An empty world around the bus terminal at one minute to six.

Then a big LeSabre, dented, patched, its trim rusted but its motor purring, swings around the corner, considerably down at the back end. It pulls up before me, Coco at the wheel, Harvey and Lester in the back seat like a pair of touring linebackers out to view the local alligator works in charge of a spade chauffeur.

Coco comes out to open the trunk and help me fit my bag in along with other assorted luggage and the dozen five-gallon cans the linebackers had loaded with daddy's high octane.

"Les wasn't so far wrong," I tell Coco. "This thing ever hits a pothole, the bumper'll drive right through the pavement."

"No potholes on the dandy highways all the way up to New York, man," says the foresighted spade. "By then, no big load to do damage."

No argument.

I get in beside Coco and we head south toward the Trail. "How much money did you turn up?" I ask Harvey.

"Fifty." He had not only taken the money daddy kept

49

stashed behind some loose bricks in the garage wall, he had taken it in the rusted soup can it had been stored in. He passes the can to me, and I haul out the soggy wad of bills. Fifty it is.

I say to Harvey, "You figured on a lot more than that."

"I know. But this is what there was."

Lester says, "There was twenty in the cash register, but we let it be. If daddy saw it was gone, he'd know for sure we backslid. He'd have the law after us soon as he *dingged* that register."

Backslid. Whatever flickering suspicion I have that this pair of Shanklins removed some of the can's contents before turning it over to the Company, that word alone anesthetizes it.

Coco says, "Poor pickings, man. We require at least three days' eating money for the four of us."

"Yeah, but don't forget Santiago," Harvey points out. "Man like that don't go around with his pockets empty."

"Perhaps not," says Coco, "but if you want to bet your million on it, that does not mean I want to bet my million on it."

"Knock it off," I tell him. "We'll make do."

"One does not make do in an enterprise like this, Mr. Flood. One takes all variables into account."

Enterprise, he says. Variables, he says. The Scholarship Grant Commission of St. Hilary could be proud of him. He was their first national project ten years ago, the first local high achiever shipped off to jolly old London University by St. Hilary's taxpayers, and he had made it at school for almost a year before getting hooked on the Black Students Union and knifing an unsympathetic bobby in a fracas at Trafalgar Square. That bobby was one of the few variables in Hubert Digby's life he had handled carelessly. He was never that careless again.

I say to Hubert Digby, "According to the Company

rules, Harvey is running phase one, and so far he's done all right. If he fouls up, you can be chairman of the paranoia committee."

What the hell, I'd put in twice as much time in college as he had, two years of Alma Mater, mother of Friends, where after tepid institutional breakfast on Sunday—beg pardon, First Day—you could, out of boredom, indulge in Quaker silent worship among believers glassy-eyed in their search for the Light. Oral messages invited, of course, from anyone who came up with a glimmer. I had the compulsion to deliver just one message there during my time, that First Day morn when stoned two inches short of the stratosphere I rose to say, "I hope all of you here realize that this is a lot of shit," and those who know what Quakers are will not be surprised to learn that I was not given the firing squad for this—heavens to Betsy, no—but was delicately eldered by a committee who pointed out that this gasp of revulsion was, in truth, a revelation of my own hungry search for the Light—a white-haired elder actually, if awkwardly, using the words *doing your own thing*—so that, like one in the embrace of a giant jellyfish, I found myself clutched even more tightly in the Quakerly embrace for having tried to act as an irritant to all that jelly. And SDS, embryo Weatherman division, embraced me even more gladly, which is how I—not uncoincidentally paralleling Coco's crisis at London U—wound up in the thick of a fire-bombing, followed by a suspended sentence and a life on the open road.

What did I say to the Movement itself when I cut the umbilical cord? I said, "I, James Flood, am not freaking out. I am not selling out. But I have examined the System closely and have come to see that it is a vast jellyfish. Its life is tedious and gray; it requires a fix now and then to make the endless tedium bearable. And our youthful role has been to provide that fix. We fling our ruthless, idealistic, shaggy beings against this pulp; we send charges of our negative current through it, giving it a sense that it is still alive; then we are engorged. But no more of this for me. No more providing shock treatment for the monster by way of headlines and TV news shows. No more waiting for bail to be met while rotting in the local juzgado where uncouth elements eye my tender asshole with hungry eyes.

"No, no, dear idealistic chums, you have started with a false premise and compounded it into a gigantic theological error. You have seen yourselves as an angelic host warring against Satan, the Establishment. But in truth, the Establishment is the Lord God Jehovah Himself, and you and I are pathetic little imps aiming tiny kicks at His armored shin.

"So, chums—ex-chums—James Flood is now joining with the forces of righteousness, is now going forth to cut himself a slice of the action. What is the measure of his calling? He will have his first million before he is thirty. One million and no less."

End of sermon.

Did I actually lay this on them that night? I did.

Because what I would not risk for a penny less than that, I would risk for a million.

Why before thirty?

Because the night of that sermon I was twenty, and so thirty looked like the end of all manhood. Now, at twenty-six, I know better. With a treasure chest under his arm, one strolls past thirty without even realizing it. And I would have the treasure four years before the target date.

"Man, what the devil are you dreaming about?" Coco says to me. "You see something out there in dreamland the rest of us don't, kindly paint the picture out loud.

Perhaps it concerns what we do if Santiago does not have a pocketful of eating money for us."

Chairman of the paranoia committee, all right, that one.

In all the monotonous length of the Tamiami Trail, which we traverse to the sound of soft rock from the car's radio—acid rock diluted with Kool-Aid—we find almost no traffic. When we turn off onto Route 94, which heads us southwest into deep swamp, there is no traffic at all. Not until we're slowed up by a happening in front of us. Half a dozen huge contraptions, their drivers perched on seats high over our heads, are lumbering along like a procession of mechanical elephants.

"Swamp buggies," Lester says. "Racing day today."

"Around our area?" asks Coco.

"No, around here. We still got more than a mile to go."

"Oh?" Coco says. "And what about these people hearing a gun go off that close?"

"It's a carbine," Harvey says. He leans forward and pinches Coco's neck between his thumb and middle finger. The size of that hand, it looks as if he could circle Coco's neck and strangle him with those two fingers. "Not a cannon," Harvey says. "Just a little bitsy popgun."

Coco suddenly stops the car and looks at Harvey in the rear-view mirror. "Mister, I do not like to be caressed without invitation."

If you know Coco, you know this is an ultimatum. He is not altogether blacksnake, Hubert Digby. No, there is a

54

strain of rattlesnake in him too. One warning buzz allowed, and this is it.

Harvey knows Coco. But Harvey, from what he had recounted about his youth on the edge of the good old Everglades, had been a laddie who liked nothing better than to tease a rattlesnake into lively spirit before bagging it and fetching it to the Miami Serpentarium for a quick cash sale. Once Harvey had teased too carelessly and was struck by the rattler, so Lester had snagged it by the tail and flogged it to death against a tree trunk.

It is a tactical error for Coco to deliver an ultimatum with Harvey's fingers pressing into his neck and with Lester sitting beside Harvey. On the other hand, it is a mistake for Harvey to think he can keep those fingers pressed into that black neck without eventually getting stung.

I like this. Like the way the tensions are building up. A guitar with loose strings makes no music. Here is evidence that the Company is ready to make music. The troops are primed for action.

I say to Harvey, "Cool it, Harve," and then to Coco, "Get moving and pull around that parade. They start turning off the road up there, they'll cut us off too long."

Harvey releases those knackwurst fingers from Coco's neck. Coco gets the car going and pulls past the parade into the clear. James Flood has spoken. When J. Flood speaks in this manner, impatiently commanding what must be done, he gets no comeback from his companions. The reason? His unpredictability. His unpredictable, sometimes uncontrollable finger hovering over The Button.

They learned that at one of those Raiford experimental group therapy sessions which we all attended, partly because it offered us a chance for Company meetings, partly because ripping off the amiable idiot who conducted them was better than another game of checkers, and it was at such a session that my interesting past was exposed and The Button discussed. No rip-off there, the facts were indisputable, the rest of the Company accepted them with respect and ever after had a wary eye on that Flood finger and its proximity to The Button.

Thus, if J. Flood is driven to the point of wasting any of his partners in the Company, he is not even likely to know he is doing it. So we are all equal indeed, but one of us—the wisest and most self-sufficient, although the most inconspicuous one—is considerably more equal than all the others put together.

So when Harvey grudgingly releases his grip on Coco's handsome neck, and Coco sullenly steers the car past the clattering procession of swamp buggies, it is evidence that they comprehend the dangerous facts of life and that the Company is soundly based and properly functioning.

A good omen.

The burned-out shanty is where Santiago said it would be. It had been a total fire. All that's left of the shanty is some charred framework. The flames had reached out far enough to parch a metal sign hanging from a post ten feet from the shanty. The sign says in what remains of its lettering *Glades Rifle Club*. In even larger lettering beneath that is *Private! Keep out! This means you!*

"Used to have a guard here," Harvey says. "Mean-looking mother with a shotgun. Pull up here, and next thing you'd have that gun shoved right in your face."

Beside the shanty is a two-wheel, deep-rutted track leading off to a tangle of brush southward. Coco swings the car into the ruts and we slowly jounce along toward the brush, the rear bumper now and then thumping the ground with a sledge-hammer wallop.

Coco says to the back seat at large, "What if Santiago and some friends are waiting for us the other side of that greenery? We are supposed to be carting four thousand dollars cash money with us. They could take us like pigeons, man."

"No way," Harvey says.

Coco stops the car and motions with his head. "Suppose you make sure."

The carbine is in a gun case at Harvey's feet. When he

57

pulls its sections out and assembles them, it does look like a popgun in his fist. He gets out of the car, ambles toward the greenery ahead, disappears through it. After a while he reappears and waves at us to move up. We do, and see that the greenery is not the dead end it seems to be. Where the track reaches it, it bends at a right angle and winds through the brush, leading us to another clearing walled off at its far end by a second stretch of tangled thicket. Again we move through a concealed opening and now are in a broad open area bordered by a canal. The remains of a wooden dock thrust out into the canal. Beyond the canal is a whole world of saw grass.

We get out of the car as the Kool-Aid rock cuts out and somebody comes on the air to tell us it is seven A.M. and all traffic lanes in and out of Miami are clear. Traffic is moving along just fine, boys and girls.

"That's for sure this time of day," Lester says. He reaches in and switches off the radio, and we all watch Harvey make his way to the dock, look up and down the canal. On his way back to us he scuffs his toe into the ground here and there and picks up muddy souvenirs. He shows them to us. Oversized cartridge cases. "Plenty more around here," he says. "Looks like this is one rifle club didn't stick to rifles."

Coco picks one of the cartridge cases from Harvey's hand. "Fifties," he says. "Heavy machine gun."

Harvey points at the surrounding greenery. "And there's rusty old barbed wire all the way along in there."

"Very military," Coco says. "Well, man, which way do you think he will be coming, road or canal?"

Harvey shrugs. "Road, most likely. If he comes by the water there, you'll know it a long time ahead. Those airboats are loud."

"But he could come by boat," Coco says.

"He could. Only thing is to cover both ways."

"From those bushes?"

"Nope, too far away. Must be seventy, eighty yards to the dock from there. Up to thirty yards, Les can hit a dime with this here gun. We just set up where the car is now, he can cover everything."

"From the car?" Coco says. "Santiago is sure to have company with him, man. You show that weapon through a car window, and it will be only a question of which of us gets blasted first."

"Not in the car," Harvey says. "Under the car."

He has, in his methodical Shanklin way, thought of all possibilities and has come prepared for the one we face. A shovel wrapped in burlap sacking is in the car's trunk. Lester does the digging, first of soft dirt, then of muck, carrying each shovelful down to the canal and dumping it into the water, until he stands waist-deep in his foxhole. "Ain't sitting down in this slop dressed up," he says. He strips naked, then squats down in the hole. His scalp is just on a level with the surrounding terrain.

Harvey hands him the carbine, then gets into the car and inches it forward over the hole. "Yo!" calls Lester when the car is centered over him, and Harvey puts on the brake. He comes out of the driver's seat and squats down to peer under the chassis. "No cave-in?" he says.

"Some," Lester says. "I got slop shoving right up my asshole. But it's no sweat."

Standing there, I can't see Lester at all. Squatting low beside Harvey, I can make out the glimmer of his eyes and the barrel of the carbine.

"Cover everything?" Harvey asks him.

"Everything from the road all the way down to that dock. You just have to keep him this side of the car. Now back up and let me loose from here until we hear him coming."

When the car is backed clear of the hole, Lester takes a bath in the canal, then stretches out naked on the dock to work on his tan. He and Harvey have that miraculous

59

capacity to fall asleep under any conditions, once they know they are faced with waiting time. I sit in the car, hunt around on the radio until I find a newscaster reporting the latest from out there in Chaos. Coco goes prowling through the brush, thicket, and saw grass surrounding us, the blacksnake slithering along on a journey of exploration, until Harvey calls him off.

"How do you know some of that wire and stuff ain't booby-trapped?" Harvey asks him.

"Why would it be?"

"Because I got a feeling this was real army stuff back a while. Cubano training stuff. Like for that Bay of Pigs mess."

"That was in Guatemala," Coco says. "What would you know about it? You were peeing in your baby pants then."

"It was here too. You think folks around here go poaching for alligators with machine guns?"

"Do what he says," I tell Coco. "Until we're out of the county, he's in charge."

"Indeed," Coco says chillingly. He is no good at all at waiting, not when faced with unpredictables. "There will be Santiago, and at least one more. They will have guns on them, Mr. Flood. With the open market in handguns down here, we could have matched them in fire power very easily."

"So what?" Harvey says. "Santiago said he's already been hijacked once too much. He said he sees any guns on us, that's the end of the deal right there. He takes off, and we wind up with a bad name if we try to deal with anybody else."

"Did it strike you," Coco asks at his snotty meanest, "that if we came properly prepared, we could have stopped him from taking off?"

Since Coco's knife is strapped to his arm and not yet in his hand, Harvey has time for a little fun. "Sure," he says.

60

"But if shooting starts, fact is I'm the biggest target around here. You stand sideways and the only thing anybody can see to aim at is that skinny black cock of yours."

I see the look in Coco's eye. So just to make sure the Company doesn't dissolve itself before payoff time, I take the carbine from the back seat of the car where Lester laid it. "Meeting's adjourned," I say, and when Coco says, "Who made you chairman of it?" I level the carbine at him through the window and sight it between his eyes.

He knows, does Hubert, that while I am in the book for two convictions for manslaughter, they were the result of plea bargaining when the witnesses against me in both cases showed a loss of nerve before the trial. Manslaughter is a very nice word for it. And, of course, he knows all about The Button too.

He cools off fast, Hubert does. But not looking to lose face, he spits hard on the ground, then turns and walks away.

"Hold it!" I call, and he freezes in his tracks, not even daring to turn his head in my direction. I put the gun on the back seat and lean out of the window empty-handed. "Now run," I say. "Fast. Move around. Don't make it too easy for me. I'll count three before I shoot."

Coco looks at me over his shoulder, his eyes staring, his mouth gaping. Then he sees I am not holding the carbine, and he goes slack all over. He stands shaking his head. "Very funny," he says. "Very funny indeed."

"I don't hear you laughing," Harvey says.

At nine-thirty we hold a Company meeting and run through the permutations and combinations of the coming event. Then Lester, grumbling when Harvey commands it, takes the carbine and settles down in his foxhole, and Harvey centers the LeSabre over him.

A little after ten we hear the sound of a machine banging and clattering as it makes its way along the rutted road. When it shows up through our perimeter, it turns out to be an old pickup truck, Santiago at the wheel, another man almost as fat as Santiago standing in back, a gun in his hands, a submachine gun, aimed in our general direction.

Santiago steers, not toward us, but along the whole perimeter, checking it out. Another good omen. If Lester was staked out in that underbrush, he would have been spotted by that close inspection sure as hell. Santiago swings the truck around and pulls up near us, the gunman covering us from about twenty feet away. The door of the truck is lettered *A & A Scrap and Salvage*, and the cargo is a couple of rusting deep freezers, roped around and laid out like coffins, and a collection of metal junk.

We stand waiting while Santiago lowers himself to the ground. He pulls a snub-nosed pistol from his hip pocket, tugging hard to get it loose, goes over to the LeSabre to take a good look inside it. Then he walks up to us smiling, the gun moving back and forth, covering us. "I hope you don't mind," he says, and gives each of us a quick one-handed frisking.

"You are a very suspicious fellow," Coco says.

"Yes. There is a bad element in this business lately." Santiago motions with the pistol at Harvey. "The money?"

I say, "You told us we could look over the inventory first."

"Did I? Well, I changed my mind. First the money." The trouble is that he's planted square in the line of fire between Lester's foxhole and the man on the truck. No use trying to take him out while that spray gun is aimed at us from the truck. I say, "You saw our money last night. So far, all I see is a couple of beat-up food lockers."

"You'll see what's in them fast enough when you pay for them."

"Everything there as ordered?" I ask. He gives me the feeling he is rooted to that spot, he is going to spend the rest of his life rooted there, blocking our play. "The real goods? No switches?"

"Only for the better. The submachine guns are Uzi, not Thompson. Israeli. You can't do better than that, and they're the same price to you. And the rifles are M-fourteens, not sixteens. There's too much heat on to get sixteens. But you don't need them when you can get fourteens."

I motion at the truck. "How about letting us see for ourselves?"

"The money, please."

"All right," I say, "the money's in the car. In the glove compartment. I'll get it for you."

"No." He waves the pistol at me. "Just stay where you are. I will do the getting, mister." He sidles toward the car, his eyes fixed on us, the pistol at the ready. He fumbles for the door handle, finds it, opens the door, then leans inside, reaching across the steering wheel for the glove-compartment knob.

"Probably locked," Coco says. "Here is the key, man," and walks to the car holding out the key. For this moment Santiago, wedged behind the steering wheel, might be a roast turkey laid out on the carving rack ready for the knife. And where is our son of a bitch redneck sniper, Lester Shanklin, at this moment? Asleep in his foxhole?

The sound of the carbine under the car is like a whip being cracked at my ankles. Coco suddenly has the carving knife for this turkey—an eight-inch switchblade —in his hand. He drives it into Santiago's back so hard that he has to strain to wrench it out for the follow-up blow. Santiago screams, struggles to get himself clear of the wheel, and I move as fast as I can to get at him and pull the pistol from his hand. I turn and see Harvey charging the truck like a rhino, clambering aboard the truck bed. The man with the submachine gun is not in sight there. Harvey looks down at his feet, gives me a V-for-victory sign. Total elapsed time: ten seconds, give or take a second.

Coco says to me, "Lend a hand. This bugger is bleeding all over the car," so I lend a hand with Santiago, who is not quite gone but is making a gargling sound with each breath as he pours blood from the rent in back of his jacket. We haul him out on the ground, where I kick him a couple of times in the crotch for being the blubbery nuisance he is and then put a bullet between his eyes. The blood on the car seat and floor Coco quickly attends to with a rag wet in the canal. After that I back the car clear of Lester's rifle pit, and Lester comes out of it smeared with muck, groaning, trying to flex his knees.

Harvey already has the ropes off the two freezers when

64

we climb on the truck. Near them, Santiago's partner lies on his back, a large bloody hole where his eye had been, part of his skull gone and spattered against the back of the truck's cab.

"One shot," Lester says, admiring his work.

"It took you long enough to get it off," Coco says.

"Because I had that fat bastard in my way," Lester says. "He blocked off the whole truck where he was standing. You were supposed to keep him clear of the truck."

"And how was I supposed to do it? I said there were too many unpredictables in your planning. That means poor planning."

Harvey says, "It came out fine, didn't it? Now lend a hand with this stuff."

The stuff is in the two freezers, weapons in one, ammunition cases in the other. Two Uzi submachine guns, five hundred rounds of 9mm ammunition for them; two M-14 army rifles, a hundred rounds of 7.62mm ammunition for them; four Colt Police Positive revolvers, six-shot .38s, with a hundred rounds for them; and six hand grenades. In the locker with the ammo is the bonus Santiago agreed to throw in, four G.I. gas masks. The merchandise is prime. Even at Santiago's steep price, it wouldn't have been a bad deal. At our price, it is the best possible deal.

I had laid out phase two from every piece of writing on the subject I could lay hands on, especially the Munich Olympic job, which was fouled up by an Arab miscalculation, something no one mentioned in all the analyses of it. That is, the nature of the hostages. A collection of semi-professional athletes, muscle men in the Shanklin class, was no emotional deterrent to the German police when it came to estimating the risk of a showdown. The nature of the Company's hostages will be different, a solid deterrent. But the odds on an assault and a siege are strong enough to mean that proper measures must be taken. Granting even a two- or three-day siege before the attackers lose nerve, we now have the weapons to guarantee a stand-off, which is all we need.

We stow the weapons on the floor in back of the LeSabre, a blanket over them, and plant the ammunition on the floor beside the driver's seat to help trim the chassis as much as possible. Then after extracting a vital two hundred-odd dollars out of the wallets of Santiago and his man, we get them into the cab of the truck, and Lester heads the truck into the canal. The murky water is not all that deep; the roof of the cab shows above it; so the Shanklins take the time and trouble to lay a mat of brush and grass over it as camouflage, although Coco is now twitching to get moving, mumbling under his breath about donkeys doing whippet work.

" 'Copters," Harvey says when he catches the complaint. "They buzz around here, and somebody looks down and starts wondering, and then what?"

We finish our housekeeping at eleven. A few minutes after one we are across the Dade County line, heading north through Broward County, and phase one is finished.

Marcus Hayworth

It is a sizable meeting for worship, the largest in some weeks—all thirteen of our members being present, as well as Ray McGrath and Lou Erlanger of the commune, and three well-dressed ladies who arrive in a chauffeured car from some resort on Lake George to, I suspect, look us over as part of their vacationing entertainment. The chauffeur himself, an elderly Negro, will not enter the meeting house, although urged on by several of us to share our worship. No doubt, like my family's one-time housekeeper Wilhelmina Snyder, he has been overly well trained in his role of servant.

But numbers, of course, do not automatically make the good meeting. Once I clear a clutter of extraneous thoughts from my head, it is the sense of gathering which makes this meeting meaningful to me, the sense of being in silent communion with kindred, all of whom, whatever the differences among us, wait in unity upon the Light which may give us understanding of our troubled selves and guidance to our otherwise uncertain courses.

Two messages are offered during meeting, one from Anna Marcy, a tender reflection on the joys of having the children among us, and the other by Uri Shapiro, one of our most cherished Friends, a transfer from Fifteenth Street Meeting in New York City, when, long years ago,

Uri left the city to manage The Mart on Front Street in Scammons Landing.

The message is, as so many of Uri's messages have been, based on a Talmudic or rabbinical admonition, in this case, *Where there are no men, be thou a man,* and it leads me to reflect on the question of manhood in a society where it is supposed to be marked by one's willingness to engage in violence. By my Light, which leads to the acceptance of the peace testimony and the tactics of non-violence as the only solutions for the world's most bitter troubles, and which had led to my three dismal years in federal prison for refusing to register for the draft in the Second World War, true manhood is best demonstrated by non-violent resistance to violence. Logic alone demands this. The advice to turn the other cheek was never intended to prepare the victim for another blow, but to provide evidence that more often than not the assaulter, faced by deliberate defenselessness, will not be able to deliver another blow.

But were those three prison years the highwater mark of my manhood? Friends are not supposed to casually use such divisive terms as Hicksite and orthodox, activist and quietist, but I use them in my mind sometimes, sorting out answers to my own questions. The Quimbys and Deborah and David were certainly activists against our country's engagement in Asia. In fact, Deborah had first met David at an anti-war demonstration she attended with the Quimbys in Washington. The Marcy sisters and Janet are just as certainly opposed to the meeting's support of anything beyond an individual concern for someone in town who needs a helping hand, and even there they take strict account of who needs the helping hand and whether the need is certified genuine.

And where do I stand? Have I become over the years what my grandfather had been, a quietist out of the last century, powerfully convinced that never mind what direction other meetings took, Scammons Landing Meeting is no more or less than a refuge from the world, a retreat for us when the surrounding world is too much against us?

At fifty-five, am I ready to undergo a transformation, help lead the meeting on the course David urges, have it enter into the town's affairs, move out into the community as part of all those hopeful associations which will tomorrow solve everyone's problems, open its meeting house to everyone in the county for round tables and discussions and gatherings?

Outreach, David and Deborah call it.

Missionary work, the Marcy sisters say. "Thee has missionary instincts, young Friends," Anna Marcy told them during one coffee hour after meeting for worship. "I do not hold with that. Friends lead by example, not by meddling."

Well, well, the Marcy sisters are dear old Friends, mainstays of the Committee on Ministry and Oversight, upholders of the old days and the old ways, and cantankerous as only proper Friends can sometimes be. But are they so wrong?

I have just planted the question mark on this question when I realize that Emily at my side is gripping my hand tightly and affectionately; the meeting is over. And then the three well-dressed ladies from their Lake George resort approach me, all apparently well pleased with their experience.

One of them gestures widely at the room. "So glad we came," she says. "So quaint."

For this moment at least, I have the answer to my question. "Is it?" I say. "It wasn't intended to be."

We walk home from the meeting house along Ridge Road, my family and the Marcy sisters and the two attenders from the commune, keeping our pace slow so that Anna and Elizabeth are not put to any inconvenience, stopping at Lookout Point, the one place along the road where you can catch a view of Lake George through the heavily wooded incline of the ridge. It is an incredibly beautiful and deeply moving view to me no matter how often I see it, spoiled only a little now by the sight of all the motorboat traffic on the lake during the July season.

We see Anna and Elizabeth to their door, then continue the quarter mile to home, where I discover we have visitors waiting for us on our porch. Two men—one small and slight, with neatly trimmed hair and beard, the other a very tall, very dark Negro, both, despite the sweltering weather, in jacket and tie—are seated there helping themselves to a pitcher of refreshment before them. Sarah Frisch's watery lemonade probably, one lemon to a gallon of water. And there are two battered valises on the porch, suggesting that these are more than passing strangers.

"Good heavens," Emily says, "it's Jimmy. Jimmy Flood."

And so it is, quickly standing to greet us, shaking hands

warmly, smiling with evident pleasure in this reunion. Introducing us to his companion, the Reverend Hubert Digby, who when he stands up is even taller than I first guessed, who shows splendid teeth in his smile, and who speaks with a melodic, liquid accent that stamps him instantly as from the West Indies. He says, "James told me that when you see him, you will instantly think, 'Oho, the bad penny has turned up again.' Well, dear people, I must inform you that this is no longer a bad penny." He hugs Jimmy's shoulders in a comradely gesture. "This is now pure gold. This is a man who has delivered himself to Jesus. A soul reborn."

I have mixed feelings about this. The ornate "delivered himself to Jesus" talk makes me uncomfortable, but on the other hand, looking at this Jimmy Flood, I have the feeling he might really have found peace for himself, and what does it matter how one does that? The sad part is that his Light appears to have been kindled by evangelism—probably Pentecostal, which is now so popular among the young—and so that has succeeded where Quakerism has failed. Jimmy had lived close to us, had shared our family life, had taken part in the meeting during his later teens, his most impressionable years, yet our example has meant nothing to him, and the aggressive ministry of the evangelicals has evidently come to mean everything.

Still, I can console myself for our Friendly failure by reflecting that Jimmy Flood is not your usual case. I would never go so far as Janet once had in acidly remarking that he was a sort of youthful Jekyll and Hyde—Tom Sawyer and Mr. Hyde was the way she put it—but there is no question that this undersized, silent, almost too polite and respectful boy so much in our presence during his adolescence had a bewildering and sometimes frightening side to his personality.

His job after school each day was to tend our grounds

73

and to help with the maintenance of the meeting-house property. He would do this with ferocious bursts of energy, then fall into a stupor of inactivity—daydreaming perhaps—always leaving part of the job undone. Talk to him about this, and he would stare at you blankly with those goatish eyes, nostrils flared, lips compressed, so that you got a feeling of seething hostility behind those neat features.

After all, one couldn't help taking into account that this was a boy who was involved in a shooting episode—a near-murder—before he was out of his childhood. Even accepting the testimony of the psychologist at the trial that this was a high-strung adolescent going through natural hormonal changes, an honor student too rigidly dedicated to success, too repressed in his social behavior, so that the episode was really an uncontrollable explosion in him—even accepting all this psychological verbiage, it was hard to get out of the mind that this child had aimed a gun and fired a bullet at an unoffending stranger.

It made me awkward in my dealings with him. Indeed, there were times when I wound up sessions with Jimmy feeling guilty for being so inept a surrogate father and then feeling resentful that I, not Donald Flood, the natural father, should be weighed down with any responsibility at all for the boy. Especially at a time when I had enough troubles trying to handle a sullen, uncommunicative eighteen-year-old daughter of my own, not to mention a ten-year-old daughter who had just discovered the power of her pretty face and winsome ways.

I suppose my initial mistake was in trying to play surrogate father under conditions where, after spending part of each day with us, Jimmy would then return to the home he shared with his proper father. Emily was wrong about Donald Flood's taking up alcohol after his wife abandoned him and her child for another man, but this is one of those romantic myths—a man drinking himself to death because of a lost love—which dies hard. In fact, Donald, a big, bulky man with an unpleasantly servile nature not too well masked by a loud, hearty manner, always had a drinking problem and had managed to hang on for years as a bookkeeper at the bank only because of my own weary patience in abiding with it.

Certainly my mistake in the matter was compounded by involving the Friends in my concern for the boy. This came at a time when the anti-war movement was growing strong, and there was a corresponding uneasiness in the meeting that we were contributing very little to its strength despite the more and more frequent messages during worship regarding the peace testimony. Only Kenneth and Ethel Quimby among us took an active part in the anti-war movement in its early days, tirelessly attending every conference, vigil, and demonstration they could get to, as far away as Washington.

So the opportunity to function positively by taking Jimmy Flood under its care came at the right moment for Scammons Landing Meeting. An intelligent, emotionally disturbed boy, a potentially lost cause who might be salvaged for better things, he made an appealing concern, or, as the Quimbys sarcastically charged during one acrimonious meeting for business, a fine dose of conscience balm. At the time, Uri Shapiro and I disagreed with them about their position and their use of this un-Quakerly language. It was only long after the event that I admitted to myself that the position, if not the language, might have been justified.

But even the Quimbys shared our concern on a practical basis, and so the whole meeting saw to it that Jimmy had all the odd jobs he could handle, was made as much a part of the meeting as he would allow himself to be. And, at considerable cost, was funded into college and through two years of it, where, ultimately, all our good intentions were blown sky-high by his joining with the most extreme, violence-prone elements of the student movement.

Why had he taken this course? The Marcy sisters and Emily firmly believed it was because he had been removed from the meeting's influence. The Quimbys and Janet—it was one of the few things on which they agreed—felt it was because he had been unfettered from his father. When I remarked to Janet that this didn't make much sense, since Donald Flood was, if anything, a bad influence on his son, she answered, "Sure he was. But he was the one person on earth Jimmy was afraid of."

Kenneth Quimby also said much the same to me, although not in Janet's condemnatory tone. Indeed, Kenneth and Ethel sometimes came very close to approving Jimmy's adoption of violence as a tactic in righting social wrongs. "Maybe," Kenneth said during one memorable coffee hour after meeting, "the kid has all the courage we only pretend to have. We Friends have been abiding in patience and waiting on the Light for three hundred years now, and look where it's gotten the world."

"Kenneth Quimby," said Anna Marcy, "thee is talking rot. There is no courage in killing for one's convictions, there is only courage in being willing to suffer for them. I cannot center down in meeting, knowing thee is seated beside me, your head full of killing."

That was a merry time of it, when during the next few weeks Anna and Elizabeth would not attend meeting but, instead, invited the rest of us to their home for midweek evening meeting for worship-sharing, and Kenneth and Ethel, seeing what was up, followed the same disruptive procedure and put us all in the most difficult spot as well as reducing First Day meeting for worship itself to no more than a Hayworth family gathering sometimes shared by Uri Shapiro. It took two months before peace reigned again, and we could put aside the bleak thought that Scammons Landing Meeting—or what was left of it—might have to be laid down.

And now here is Jimmy Flood back among us.

It turns out, as I suspected, that Jimmy and his mentor, the Reverend Hubert Digby, are very much involved in the Pentecostal movement. Their church is in Florida, but with a couple of other members of it who are providing the transportation, they have been attending to churches in Canada and are now on their way home. They had stopped at Scammons Landing on their way north so that Jimmy could visit us, but he was so unsure of his reception that he lost nerve and simply continued on his way. On the return trip, however, the Reverend Digby made an issue of this. When a sinner has come to Christ, he told Jimmy, he has not merely the right, but the duty, to stand proudly before the world and declare himself.

So here is the new Jimmy Flood declaring himself, and more than that, putting in a bid for our hospitality. "The brethren with the car," he says, "are doing some sightseeing for the day, but they'll pick us up first thing tomorrow. I wonder if you could put us up for the night. Of course, if it's inconvenient—"

"Not a bit of it," Emily says firmly. "Sarah Frisch told us about your being in town last month. We've been feeling awful that you didn't drop in to say hello."

We, she says, using, as Emily would, the courteous

plural. But I find in myself reservations about having even the new-model Jimmy Flood as a house guest, and from the expression on Janet's face, I surmise she has a great many reservations. The others, however, David and Deborah and the two communards, seem much intrigued by Jimmy's presence and manner. And, no question, having the very Negro Hubert Digby as a house guest makes up a little for the unpleasantness of that scene before meeting for worship when the Negro chauffeur, faced with the stony eyes of the three tourist ladies employing him, refused to enter the meeting house with them. Tempted he was, I am sure, but those eyes gave him a distinct signal to remember his place.

So we have a large party for lunch, Ray McGrath and Lou Erlanger of the commune, apparently approving of our two house guests, joining us, and the longest grace ever to preface a meal at our table. It is our way to simply clasp hands around the table and share in brief silent thanks for our benisons. What we are now offered is a sermon by the Reverend Digby, an interminable discourse on the last supper of Jesus and the communion it denoted and the sacrifice it preceded, on and on in that lilting West Indian accent, musical but monotonous, so that my thoughts eventually wander far afield, a sign to me here, as it sometimes is at meetings for worship, that the voice of the messenger is outlasting his message.

It goes far better during lunch when Jimmy, engagingly open for the first time in all my acquaintance of him, brings us up-to-date on his experiences during the past few years. A painful account it must be for him, because he doesn't hedge on any detail, and what emerges is a record of petty crime, a loss of all self-respect, until, during the last of his several confinements in prison, he became the concern of the Reverend Digby, a prison visitor. Had, indeed, been brought to Jesus right there in prison and has never looked back.

We are a long time at lunch, and then, after a talky afternoon, again at dinner, although this time without the company of Ray McGrath and Lou Erlanger, who have their commune to attend to, and Janet, who without a by-your-leave simply departs from the table early in the meal and then stays out of sight in her room for the rest of the evening. In a way, it is just as well she does. Her manner toward Jimmy throughout the day had been openly contemptuous, her verbal shots at him sometimes rude enough to make me flinch, although he bore up under them good-naturedly.

At bedtime, without telling Emily, who always puts her foot down on what she regards as my excessive concern for the children, I go down the hall and tap a finger on Janet's door. She opens the door in robe and slippers. Inside the room, I have to nerve myself to say it, her expression is so forbidding. "Is anything wrong?" I ask.

"No. Why?"

"Because of your behavior toward Jimmy all day long. And then that business of walking out at dinner. He must have felt it was aimed directly at him."

"It was."

"Then there's no reason for any of it," I point out. "It's obvious that he's changed."

"To what? A Jesus freak? That's this year's transformation. Come back next year and see what's left of it."

"Janet, back in the old days when Jimmy was around so much of the time, did something happen between you two to turn you against him so violently? Something I don't know about?"

"Nothing happened."

"I don't believe you, Janet."

She studies me with narrowed eyes. She gives me the same painful feeling I have known before during such scenes with her, of a bitter hostility toward me for no reason I can comprehend. At last she says, "You're right.

In polite language, we went to bed together. It turned out he wasn't really ready for the experience."

I say incredulously, "You mean a sixteen-year-old boy could persuade you to—"

"Don't be foolish. I asked him to screw me and he did. My mistake. Afterward he was working up to some petty blackmail, but I settled that on the spot, thank you. And there's no use standing there and looking at me like that. If you don't want honest answers when you cross-examine me, just don't bring me into court. Now goodnight."

"Janet—"

"Goodnight!"

James Flood

Coco is getting edgy, prowling the bedroom in his underwear shorts as if he is back in his cage at Raiford. Now and then he checks the midnight blackness outside the window through a slat in the Venetian blind.

I finally say to him, "Hayworth House. A deluxe room, twin beds, private crapper. And free. What the hell more do you want?"

"Man, I want to know for a certainty that Harvey and Lester will pull up here at five-thirty A.M. I would like to know where they are now. If they are somewhere getting stoned—"

"You know them better than that."

"After three days' touring the Eastern Seaboard with them, I know they are remarkably stupid."

I say, "So far they've delivered the goods. For that matter, you weren't so bright yourself today, the way you overplayed the Reverend Digby act. You've got the wrong audience for it here."

"It was well done, Mr. Flood. It sold the customers the goods. That is what it was supposed to do."

"You laid it on too thick. You were supposed to run interference for me, not lead a revival meeting."

Coco says, "The only one not buying it is that Janet woman. You cannot lay this on me, laddie. She would not buy James Flood if he flew in on angel wings with a halo over his curly head. She is a mean, skinny bitch who thinks you are poison. Why is that? You made so much about all the pussycats gathered here. You never said one of them would be a tiger. That was a miscalculation."

"Not the kind that matters."

"It could be, man. You planned on female hostages who could be counted on for some crying and some praying and no complications. Easy handling of them, easy transport out of the country, they all get released in prime condition. That might not apply to tigers."

It had been a miscalculation. In my Scammons Landing reconnaissance last month, I had picked up word that one of the Hayworth girls had gotten herself married, and I had somehow taken it for granted that it was Janet. Not altogether my fault. The last time I had seen Deborah, she had been a little kid in jeans, sometimes getting underfoot and making a nuisance of herself, always stinking of horse manure from her riding lessons. But Janet was eighteen to my sixteen when I first came to the house, hot-looking for all her boniness, tough-talking as any man down in the south end of town. A standout among all those mealy-mouthed Quakers. I think she scared the hell out of the family. I know she scared the hell out of me.

Especially the day when she pulled up in the car beside me where I was filling potholes on the road with a wheelbarrow of gravel. "Come up to the house," she said.

"Why?" Nobody else was home, the old man at the bank, the rest of them, including the maid, gone off shopping to Glens Falls, and the last thing I wanted was to be getting orders from Janet. "Anyhow, I have to finish this job."

"Later. Right now I want to see you at the house."

She drove away fast, spraying gravel all over me, and I waited awhile, just to show her I didn't jump when she snapped her fingers, then I dragged ass up to the house. She was waiting for me in the foyer, puffing hard on a cigarette and looking all wound up and ready to explode. I had done something wrong, I had goofed off on some job, what was it her business? The old man gave me my work orders, the old lady told me not to get overtired tending the place, so what was this one stepping in for now?

But she wasn't offering explanations yet. She was piling up the mystery. "Upstairs," she said. The court had given me a year's probation, and I still had six months of it to go. It was the old man's lawyer who had made the deal with the judge, and the old man who had signed all the papers. I didn't say no to any Hayworth.

It was when I followed Janet up the stairs, watching the motion of that flat little butt in tight shorts, that I had the first inkling that maybe this didn't have to do with hauling furniture around for her or getting a window unstuck. Put it all together, the way she was acting, here we were alone in the house going up to the bedroom floor—hell, wild as the thought was, it wasn't that wild.

She led me into her bedroom, locked the door behind us. She said without looking at me, "Have you ever made love to a girl?"

"What?"

"You heard me." She still wasn't looking at me. "Have you ever fucked a girl?"

"No." Twice I had fumbled around with girls to a point where I suspected I was being offered the whole works, but neither time had nerve to test the offer.

Now Janet did look at me, her face angry. "But you'd like to, wouldn't you?"

Lying about it might only make me sound like a freak. Telling the truth, as far as I could see, wouldn't be violating my probation. The funny thing was, I had already gotten these same questions from the psychology genius the law had put on me to find out what made me tick. "Yes," I said.

"All right then," Janet said, and next thing she was peeling off her clothes. What she had to show me was even less meat than either of the schoolkids I had fumbled around with.

That was my seduction, a deliberate humiliation from start to finish, a kind of clumsy struggle in bed where I was made to look foolish from the opening bell. Foolish enough anyhow to stay turned off women completely until I was in the Movement in college and found that with someone other than Janet Hayworth, it was only a case of doing what came naturally.

So here I am standing in the bedroom across from hers ten years later, considering her, and I can't help shaking my head at what lights up in it.

The odds were that I had been seduced by a dyke who was going to give the male animal a try before making the final decision on which way she was headed, and I happened to be the handiest and safest male animal around. Never mind the damage this could do to her guinea pig, this butch was going to settle her own problem.

Well, it's my turn now. Comes the dawn, and comes the Shanklins, and Janet will find out that life is not all fun and games and guinea pigs.

Coco says peevishly, "Man, you are at it again. I talk to you, and you are in Rio spending your million dollars."

"All right," I say, "talk."

"I was asking about that other one. That David. He is as new to you as he is to me. Another unpredictable element."

"He's one of this crowd. You got a good look at them today, including those two scarecrows from down the road. Peace at any price, that's the slogan."

"You intend to keep David here with us just to make sure of that?"

"No. He goes along with Hayworth. The three women are what'll pay off for us, not counting in the maid. Even if we have to waste one of them, Hayworth'll pay the same money for the others."

Coco says, "What do you mean, waste one of them? When I talked to my contacts in St. Hilary, I assured them there would be no such thing. I assured them all the women would be kept safe, although I guaranteed nothing about any police or federals who got in the way. That is the understanding. I do not want phase three wrecked in advance because you are going to go crazy and foul up phase two."

"Nothing will be fouled up. I'm just trying to get it into your thick head, Mr. Digby, that no matter what happens in here, Hayworth only has two options. Either way, the police and FBI will move in. But one way he can leave it all to them, and they can take their chances on blasting us out of here while we're holding guns on the women. The other way he can use the pigs to make everything easier for us."

"Will he want to keep them from blasting?" Coco says. "Now that I have met him, I don't know. He seems very tight-assed to me. Very law and order."

"All right, if he turns them loose on us, we hold them off until the pressure is all on them. That's why I want only the women in here. Mix men in with the hostages, it takes the edge off it. Only poor helpless women whose lives are in danger, that's the stopper. Those fucking FBI heroes are always thinking about their public image. They'll be half crippled to start with by the kind of public image we can plaster them with."

Coco thinks it over. Then he says, "But no wasting anybody. None of the women, I mean. You do that, it would be a serious mistake. When Harvey and Lester are about, if they ever get here, I do not want you to even mention it. They are very impressionable."

It looks like he and his St. Hilary pals have their public images heavy on the brain too.

We can't risk trying to stay with it until five-thirty and then falling asleep just when the Shanklins are due to show up. And for all we need whatever sleep we can scrape together after that three-day run from Florida, there is no other way to guarantee we'll be up and functioning as greeting committee than to spell each other at sleeping, one hitting the sack while the other stays on watch.

I take first watch, and when it comes my turn to crawl into bed, all I can do is lie there and keep grinding the Company's options over in my head. We risked time heading north just to stop at the out-of-town newspaper stand on Times Square in New York and get the latest *Miami Herald* instead of holding tight to the expressway, but there was nothing in the paper to indicate that Santiago and his partner were listed among the missing yet. And if the Shanklins' daddy has gone to the police about his erring boys and his car, it didn't rate any space in the paper. But that doesn't mean Harvey and Lester, with orders to cruise around away from Scammons Landing, haven't run into local problems and might not show up on schedule.

Question. In that case, can Coco and I make it on our own? There are two doubles and a single in three bedrooms upstairs, each with a phone on the night table, and a single, the maid, in her room off the kitchen downstairs, and there's a phone right there on the kitchen wall. Any little slip, and the lid blows off with a bang.

Get outside now and cut the phone line into the house? Next thing, the way it works in a town this size, a repairman will be up here knocking the schedule apart. Word would be out and the police will be in before we even have Hayworth set up to deliver the money. And unless I want to handle all the negotiations close up, I need that phone line open.

Worse, the only weapons Coco and I have with us are two of the Colt Police Positives. I have a picture of Hayworth and David and a phone repairman locked inside here with the women, while the local pigs and an army of FBI heroes outside are doing business their own way, and—if we slice up one of the hostages to show we mean action—having them use this as an excuse to blast the house down. Who the hell can forget Attica? The excuse is all they're looking for.

So, no Shanklins, no show. No Shanklins could also mean Harvey and Lester are having that arsenal in the car checked out right this minute by some state troopers. They might hold out a long time under questioning, Harvey and Lester, but even so, it means that first thing after breakfast here, Coco and I would have to get a lift into town and there say goodbye to each other and take off in opposite directions. While the Monday-morning money which is unloaded on the bank from half the hotels around Lake George and Hayworth's three other bank branches in the county who use this Scammons Landing bank as their deposit point—well, all that money would be just as usual unloaded into armored cars and deposited in whatever warehouse in New York that Friend Hayworth has piled to the roof with his money.

That sanctimonious son of a bitch could sink four million in the lake and never miss it.

I fall asleep angrily thinking that, and when I suddenly come awake, it is the first thing in my mind, the resentment along with it.

Then I realize Coco is poking me and whispering in my ear, "It's time, man. It's time. And the car is coming."

Just light enough now to show outlines but not colors. In the break-of-day silence—the crickets having tuned out and the birds not yet tuned in—I can make out the sound of a car moving along in low gear, the gravel crunching under its tires.

Coco is already dressed. I put on slacks, shirt, and sneakers, shove the gun into my belt, buttoning the shirt over it. The only other equipment necessary are the already measured lengths of Venetian-blind cord, the roll of adhesive tape, the extra handkerchiefs, and the knife, all of which I work into my pockets.

The trick in going down a creaking staircase under such conditions is not to make a big deal of it. It is the surreptitious nature of sounds being made too carefully which cuts through to the unconscious. An even, light-footed walk is what is called for, and that's how Coco and I make it down to the inside foyer. I open the bolt on the front door almost noiselessly, and we go out on the porch just as the LeSabre pulls up.

Harvey and Lester get out, leaving the doors open, and with a finger to my lips I wave them into the house. We've charted this out, step by step, rehearsed it so many times, no one has to say a word, and no one does. The three of them wait there at the foot of the staircase to the

94

second floor while I go down the hallway to the kitchen. The door of the maid's room opens from the kitchen, but open is the wrong word, because when I try it I find it's locked. No surprise. I allowed for this.

I knock on the door panel with one knuckle and wait. We are still not past the point of no return. If anything goes wrong, we're in a position to introduce the Shanklins as our traveling companions come to pick us up earlier than expected. Depending on how wrong things might go, that leaves us free to either take off or stay with it.

I almost rocket through the ceiling when I feel a pressure on my shoulder. A hand. Hell, Coco's hand. Trust him to count three and start worrying. Count three more and come to check up. I shove his hand away and wave him out of the kitchen so violently he must know he was close to blacking me out. He holds up both hands in a placating gesture, then moves out to the hall again.

I rap on the door once more, and this time hear the sounds of someone moving around in a bed which creaks as wickedly as the staircase. "What?" I hear the old biddy say. "What is it?" From her voice, she's still half asleep.

I put my mouth close to the door. "It's Jimmy, Sarah Frisch. I'm sick. Do you have the doctor's number?"

"Number?"

As she unlocks the door I pull the gun out from under my shirt, heft it by the barrel. It has to be handled quick and clean, this particular part of the operation, so there's no use menacing her with the gun. The first thing she'd probably do if she sees it poked at her is let out a yell. And no sense trying to take her out by slamming her with the barrel, because there isn't enough heft in it to guarantee the knockout. Anyhow, I hadn't specified to the Company how I would do it. I just said it would be done without damage, and damage is a relative word.

So when she opens the door and stands there, I slam the butt of the gun on her skull, and down she goes. I grab at her, trying to get both arms around her, but she slithers through them, her nightgown pulling right up to her skinny shoulders as she hits the floor.

I haul her into the middle of her bedroom. There is light enough now to get a good look at her face, and for an instant I think I have by some freak caved in her whole jaw with that wallop on the head. Then I realize she had come to the door without her teeth in—they're in a glass of water on her dresser—so the only damage done is the knockout itself. I don't have to check her pulse to know she isn't finished off. Her loud breathing, a kind of slow, heavy snore, tells me that.

I use a handkerchief and plenty of tape gagging her while she is stretched out there on the floor, then get her into the bed, tie her wrists behind her, bind her ankles, and throw the cover over her.

We have now passed the point of no return.

Marcus Hayworth

Emily, as usual, is sound asleep minutes after I turn out the light, but I lie there beside her wide awake and sick in spirit to brood over Janet's revelation of that ten-year-old episode with Jimmy Flood.

All right, no harm done to her or the boy. A boy of sixteen, as I can vividly recall from my own youth, which doesn't seem that long ago, is ready and rampant for sexual experience. A girl of eighteen, well, she probably is curious enough about it to at least want to experiment. But to Janet at eighteen, tall, not unattractive, seemingly sophisticated, this undersized sixteen-year-old boy must have seemed a child. Was she that much afraid of the full-fledged men who, on occasion, used to show up at the house seeking her company?

In recent years, since she got her degree at Wharton and came to work as my assistant at the bank, there have been very few men showing up for that purpose. I pitied her for it, worried about it, but now I'm not so sure. If she could keep that ancient secret about Jimmy locked in her so tightly, how can I know what goes on when she's away from the house for any length of time? Those trips to Europe, those week-long visits to New York and Philadelphia to renew acquaintance, so she says, with classmates and teachers who are just names to me, are these the manifestations of a sexual life the family isn't supposed to know about? Or, most infuriating thought of all, am I alone not supposed to know about it? Do Emily and Deborah and even David share a secret I am not privy to? Am I regarded as some kind of caricature Victorian who would fling his unmarried daughter out into the cold because she has perfectly normal instincts?

Do I really project that image?

Well, if I do, it is not my fault. It is the fault of a world off-center where anyone who believes in marital fidelity and who is repelled by sexual license and its porno-graphic, orgiastic trimmings is made to look an utter damn fool. A doddering, antiquated prude.

On the other hand, can I be imagining all this? Is it simply that Janet, hair-triggered when it comes to questions about her personal life, was bound to feel especially sensitive about that episode with Jimmy, was driven to hitting out at me as hard as she could for my unwittingly rattling that skeleton in her closet?

Even as a child she had been the difficult one. Deborah had been the chatterbox, the noisily confiding spirit in the house. Janet had been silent and remote, her own hardest taskmaster, fanatically neat and orderly in her ways, a supervisor of the children in First Day School when she was hardly older than they were. Born like that? Made that way because Deborah, eight years younger, was plainly destined from infancy to be the family pet?

I am in a trap of my own devising. I am no happier in Janet's company than she is in mine, yet the proper solution, her going off to marry and make a home of her own, seems to be thwarted by her place in the bank. I had wanted a son who would be the fourth generation of Hayworths to take over the family business, but I had gotten a daughter, and then after a long barren period another daughter. Which meant that the elder would have to be, to use David's term, the birthright banker, and she became aware of that, I think, as soon as I did.

So there is not only our uncomfortable proximity in the house, but also during working hours, too much of it, in fact, and no escape from it.

I fall asleep with this thought futilely circling around and around in my mind.

I wake up in the light of dawn and see, incredulously, that Jimmy Flood is standing at my bedside, one finger to his lips gesturing silence, the other hand holding a pistol aimed at my head.

It is not the first time I ever had a gun aimed at me.

Once while I was serving my wartime sentence in prison as a conscientious objector, a guard, drunk with alcohol and rabid patriotism, had wound up a harangue of me by drawing his gun and threatening me with it.

Another time I had intercepted a couple of hunters trespassing in the woodland on the western slope of Scammons Ridge, away from the Lake George side. This was not only my property and conspicuously posted against hunting, but the entire ridge had, over a couple of generations, become a sort of unofficial game preserve, and the few deer which still inhabited it were as trusting as cows in a barnyard. The two interlopers, both done up in gaudy Abercrombie and Fitch big-game-hunter style, reacted to my explanation of the situation as if I had threatened to assault them. In effect, I was warned off my own property, and when I refused to move, was threatened with a rifle leveled at my chest. It was a frightening moment, but trusting in the theory that if one behaves bravely, he will seem brave, I held my ground, and in the end it was the hunters who departed downhill to the highway where their car was parked.

But in both these cases I was the only possible victim if the trigger were pulled. And in both cases I sensed that I only had to survive a bad minute or two. Tempers were high, but given a few ticks of the clock, they would cool enough to let logic prevail.

But this is different. I am not alone. Emily, soundly sleeping beside me, might be the victim if I make a false move. And I am not confronted by a case of bad temper. I am confronted by a smiling young man who looks as if he waked me up to give me news about good weather ahead. As if this is some kind of game we're playing.

A false impression. I start to sit up, and next instant Flood jams the muzzle of the gun brutally hard under the angle of my jaw, shoving my head back on the pillow. He bears into the jaw steadily, as if he intends to thrust that steel right through the flesh—the pain is agonizing—and then slowly withdraws the gun.

No game. No magical religious conversion either, because in the doorway appears the Reverend Digby— the supposed Reverend Digby—gun in hand. A hoax. An elaborate, deadly hoax.

Digby says in a loud whisper, "The girl's room is locked. The other was open. They are out in the hall now."

Flood says to me, "Do you hear that?" and I nod. He says, "There's another man out there with them, Marcus. A bad man. You won't try anything foolish, will you?"

I shake my head. Then I realize that Emily's eyes are open and staring at me fearfully. I say to her quickly, "It's all right. Don't move. Don't make a sound. There's nothing to worry about."

"Wrong," Flood says. "There's plenty to worry about." He aims the gun at Emily's head. "It's ready to go off," he tells me. "Make a sudden move, and it will. Got that straight?"

"Yes."

"All right, out of bed, both of you."

He backs away a couple of steps, the gun still pointed

at Emily, as we get out of bed. I am enormously relieved when Emily says to him in an even voice, "Do you mind if I put on a robe?" Obviously she is in complete possession of herself. She always did have a good, quick mind, and despite her gentleness, a certain toughness of spirit.

"Put it on," Flood says, and when she has he motions us both out of the room. I am due for another shock in the hallway. Deborah and David are standing there in their nightclothes under guard, both of them gagged and with their arms bound behind them. I have an impulse to sharply protest this, but the sight of the huge, powerfully built, vacuous-faced man guarding them, gun in hand, strikes me dumb. That vacuous expression especially, and the stoniness of Digby's features and the malevolent coolness of Flood give me a despairing sense that they aren't human. Are, in the deepest sense, unfeeling. In the face of that, all one can do is play the game their way, yield every point, trust that in the end they will depart without hurting anyone. Without killing anyone. That's what it really comes down to, without killing anyone.

Flood gestures at the door to Janet's room. "Get her up," he says to me. "But easy."

I knock tentatively on the door, put my mouth close to it. "Janet?" No response. I stand there uncertain what to do next, and Flood says, "Go on. Try again."

I do, knocking harder this time, but still drawing no response. I sense the mood of our captors changing, becoming a little uneasy, and it is even more menacing that way. Digby says to me, "She did not go away last night and lock that door behind her, did she?"

"No," I answer, "sometimes she has trouble getting to sleep. She takes a barbiturate for it. She probably took one late in the night."

"Downers," Flood says contemptuously. "Stoned out

of her head until it's time to punch in at the bank, right?"

Digby says to him, "Perhaps not, man. Perhaps she is on the phone in there right now. I told you these upstairs phones had to be knocked out first thing."

"How?" Flood says. "You'd have to knock out the whole house to do that." He turns to me. "Do you have a key to this door?"

"No."

Again he smiles at me. The smile gives him the look of a bearded death's-head. "I don't believe you, Marcus."

My throat constricts as I watch Digby press his gun against Emily's head. I manage to say, "I don't have the key. But you can break it open. Break it open, for God's sake."

Flood turns to the huge man guarding Deborah and David. "You hear him, Harve? But no dry run."

It takes just one blow of that massive shoulder to accomplish the job, the slide bolt inside snapping clean off as the door flies open and smashes back against the wall with a noise to wake the dead. But it does not wake Janet. She lies there naked, bedraggled, beaded with perspiration, in a twitching, apparently uncomfortable sleep. Maybe the noise we made intruded into her dreams, whatever they are.

Flood lifts one of her arms as if hefting it. When he releases it, it falls back limp. He stands looking down at her, shaking his head as if baffled. Then he slaps her hard across the face.

"Oh, please!" Emily cries out, but when Digby thrusts the gun hard against her head again, she has sense enough not to make any further protest.

The blow stirs Janet out of her lethargy. She mumbles something unintelligible, tries to raise her head from the pillow and fails. Flood turns to the big man. "Wake her up, Harve. Get her under a cold shower."

"We are wasting time," Digby says to Flood.

"No sweat," Flood says. "She has to be in on this from the start so there won't be any mistakes made."

Harve picks up Janet as if she is weightless and carries her into the bathroom. Flood motions at the rest of us. "Downstairs," he orders. "Into the kitchen."

As we move to the head of the staircase, I see in the foyer below still another man at least as big and heavily muscled as Harve and with a striking resemblance to him. Both have the same neat features in a face which seems too large for them. Both have shoulder-length blond hair. The effect is grotesque, as if female heads have somehow been transplanted onto those powerful bodies.

The man in the foyer is laying out weapons and ammunition cases on the floor, an arsenal of them. For a robbery? What sense does that make? I have been sustained by my idea that this is a robbery, that once this gang gets whatever it wants from the house, that will be the end of it. But now I have the chilling thought that this is no mere robbery, and that we are far from the end of it.

Flood says to the man, "Everything inside?"

"Uh-huh. And I put the car alongside the garage. No room inside."

"We'll take care of it later," Flood says.

He herds us down the stairs and into the kitchen, his gun and Digby's close at our backs every step of the way. The sun is up now, but the kitchen, its shades drawn, remains dimly lit. Flood switches on the overhead light, leaving the shades drawn.

For the first time I think of Sarah Frisch in her room off the kitchen. There is nothing that Flood—this man who had been little Jimmy Flood—doesn't know about the house. He must know that there behind him is the door to Sarah Frisch's room. She is a spry and gingery woman for all her years, yet faced with this invasion, she might panic. All it needs for disaster is to have a finger involuntarily tighten on a trigger.

I say to Flood, "Sarah Frisch is in that room. If you want her out here, let me take care of it."

He studies me from head to foot. "I didn't give you permission to speak, Marcus, did I?"

"Jimmy, be reasonable. You can see we're doing whatever you want us to do, but that woman in there—"

My appeal dies in my throat as he raises his gun and levels it at Deborah. She closes her eyes against the sight. I say explosively, "All right, no, you didn't give me permission to speak."

"That's right," Flood says. "So if you want permission, just raise your hand first."

I know I must sit loose. I must be gentle in my manner. I must not make a blood-spattered tragedy out of this nightmare.

I raise my hand, and Flood says gravely, "Yes, Marcus?"

"I don't want Sarah Frisch alarmed. I'd like to explain this to her my own way."

"Go right ahead, Marcus," Flood says, and motions at Sarah Frisch's door with the gun.

I hesitate, wondering if he's just baiting me, then go to the door and open it. Sarah Frisch is asleep under her coverlet despite the disturbance going on around her. I rest a hand on her shoulder and whisper, "Sarah Frisch," but get no response. Then I realize that it's not the coverlet drawn up almost to her nose, but a gag. I pull back the cover and see that her wrists and ankles are bound. And she is still not moving. She is plainly unconscious, breathing heavily and unnaturally.

I wheel to face Flood. "What did you do to her?"

Flood holds up his gun by the barrel, displaying the butt to me. "This." Then he sights the gun at me, squarely between my eyes. "But if I had to, Marcus, it would have been this. Loud and conclusive. You believe that, don't you?"

I don't have to answer. He must know from my expression that I believe it.

By the clock on the kitchen wall, it is twelve unnerving minutes before Janet is brought down to join us, the man called Harve hustling her into the room with a grip on her upper arm that has her wincing with pain. She is in a robe and barefooted, her hair dripping water, her lower lip swollen, her cheek bruised. From her look of bewilderment as she takes us all in, I can see she has not yet been given any explanation of what is going on. And her expression when she observes Flood standing there, gun in hand, is what mine must have been when he woke me with that gun. Utter incredulity.

She tries to wrench herself free of Harve's grasp, but small chance of that. "What the hell is going on here?" she demands of Flood.

He gives her that familiar death's-head smile. "What a way for a Quaker to talk. Shocking, baby."

Digby says angrily, "Enough palaver, man. We have business to take care of." He shoves Emily and Deborah toward the kitchen table. "Sit down there," he orders, then says to Harve, "That one, too."

Harve thrusts Janet down on a chair. She says to Flood, "Little Jimmy with the big gun. You haven't changed any, have you?"

Digby goes to her, grips her chin, turns her face up

toward him. "Behave yourself, woman, do you hear?" He digs his fingers into her jaw hard enough to make her groan, and, unthinkingly, I move toward him, a hand out in protest. The next instant Harve drives his fist into my belly. It is like being struck by a sledge hammer. All the breath is slammed out of me and can't seem to return. Gasping, struggling for air, I go down on hands and knees.

I am aware of someone screaming, someone else crying out "Stop it!," both sounds instantly cut off, and then Harve drags me to my feet. I am not a small man, but he hauls me over to the table and drops me into a chair as if I were a rag doll.

Digby leans over Janet. "Now do you understand?" he says. It almost sounds as if he is pleading with her. "Now do you see what will happen if you do not behave properly?" and Janet, all color drained from her face, nods her head.

Flood is watching this narrowly. "You're sure of that?"

"Yes," Janet whispers.

"Good." He turns to me, abruptly all cold business. "This is Monday. Which means that around eight o'clock the Champlain armored-car service pulls up at your bank in town here with the weekend cash from those hotels around the lake. And with last week's surplus from your bank branches. About ten o'clock Wells Fargo picks up the whole load to bring down to New York. That's how it works, right? Just say yes or no."

"Yes."

"Putting it all together and adding on the cash you keep in the main bank here, it means that for two hours—between eight o'clock and ten o'clock—you'll have over a million and a half right here in the bank vault. Yes or no."

"Yes."

110

"And how about the three branch banks? How much cash is in their vaults right now?"

"Eight hundred thousand in each. Around two and a half million altogether."

"So between the main bank and the three branches, you can lay your hands on at least four million dollars in cash this morning. And you know what, Marcus? That is what you are going to do."

I try to comprehend this. "You mean you want me to turn over every penny of the bank's cash to you? All of it?"

"No. The pennies are all yours. The green stuff is all ours. It makes it that much easier to divvy up."

"Jimmy, it can't be done. You must see that. There'll be at least a dozen people involved in any such thing. They'd know something is wrong. It'll be impossible to keep the police out of it."

Before Flood even answers, I suddenly understand the reason for all those weapons laid out in the foyer. He reads in my face that I understand. "That's right, Marcus. You're a weighty Friend. An elder of the meeting. You wouldn't want to start World War Three right up here on the ridge, would you?"

"Jimmy, listen to me. You're asking me to do the impossible." I try to get my thoughts straight, to do some simple arithmetic. "Look, what I can do is get you enough cash so that no one will take notice until after you've gone. Two hundred thousand from my account and some others I can cover with my personal notes. It won't be easy, but it can be done. That should be worth it to you. And it means no risk to you."

Flood shakes his head. "Four million, Marcus. The whole load."

"But then the banks will have to be kept closed. My God, we'll have a panic in the whole area. No matter what explanation I try to make, the authorities will move in immediately. Treasury men and FBI men will be up here as fast as they can make it from Boston and New York. Then what?"

"Then, Marcus, you will point out to them that we have four hostages in here. Four funerals for the papers to write up if anything goes wrong. Get it into your stupid banker's head, Marcus, that they might not want headlines about a massacre on Scammons Ridge any more than you do. That is clout. Heavy clout. Use it right, and maybe there won't be any massacre. So it's the whole four million, Marcus. All or nothing."

"Jimmy, you're not making sense. Do you really expect to get away from here with that money with every road closed against you?"

"That is part of the package you'll be handing over, Marcus. Transportation down to the airport at Glens Falls, then a plane to Boston, then a long-distance jet waiting there. With all the comforts. Because, just to show you how much sense I can make, the ladies will be going with us right to the end of the line."

"Man," Digby says to me, "understand it. If everybody cooperates, there will be no harm done to any of you people."

If everybody cooperates. Bob Daniels who runs Vista Airways out of Glens Falls can charter me a plane to Boston. But what airline at Logan Airport can I appeal to? How do you shop for a plane to be hijacked? And the authorities themselves would have to cooperate in this insane business. The police here. The police in Boston. The FBI all over the place. Cooperate? With a kidnapping and hijacking?

Do they have a choice? Do I have one? Any choice?

"Look," I say, "the armored car from upstate will have seven or eight hundred thousand in it. I'll add two hundred thousand to that. You'll have a million right there. Drive me down to the bank in the station wagon, and I'll see that the money is loaded into it without anyone interfering. You get the wagon and the money and a head start to wherever you want to go. A million dollars and no trouble. You can't ask for a better deal than that."

It shakes them up. I can see that. At least, it shakes up Digby and Harve. They are thinking hard, Harve slowly wiping his hand back and forth across his mouth, Digby nervously spinning the cylinder of his gun with a thumb again and again. Only Flood does not react. He waits as if timing his answer for better effect, then shakes his head. "No," he says flatly.

"Look, man," Digby says to him, "I want to talk about this."

"Why? How far do you think we'd get that way?"

I say, "I'll go with you as hostage as far as you want."

Digby says stubbornly to Flood, "Harvey and I both want a meeting about this," and Flood looks at Harve and says, "Is that a fact?"

Harve looks embarrassed. "Whatever you say, Jimmy."

"I have a say, too," Digby raps out.

Suddenly the gun in Flood's hand is aimed at Digby. Flood's teeth show. His eyes—somehow they give the impression of having horizontal irises like a goat's eyes—are very wide and glassy. Digby takes a step back—I think without even knowing he is doing it—and says in open alarm, "Man, you are getting yourself worked up for nothing."

"You wanted a meeting," Flood says. "This is it."

Digby tries to smile. "Yes, of course. And it's over now. Everything is settled, Jimmy. Have it your way."

"My way?"

"The Company way."

"Good," says Flood. "We'll put it in the minutes." His gun moves from Digby, takes unwavering aim at Emily.

He nods up at the clock on the wall. "You've got thirty seconds to make up your mind, Marcus. Twenty-nine. Twenty-eight—"

What choice is there?

"All right," I tell him, "I'll do what I can."

Apparently we have arrived at a truce.

Not ungently, Digby removes the gag from Deborah, unties her wrists. With somewhat less gentleness, he does the same for David, saying as he pulls the cord loose, "You will not get any tricky ideas in your head, do you hear?"

"What I've got in my head right now," David says, "is this talk about four hostages. Don't I make number five?"

Flood says, "You're not wanted in here, Davy boy. You're going along to back up daddy. If he has trouble convincing people all this is for real, you convince them."

He leads the way out of the kitchen, Digby following us, gun at the ready, Harve left in charge of the women. In the foyer, all the weaponry is now laid out in an orderly row. In the living room, the other big man is at work pulling the heavy storm shutters closed over the windows and bolting them. Preparations for a siege.

Flood says, "The same for every room in the house, Marcus. We're buttoning up tight. And remember, whether it's bullets or gas anybody wants to try on us, the women don't get shipped down to the cellar out of range. They stay right up here and take what we take." He picks up a gas mask from the floor. "Too bad we don't have extras on these, Marcus. Nothing in a lady's size."

I say, "I'll do everything I can to keep the authorities from interfering. But what if they do? You must understand it won't be my fault."

"It won't matter whose fault it is, Marcus, the payoff is the same." He points at the front of the house. "Those grounds out there are no man's land. After you two leave here, the only one who can come back up that driveway is you. You, all alone. Nobody else. You park out there on the road and walk to the house. Anybody else gets blasted on sight. And no helicopters over the house, nothing that might make me nervous. There'll be somebody watching from that sun deck on top of the house twenty-four hours a day, if it stretches out that long. Make the police know all that. Get it through to your pet cop Duffy that if we have to speed up the action by killing one of the women, we'll do it. Understand?"

"Yes. But you're talking about time pressure. How much time do I have to take care of everything? It'll take hours just to get the money from the branch banks. And travel arrangements have to be made. If I don't have enough time—"

Flood glances at his watch. "It's about six now. You'll be at the bank at six-thirty. You'll use the phone there and get all your branch managers out of their beds. You'll tell them that when the Champlain armored car stops by, they're to pile everything into it, every piece of green money they've got locked away. Just sack it up and throw it in the truck. The truck usually makes it to Scammons Landing about eight, but I'll allow plenty of extra time for it, another three hours. You'll be taking the station wagon into town, you'll unload everything from the trucks right into it. Everything. Got that straight so far?"

"Yes."

"Good. And twelve o'clock is your deadline. That means that at twelve o'clock, and no later, you park the wagon out there and bring every sack of cash into the house by yourself. We count the money in here. Then if it adds up right, you load it back into the wagon, we all pile in with the ladies, and you take us for a nice ride to Glens Falls airport, where you have a plane waiting. Simple, isn't it?"

"Jimmy, if anything goes wrong while I'm away from here—"

"Any complications come up at your end, I'll be waiting at the phone to untangle them. Now upstairs, both of you, and get dressed."

David and I are given turns at dressing, Flood and Digby standing there to supervise the process, and on our way downstairs again I am tempted to ask Flood if we can't see the women before leaving, but the thought seems so much as if I'm arranging a morbid farewell, I put it aside. Then another thought, a troublesome one, strikes me.

I say to Flood, "You mentioned complications. There may be one very soon."

"What kind?"

"Those people who run the commune—those two you met yesterday, McGrath and Erlanger—know they're welcome for breakfast here. They sometimes drop in without notice."

"Then just make sure they don't," Flood says. "Dead sure."

Digby brings the station wagon out of the garage, and David, evidently recognizing that I am in no condition to do any driving right now, gets behind the wheel. As the car goes into motion along the driveway, Flood leans in at the window on my side and points meaningfully at his wristwatch. "Twelve o'clock, Marcus. That's deadline time. One minute after twelve is trouble time," then we are away from him and Digby, making the loop along the driveway, jouncing onto the road.

It is a strange feeling being away from those two, a mixed feeling. Relief at no longer being under those guns, qualms that I had not chosen to see Emily before leaving to at least offer her some reassurance that all would be well, guilt that I have departed without insisting we take Sarah Frisch along for medical treatment. But it had all been too much for me, too suddenly. And now there is the sickening question of what lies ahead even when I give Flood all he wants. If I can give it to him without murder being done. The women will still be carted along to some unknown destination perhaps halfway around the world where the authorities might be more anxious to capture Flood and his men than to save the hostages. I have faced trials and terrors and crises before in my lifetime. Nothing in them has prepared me for this.

A beautiful morning. A golden sunshine, a scattering of clouds, a mild breeze stirring the greenery along the ridge. And my home on the crest of the ridge an armed stronghold, my family captives in it. Impossible to comprehend. Impossible to sort out the fear, anger, frustration in me.

I take a last look at the house before the car moves into the wooded area that lies between it and the commune half a mile away, and then we are in the woods, and the house is out of sight. I find myself, not weeping, but gasping for air in long, shuddering breaths, each breath a knife-thrust between the bruised ribs where I had been punished for my one feeble act of protest.

We are halfway through the woods when David brings the car to a halt. I hastily say, "I'm all right. Just get to the commune fast. We must let them know there's to be no visiting."

"Not yet," David says. "First a meeting."

"A meeting?"

"Sit loose, Friend. A minute in silence, and then a meeting for business."

"David, we don't have time for this!"

"We'll make time for it. Because what you intend to do, Marcus, must be held up to the Light."

So we enter silence, and I find myself desperately in prayer. I am not one for prayer, never have been since that time in my youth when I discovered that petitioning heaven for favors embarrassed me. Unlike my father, who worshipped a sort of divine tax examiner, I early settled, as Elias Hicks had done, for the belief that true divinity is wholly spirit and is manifest, in greater or lesser degree, in every human being.

Now here I am supplicating that spirit, feeling, as I do, the comforting I sometimes get from meetings for worship. I am grateful, too, that this man beside me sharing my crisis is a better Quaker than I am. Struck by calamity, I did not think of waiting on the Light for strengthening and guidance, but he did.

True, he was lately hardened in the crucible, while I might have grown brittle with time. He had given up a career in business to search for some meaning to his life among ashrams and communes and groups addicted to Zen practices, had been a community worker in New York, and had, through his acquaintance with Friends in those movements, been led to attend our meetings. Then, just before his marriage to Deborah, he had joined our meeting.

That was two years ago. I suddenly feel I know more

about my son-in-law now, have a deeper affection for him now, than in the whole two years of our sharing the same house.

It is David who breaks the silence. He says abruptly, "It can't be done Flood's way, Marcus. You were right when you told him there were too many people involved that way. You'll never be able to control them all. That means there will be killing before this is all over."

"I can try to control them. I don't have any choice."

"You have. Flood is ready for every contingency except one. That's the one to face him with."

I say in bewilderment, "An assault on the house? With the women in it?"

"I don't mean that. Matter of fact, I have the feeling Flood wants an assault on the house. He wants to prove to the world how tough he is. He's machismo gone crazy. But he's not so crazy he won't settle for the money and everything that goes with it, including the glory. Those are the alternatives he sees. But there's still another."

I am completely lost now. "I don't see what you're getting at."

"Simply that Flood's gang is not any squad of fanatics. They're not out to martyr themselves for any cause. They're not freaked out with the Kamikaze spirit. I think they would have settled on the spot for what you offered them, a lot of money and a chance to get away with it, but it was Flood blocked that. If they're faced with some heavy trouble they don't expect, they'll count that against Flood. I say we have to face them with that trouble."

"But any move we make against them—"

"Marcus, that's what I'm getting at. We don't make any move against them. Try to understand. Their weapon isn't really those guns piled up in there. Their weapon is communication. It's the ability to make the rest of the world know about those guns and react to them. They're practicing violence just by threatening it, and they expect a violent response to it. But if there is no such response, if we only stand in peace, not responding in any way—"

"While the women are in there with them?"

"Yes. Because the women are our hostages as well as theirs. Don't you think they know what'll happen if they kill one of those women? It'll blow their whole big deal. It'll wipe out any control you might have over the police. Flood can't risk that, with those men watching him and waiting for their money."

"There's a chance he might."

"There's a lot better chance of murder sooner or later if you try to do things his way. Marcus, listen to me. We can isolate that house. If we can get some help, we can completely cut off Flood from the outside. The police won't know what's going on up here. Nobody who might react the wrong way will know. Put yourself in Flood's place under those conditions. Nobody shows up at noon with the money, but nobody shows up to attack the house either. Nothing at all happens. Twelve o'clock, one o'clock, it just goes on like that with nothing happening. What do you do then if you're Flood?"

I try to make sense of this. "I don't know. I suppose I'd phone the bank to find out what's happening. Call the police, for that matter. I'd threaten to kill one of the women if my orders weren't followed."

"But the phone will be dead. You can't threaten anyone."

"Then I'd take one of the women with me, a gun at her head, and go out to see what's happening on the grounds. If there's no threat, I'd settle down and wait."

"But what you find on the grounds," David says, "is that this one road you can use for a getaway by car—still taking your hostages with you—is blocked by, let's say"—he points ahead—"by that tree which is down right across the road. And if you try the other direction, there's a tree across the road there before you get to the

Marcy sisters' place. Meanwhile, there are no police around to bother you, nobody to threaten you, nothing to worry about except that as loud as you yell, there's nobody listening. Now what do you do?"

What would I do? How would someone like Flood respond to any such situation? "I don't know."

"That's right," David says. "And Flood can't afford not to know. So far, he's made good on everything he must have promised his gang. But when they realize he's made a serious mistake, that he's gotten them into something he can't cope with, his authority over them ends."

"They'll take it out on the women, David. Certainly Flood might. You said yourself he's dangerously unstable."

"Granted. But do you think armed police moving up on the house will make him any more stable? He'll use those guns of his at any provocation. World War Three up on the ridge, he said. And the women in the middle of it. Do you really believe they'll be any safer that way?"

"I don't know. I still don't know. And there's the waiting. When does it end? How does it end?"

David slowly shakes his head. "That must be their decision to make. Only theirs. If we try to influence it in any way, show our presence so we can negotiate, then they've got their real weapon back. The open line of communication. The threats, the demands that can be sent over it. And we can't risk that. We'd have to stay out of range until they make their decision."

I say, "What if they take the women—just one of the women—and get away on foot?"

"They might try that. I don't think they'll use the road once they find it's blocked. For all they know, there could be an army right on the other side of those roadblocks. But there's the trail in back of the house down to the highway. Flood would know about it, wouldn't he?"

"Yes."

"If the pressure builds up enough, he might take a chance on it."

I say, "It wouldn't be hard for us to block that way out too. It's almost two miles to the highway through those woods."

"No. We don't block it. It stays open. When I was coordinating peace demonstrations, the one thing I tried to get across to the police was never to block every possible way out for our people. Pen a crowd up completely, and things could get ugly. Leave some way out, and there doesn't have to be any trouble. It worked, Marcus. It can work here too."

Is this beginning to make sense, or am I grasping at straws? I say, "What about the women? We'll be putting them through a brutal ordeal, David. They won't know what's going on any more than Flood will."

"They'll know before he does. Marcus, if they could hear us right now, what do you think they'd tell us to do?"

Emily. Deborah. Janet. What would they tell us to do? No.

What would they tell us *not* to do?

"All right," I say to David, "what's our first move?"

A world of sleepers at the commune. Under blankets or in sleeping bags, most are ranged along the porch, a few are on the lawn. As David and I get out of the car, two youngsters—boys of about seven or eight carrying crude fishing tackle—come through the screen door of the house and start toward the road. If they are headed for the commune's favorite fishing water, the pond on the other side of the meeting house, these children will be walking right past my home. Flood's armed fortress.

I call out to the boys, "Wait. Hold on," but mine is the voice of authority to them, and as McGrath has boasted more than once, the children here have been brought up to despise any authority, even when it makes sense. Now they only move faster to indicate that they hear me and are putting me in my place. Luckily David catches on at once. "Hell," he says in alarm, "they'll be going by the house," and sprints after them. He finally collars them both, and it is their squalling and struggling against his grip that rouses the sleepers.

A few only sit up to see what is going on, but some get to their feet and walk over to David, who is by main force hauling the boys back toward the building. "Hey, man," a young woman says angrily to David, "what is this?" and a tangle-haired, heavily bearded boy says, "Busting babies now, Dave? That is a real downer," but no one attempts to release the children from his grip.

"Nobody's busting any babies," David says. "Just get Ray out here. Right now."

The grim note in his voice makes it plain he is in deadly earnest. One of the men goes into the house, and a couple of minutes later Ray McGrath appears through the door. Lou Erlanger is not far behind him. Heavy-lidded, squinting against the sunlight, both of them take in the scene. McGrath says, "What's it about, Dave?"

"For one thing, it's about keeping these kids close to the house for a while. All the kids you've got around here."

"You know we don't do it that way," McGrath says.

"There's a reason. I'll tell it to you in private."

In private means a fair distance from the house, where the four of us gather in what had once been one of my late mother-in-law's cherished gardens but which is now only a weed patch. Here, David describes the situation down the road, and it amazes me that neither McGrath nor Erlanger displays any strong reaction to what they are hearing. They listen, and that is it. Erlanger remarks, "Like some of them out there won't let us find peace wherever we are, will they? Even in Utopia."

"Flies to the honey," McGrath says. "Buzzards to the money. Now how do they figure to handle that much cash? They'll need a freight car for it."

"No," I say. "It doesn't make that much of a load."

"Live and learn," McGrath says. "Well, I'm glad you told us about it before our kids go running around there. We've got this boy Mike Roos who's kind of a Pied Piper to them. He'll see they stay put until you give us the all-clear. And if you want to use the phone to call in the police now, not that I ever thought we'd be using it for calling in the fuzz—"

"We're asking for more than that, Ray," David says.

"A lot more. We don't want the police in on it. We want you in on it. All of you."

McGrath and Erlanger look puzzled. Erlanger says, "Being a posse is not our thing, Dave. You know that. You get ripped off by the black-hats with guns, you ask the lawmen with guns to even things up. Not our kind of people."

"That's it," David says. "We don't want any more guns in this. That means we can't let the police know about it. No confrontation at all."

Erlanger says doubtfully, "That also happens to mean you can't let anybody in the whole town know about it."

"Except you folks," David says. "And the Friends. We'll need them too."

I say to McGrath, "Be honest about it. Can you keep your people from spreading the word?" but it is Erlanger who says, "We'll have to tell them about keeping the kids close to home anyhow. Once they hear what it's all about, it's all for peaceable ends, they could go along with it. Like, keep it bottled up. They won't if anybody just orders them to do it."

"Well," McGrath says to me, "you heard him. You want to settle for that, it's all right with me."

I don't want to settle for it. I am depressed by the very look of these superannuated ragamuffins, by the blandness of their manner. To leave a crisis in their hands? I have the eerie feeling that five minutes after David and I are out of sight, they might forget the whole matter. If they would only react like human beings, show some emotion. Show a light in those vague eyes. But David seems to have all the faith I lack. "We'll settle for it," he says. "But it means involvement for you. A lot of it."

"How?" McGrath asks.

"We have to isolate Flood and his men in the house." David picks up a twig, squats down, sketches a crude map in the dirt. Ridge Road, my home midway along it, the commune to the south, the meeting house to the north, the Marcy sisters' place between the meeting house and my home. Winding down the ridge from the meeting house to town is Quaker Lane. From the Oates' house—the commune—to town is the twisting line of South Lane.

As the lines take form, I can appreciate how cannily Flood has chosen his victims. Not only had he absorbed from his father over the years much about the bank's operation, but in the military sense he's chosen an objective where he can settle in securely. The house stands on the highest point of the ridge. Any assaulting force leaving the concealment of the surrounding woodland can easily be detected. Long-range attack on the house is out of the question while the hostages are in it, which leaves only direct assault against the building across open ground. And worst of all, John Duffy, our chief of police, is exactly the sort of rigid, pompous, trigger-happy man who would welcome the chance to order such an assault. And Flood seems to be inviting it.

David slashes two marks across the map. He says, "Right here in these two places, between the commune and the house, and the Marcy place and the house, we have to cut the road off so they can't get away by car. If they're able to use a car, they'll pretty sure take the women along with them, and we don't want that. What we'll leave open for them, if they want to get away on foot, is the trail from in back of the house down to the highway."

"They can take the women that way too," Erlanger points out.

"I don't think they will. Marcus says Flood knows that trail, so he'd know what a tough climb it is, even downhill. Push him to where he just wants to get away fast, there's a good chance he won't slow himself down taking hostages along. Look at it from his angle. He'll be out there in the middle of the woods, not knowing who's around him behind all those trees, and that's no time to be dragging ass."

McGrath is getting interested. He studies the lines in the dirt. "How do you figure to block the road?"

"Trees," David says. "The kind it would take a block and tackle to move once they're down across the road. Would you know how to fell trees that size?"

McGrath shrugs. "I know how, but I'd sure hate to do it. These real big trees have been here a lot longer than we have."

"Is that all that worries you?" I demand. "The trees? Not the human lives involved?"

McGrath shrugs again. "How do we know this whole thing will work out? And if it doesn't, we're back where we started, except that there's a couple of great and beautiful trees gone which can't ever be put back again."

"How about cars?" Erlanger suggests. "We must have maybe ten, twelve of them around here. And that old school bus clunker parked in back. We could get it going enough to block this end of the road with it, and pull a couple of the cars around to block off the other end."

"Better than the trees," McGrath says.

"All right," David says, "cars will do fine. The other thing is to put the phones in the house out of commission."

"Easy," Erlanger says. "There's only one line along the whole ridge. We cut it, and the house is cut off."

David says, "Except that then the phone company would move in to find out what's wrong. Best way is to have the company itself cut off service to the house. Which also means cooking up some story you people will back up if anybody starts asking questions. I don't mean only the phone company. I mean everybody who isn't in on this."

"Well," Erlanger says, "how about letting it out that

you and the family just shut up the house and went on a trip?"

"That won't work," I say. "There's the bank to attend to. We've got too many friends who'd never believe we'd go off without notice. It's too implausible."

"An accident to somebody," McGrath says. "A bad one. You had some big doctors up from New York in the middle of the night, and they're on the job now. Working up to a brain operation maybe. Meanwhile, no phones working, no visitors, no anything."

"Well—" David says. He doesn't seem any more satisfied with this than I am, but like me, he can't seem to come up with anything better.

"All right, then," McGrath says. "Now who'd the accident happen to? Emily?"

I say, "If it were Emily, I wouldn't be at the bank, but Janet would be there taking over for me. It's happened before when Emily was very sick. So it should be Janet. It'll explain why she isn't at the bank. But what about the meeting? The Friends will want to close around us. Do we tell them this same story?"

"No," David says. "When Anna and Elizabeth find the phone is out, they'll certainly walk over to the house, and they'll find the road blocked too. They'll have to know the truth then. And if we tell them the truth, do we separate them from the rest of the meeting?"

No, we don't. And yet we must have the meeting close around us. Uri Shapiro, who runs The Mart, and Kenneth Quimby, who owns a boatyard on the lake, deal with a great many people in town, and whatever story they circulate will be believed. As true about Ethel Quimby, who has a wide circle of acquaintance, and Anna and Elizabeth Marcy, who spend so much of their time on the phone. But one of the earliest titles for the Friends was the Publishers of Truth, and more than a few had been jailed and hanged for publishing it. Am I now to make my meeting the publishers of an elaborate lie?

David reads my thoughts. "What bothers you? That the Friends have to be involved in this kind of deception? It won't work otherwise, Marcus."

"Maybe it will have to, David. I don't see how I can impose this on the meeting."

McGrath looks me over curiously. Then he says, "You imposed it on us. It's kind of a rip-off being told we don't rate up there with the Friends in the purity department."

I think—I am almost sure—he means it in a joking vein, although God knows this is no time for jokes. But there is too much painful truth in it to be funny. Too much painful self-enlightenment offered me by it. And all this piled on the stomach-churning awareness that so many lives are right now dependent for their safety on a hair-splitting, panicky reed named Marcus Hayworth.

I say to McGrath, "I'm sorry. I know what you mean, and you're right. If you—"

"Man," he cuts in, "you don't know what I mean. I'm putting you on. I think what you're doing is beautiful."

Beautiful?

Of all the words to describe a course where the hoped-for end must justify a hateful means, that is the last one I would choose.

The phone is in·the inside vestibule of the house, and while I am on it Erlanger goes through the building advising the commune's members of a meeting on the porch. Curiosity is not one of these people's vices. They move by me to the porch without seeming to take any notice of me at all.

My bad luck it is Anna Marcy, the more argumentative of the two sisters, who answers the phone. When I tell her I have a critical concern I must share with the meeting at once and ask if it is all right to gather in her home, she says, "Yes. But I don't like the sound of this, Marcus. A called meeting so early in the morning? It is only ten minutes after seven now. And on such short notice? What is the concern?"

"I can't explain it now, Anna. I'll tell you at the meeting."

"Is someone hurt? Is it Emily or one of the girls? Let me speak to Emily."

"You can't speak to her right now." And then, before she can continue this maddening inquisition, I burst out, "Don't be a stubborn old fool, Anna Marcy. Don't ask questions. Don't, whatever you do, call my home. Just you and Elizabeth wait prayerfully, and we'll all be there very soon."

I hang up on that, instantly sorry that I spoke in this tone and apprehensive that Anna will take it into her willful head to phone my house anyhow. It goes better with Uri Shapiro. Roused from sleep by my call, he comes wide awake at my words and simply asks, "Is it very bad, Marcus?" "Very bad," I say, and he says, "All right, I'll be there right away."

Ethel Quimby is as mercifully brief, then pulls me up short by adding, "But I'll have to bring the kids. That's okay, isn't it?"

It isn't. Three of them, all little pitchers with big ears, all used to being among us even at meetings for business, where, no matter how rambunctious they occasionally are, they have things much their own way. They would not only be completely out of place among us now, but extremely dangerous. Back in town, what would stop them from letting slip to any outsider whatever they pick up at the meeting?

As subtly as I can, I try to suggest this to Ethel, and she says, "Well, it's too early to get someone to baby-sit. Ken will just have to go without me."

"No. I want you both there."

"Marcus, you're scaring me, the way you sound. Look, don't worry about the kids. We'll be there without them as fast as we can make it."

When I put down the phone, David at my shoulder says, "All right?" and I answer, "Yes. So far."

So far.

We go out to the porch, where the gathering seems to have resolved the question before it. McGrath says to us, "Some don't want any part of it, but they'll keep buttoned up about it. The rest of us will do what we can to help. Mike Roos there"—he points to a young man, not bearded but with long hair down his back in a pigtail—"doesn't think he can keep the kids tied down to the house all day, so he'll take them to the lake for a picnic or something."

Mike Roos, I remember, is the one the commune designated as its schoolmaster, the one for whom they had applied for some meeting funds so that he can get in his required college courses. I say to him, "I'm grateful to you for your help. You know, the money that's needed for you—" and he abruptly, almost angrily, cuts me off by saying, "Fuck the money. You want to pay for this, I'd just as soon not go along with it."

"Cool it, man," McGrath tells him, and then says to me, "We can talk about all that later. Meanwhile, you know what it means once those roadblocks are set up. No more getting from here to the meeting house by Ridge Road. You'll have to go a long ways roundabout through town and up Quaker Lane. That turns two miles into maybe five or six. So if you want to stay in touch here, make sure you've got somebody standing by the phone in the meeting house."

"The Marcy house," I say.

"Anna and Elizabeth in on this too?" Erlanger asks.

"They will be. We're meeting over there right away."

Erlanger says doubtfully, "A couple of old people like that, I don't know. Best thing would be to get them away from here altogether."

"You don't know that couple of old people," David says.

"They wouldn't leave even if we wanted them to," I tell Erlanger. "As for our keeping in touch with each other, there's one thing more I'd like you people to do. Try to keep watch on the house from the woods without being seen. And on the trail in back of the house. After David and I get things settled with the meeting, we can take care of that ourselves."

"No sweat," McGrath says. "Some of our women use the woods for mushrooms and salad stuff. They know their way around the whole ridge. They'll take care of it."

"But always out of sight," David warns. "They have to keep under cover no matter what. We all do."

Erlanger says, "Even so, Flood must be smart enough to figure somebody's most likely keeping an eye on him."

"But we don't give him evidence of it," David says. "That's the name of the game. He has to be totally isolated until the structure of the gang breaks down."

"And how long will that take?" Mike Roos asks caustically. "Man, you are dealing with hard cases. And they are fixed up with food and probably pot and pills and, for a sure thing, women. And the longer they hold out, the meaner they'll get."

"I don't understand," I say. "I thought you were with us."

"Sure. But you have to set some kind of time limit. Daytime might be all right. Nighttime, when I bring the kids back here, that gang could come walking right in on us out of the dark, and then what happens? You talk about them not communicating with the outside. But sooner or later they'll have to communicate, and we've got a phone here, and our cars handy for them, and, man, we are just wide open for disaster. So I say you have to set a time limit when you start communicating with them and leave us out of it."

I look at David. "He's right about that."

David shakes his head. "I don't believe they'll try walking along the road past any roadblock, and that's the only way they can get here."

"But you can't be sure," Roos argues. "And what happens if this thing keeps up tomorrow? You really think you can stand up under that much pressure yourselves? Like wondering just how pissed off Flood is about being all fouled up, and how much he'll take it out on the women?"

"Shit, man," McGrath says. "That kind of talk doesn't help any."

"Because I am telling it like it is. All right, it's worth a try. But taking a chance our kids wind up hostages too, and doing G.I. reconnaissance with guns aimed at you out of a window—this is heavy involvement, man. I don't like the fuzz any more than anybody here. Especially I don't like Mister Tight-ass Police Chief Duffy and the way he runs this tight-ass town. But I say comes the moment of truth, and it's his business to put down Flood."

"There's time for that," David says.

"You'll be surprised how fast time can go," Roos says.

This is what I take away with me when David and I get into the station wagon and head down the road toward town. The echo of those words, and the lip-curling delivery of them.

136

When we pull up to the bank Herb Hill, the manager, is at the door, the night watchman opening it for him. Mondays, when the armored trucks make their early deliveries, I am always at the bank eight o'clock on the dot, and Hill is always there ahead of me. Now he raises his eyebrows to indicate surprise that I am fifteen minutes ahead of this rigid schedule, but says nothing as David and I follow him into the building.

He's an old-timer, Hill, has worked his way up from teller, a competent and reliable man, but a little too affable for my comfort, a little too much the back-slapper of the favored customer for my taste, though it seems to go down well with the customer. However, we have worked side by side for almost thirty years, so I must brace myself to get it out. "You'll have to take over for both Janet and me today, Herb. Neither of us will be here."

"Just like that? Something wrong at home? You look like it, Marcus."

"I suppose I do. Janet's been hurt. An accident. Very serious."

"That's terrible. In the car?"

"No, a fall downstairs. We managed to get doctors up from New York in the middle of the night. Possible brain damage, they say, and they can't even risk moving her."

"My God, Marcus, if there's anything I can do—"

"What you can do, Herb, is check my desk calendar. Postpone or cancel any of my appointments you can't handle personally. The same for Janet. Above all, make it clear to everybody that there's to be no phone calls to the house, nobody visiting."

"No phone calls. No visiting."

"None," David says. "Matter of fact, we're having the phone service to the house discontinued for the time being."

"You can have your calls transferred here," Hill says. "I can take them, at least during bank hours. And stand by here after that if it's necessary."

"No," I say, "better to just have the service cut off. Will you get the phone company on that right away, Herb?"

"Can do." Hill frowns at a bothersome thought. "I suppose Doc Jeffries is up there, isn't he? How does his office reach him, once the phone service is out?"

Orin Jeffries. Our family doctor. Who of course would be up there in such a case. It is David who saves the situation while I flounder speechlessly. He quickly says, "We didn't call in Jeffries, Herb. He's strictly country style, and this is neurosurgical stuff. Way beyond him, the operation and all."

"Oh, sure," Hill says. "Of course. Well, just leave everything to me. I'll get hold of the phone company right now."

I am sick with tension leaving the building. Outside, I say to David, "If this gets back to Orin Jeffries—"

"It will. Meanwhile, get it out of your head. One problem at a time is enough."

Sometimes too much.

James Flood

No problem about the command post; it is wherever I am. The observation post is something else.

I issue Lester one of the automatic guns and Coco's binoculars and lead him up to the attic, where it still looks like no Hayworth ever got rid of a piece of junk from the time the first one grabbed this land and built the house on it. The ladder to the roof is in the middle of the attic. I go up, shove open the hatch, and climb out onto the roof. Nothing has changed. I am on the same old sun deck with the low railing around where I used to hide out when the family got too much on my neck. Lester squeezes through the hatch to join me. From where we stand we have a view all around the building: garage, stables, springhouse, lawns and gardens, and beyond them, the deep Adirondack woods. Ridge Road in front of the house emerges from the woods on one side, disappears into them on the other.

Lester gauges the distance to the road. "Runs from about two hundred yards in front to maybe eight hundred at the ends," he says. "Rather have one of the M-fourteens up here for that distance."

I say, "Not if they come in bunches like bananas. First job is to pin them down. You can do it a lot better with the spray gun."

In the opposite direction is the long slope down to the highway, and from here the trees on it look impenetrable. Lester says, "Not much chance of them coming from that side, I figure."

"Not too much. But there's a trail from Highway Nine up to the back of those gardens. Anybody willing to haul himself up can get you in his sights from right there."

"You, too, when it's your turn up here."

"Sure. We'll all be taking turns up here. Nobody's trying to dump any extra load on you. All I'm saying is that you have to cover the back of the house as well as the road. You see anybody except Hayworth, just give him a burst at his feet, then get down the hatch."

"One hour," Lester says. "Nobody shows up to take over, I'm still coming down in one hour."

"One hour," I agree. "The ladies'll have breakfast waiting for you."

I take a good look at the trail-head beyond the gardens before I start down the ladder. After that bedtime session with Janet ten years ago, after my sixteen-year-old ineptitude was laid on the line for her the way she wanted it to be, I had to do something about it. No .22 rifle for this, the way it had been for the garbage man. Nothing that obvious. But something that might hurt as bad as a .22 short without anybody even knowing who or why.

The last time I had been up here was while I was laying shingles to replace the ones wrecked by a heavy winter. I had watched from here as Janet disappeared through the bushes concealing the trail, a beach bag in her hand. Three times within the week. Someone waiting along the way down the slope to service her. Obviously someone considerably better at it than I was.

One day, when she was away from the house on a shopping trip, I checked out the trail. A rough walk, steeply downhill, over a mat of pulpy, slippery dead leaves which concealed razor-edged rocks and twisting tree roots. A hundred yards down the slope I found what had to be Janet's lair. Off the trail, water trickled between rocks and curled over a five-and-dime little waterfall. The grass was matted here, some cigarette butts showing in it.

The next time Janet hit the trail, beach bag in hand, I was ready. I gave her a long head start, and then, camera in hand—it wasn't much of a camera, but it was a camera—I followed along. Get a few pictures of her having a blanket party with some man, and she would be one sad girl. I moved down the trail as silently as an Indian after wary game, then cut into the woods and worked my way down toward the waterfall between the trees. When I was about twenty feet away from it I saw Janet, not with a man, but almost as good, without any clothes on. She had slipped out of her jeans, shirt, and sandals, and was stretched out on a blanket reading. I sighted the camera on her, squeezed the shutter, then either that click of the shutter or a flash of sunlight on the lens caught her attention. Suddenly she sat up and shouted, "Hey!"

I was frozen there. I could have run, but even in my panic I realized that unless I just kept running right out of town, there was no sense to that. And Janet herself didn't show any signs of panic. Taking her time about it, she got into her shirt and jeans and made her way up the slope toward me. She took the camera from my hand. "What's this about?" she said. "Nature study?"

"I just like to take pictures," I said. "Nature, water-falls, anything. Honest to God, if I knew you were here like that, I wouldn't have even come down this way."

"I'll bet," Janet said. "You know, you may not believe this, Jimmy boy, but if I thought that picture you just took was for your private album, I wouldn't even mind. After all, you can't say we're complete strangers, can you? But since it's likely to wind up with a bunch of kids in town having a good time over it—" She opened the camera, pulled out the spool of film, and shoved it into her pocket. She handed me back the camera. "I owe you for that roll of film," she said.

That was it. She owed me for it, but she never did pay me for it.

Not yet.

Now here she is in this kitchen, she and her mother and sister moving like three ghosts between stove and sink and table, laying out breakfast for Coco and Harvey. It's the first time I've ever seen Janet when she doesn't give the impression she's in charge of whatever is going on. She figures to be twenty-eight, but with those bleary eyes, and swollen lip, and stringy wet hair, she would never pass for it. She looks like someone in the final stages of something fatal.

Before I can sit down at the table, Emily says to me, "Jimmy, don't be angry. But something must be done about Sarah Frisch. I think she's badly hurt."

"She'll get over it."

"Please, Jimmy. You're getting everything you want. Don't be cruel about it."

I go into the bedroom with her. The old lady must have flooded the bed, because the room stinks of piss. She has her eyes open now, and they shift back and forth between Emily and me as if trying to figure out who the hell we are. Those beady little eyes moving around like that and those toothless skinny jaws make her look like a worried turtle.

I say to Emily, "You can see there's no bleeding. It's just concussion. She'll be all right."

"Would you mind if I untied her? And cleaned her and the bed?"

"I'd mind if you untied her. I don't want her rambling around here getting in everybody's way. If you want her cleaned up, tell Janet to do it."

"I'm perfectly willing to do it."

"If you want it done, Janet will do it."

So Janet does the dirty work while I watch from the doorway, the stink not improving my appetite for breakfast any. When it's all done, right down to getting rid of the wet linens, and the old lady is stretched out on the bed again, mumbling to herself, Janet says to me, "Is it all right if I feed her?"

"Your mother can take care of that. You feed me."

No protest. Janet takes over as short-order cook and waitress for me while Emily handles the nursing department and Deborah does pan-scraping and racks the dishes in the dishwasher. After breakfast I line up the women in a neat row against the wall and say to them, "You know the rules by now. Anybody gets out of line, somebody else gets hurt for it. I mean, hurt very fast and very painfully. The kitchen and the old lady's room and her toilet are your territory, and there's never to be any doors closed here, including the toilet door. Get it straight that is a capital crime. Harve here will be in charge of barracks to start with, and he's the one who judges how the rules are being kept."

"The telephone," Coco reminds me.

"That's right," I tell the women. "Any time the phone rings, none of you answers it until I'm standing there next to her. Then you answer it nice and friendly and let me know who it is. Then we play it by ear. Otherwise, you never go near any phone in the house."

"You see," Coco says to them, "we want everything clear so there will be no mistakes. This is a dangerous time for all concerned, so there must be no mistakes.

Once the money is delivered, and we are all on the plane, it will be inconvenient for you, but no more than that. Until then, remember the word danger."

"End of sermon," I say. "Any questions?"

"Yes," Emily says. "Can't we at least get dressed instead of going around like this?"

"As long as your bedroom doors are kept open," I say. "Harve will keep an eye on yours, the reverend will supervise Deborah. You feel an attack of modesty coming on, you can use your closets."

"What about Janet?" Emily asks.

"She'll get her turn when you and Deborah are back down here."

I can see Janet's ever-loving mamma doesn't like that, but there is nothing she can do about it. When Janet and I are alone in the kitchen I say to her, "Sit down," and she drops into a chair, not seeming to care much how her robe gapes open. Deborah has developed into juicy all-female over the years. Janet, from what I can see, is just where I had left her. I say to her, "Now why do I think that right about this time, every day, you need a handful of pep pills to break the spell?"

"Because you're such a smart boy, Flood."

"I am. And what makes the spell every night? Nembutal?"

"Seconal."

"And for the ups at sunrise?"

"Crystals."

"Got a crock of them tucked away in your room?"

"Enough."

"Want a handful now?"

It sticks in her throat but she finally gets it out. "Yes."

"Well—" I pretend to think it over. "No, better to have you down and dopey than up and sharp. You seem a lot more reasonable this way. A lot more Quakerly."

She takes a deep breath. "You always were a freaked-out little bastard, Flood."

"How about you, doll? Still going down to the high school to pick cherries?"

Janet studies my face. She says unbelievingly, "Is that what's on your mind? That I destroyed your precious innocence? Come off it, Flood."

I say, "What was it all about that day? Why me? Wasn't it because you found you were going butch and started to panic about it? And I was the easiest way to find out how far you were gone?"

"Oh, listen to Dr. Freud. You mean it never entered your mind that you were the first time for me too, Flood? That I might just have gotten fed up wondering what it was all about?"

"So you picked a kid?"

"You weren't that much of a kid."

"I was a kid. And you picked me because any grown man that got near you smelled dyke."

"You're wrong. You're wrong. You are wrong." Janet takes on a puzzled look. "But if I thought—"

"Yes?"

"—if I thought that this whole crazy business—getting these men in here, terrifying everybody, robbing my father—if I really thought it was to rip me off for some imaginary wrong I did you—"

"Now you're the one getting Freudian, doll. That's all right. I hear all dykes are strung out on Freud."

"—if I thought that was behind all this, it would be a killer, Flood. My own personal low."

"Don't let it be. Just take a good look in that glass, doll. It'll tell you to avoid such ego trips."

That shuts her up.

148

Both the other women are in jeans and shirts when Coco and Harvey bring them back to the kitchen. "All right," I say to Janet, "your turn."

She stands up, clutching her robe to her at the neck—what she hadn't minded my seeing, she obviously doesn't approve of her mother and sister seeing—but Coco says to me, "Hold it, man. I want to show you something first."

I follow him down the hallway past the dining room and into the living room. With its shuttered windows, it's hard to see anything in it. Coco switches on the lights, and I look around. "Show me what?"

"That was just an excuse, man. What we are here for is a little private confabulation." There are a pair of armchairs facing each other in front of the fireplace. Coco points at them. "Sit down and listen close."

I sit down and he stretches out in the other chair. He slides his gun from his belt and dangles it by his middle finger through the trigger guard. "Quick-draw McGraw?" I say.

Coco says, "Remember, man, I was at those group shit-tossing sessions in Raiford when your little mental quirks—you know what I mean?—got analyzed by that nice doctor. Blackouts—right?—where you are not responsible for what you do. But sometimes I wonder about those blackouts. Maybe yes, maybe no. If they are the genuine thing, why were you not just put away in a psycho ward?" He spins the gun once around his finger, then levels it at me. "Either way, try not to have one of those fits now because of what I am going to tell you."

"What the hell are you talking about?"

"I am talking about phase two. I don't like the way it is being handled."

"You said the same about phase one, but it worked out fine. Phase two is working out just as fine."

"I will argue that. For example, you put me down in front of those women. With a gun. Let me remind you, Mr. Flood, that I am a partner in the Company, not a field hand on your plantation."

"All right, I'm sorry I hurt your fucking black feelings. If that's your complaint—"

"There is a more serious complaint. Your action showed you do not appreciate that I am right now the one indispensable man. Because all the loot we collect will be only bags of scrap paper if phase three is not attended to properly. And I am phase three."

"We're not there yet."

"We are moving close to it. And you can screw it up very handsomely if you keep to that collision course you are now on."

"Collision course with you, Coco baby?"

"Not me. That girl. That Janet. She is under your skin, man. She gives you the itch. I don't know why, because a scarecrow like that could not turn me on, but I think you are trying to move in on her. Can you tell me that when you take her upstairs now, you will not ask her to open up for you?"

"I can tell it to you. Would you believe it?"

"No. What I believe is that when you tell her to lay

down and give, she might try to fight it out, and then she could get hurt. Or worse."

"Killed?"

"Yes."

I laugh. "You seem to be picking up where that shrink in Raiford left off."

Coco says coldly, "It is no laughing matter. Already you took out that old Sarah so hard, it's lucky she is not dead. Phase three depends on bringing the hostages into St. Hilary in sound shape. Certainly none of them must be lost in action along the way. Otherwise, there is no phase three."

"Explain that. So far all you've let out about St. Hilary is that everything's under control there. I'm starting to wonder just how much under control."

"No need to wonder, Mr. Flood. And no need to go into details until the time comes. That is the safest way."

"Not for you." I stand up, draw my gun and aim it right between his eyes. And I don't just let my thumb rest on the hammer as he is doing, I cock the hammer. He doesn't follow suit. He sits there, his gun wavering a little in his hand. "Jimmy, don't be a fool."

I say, "Put that thing away, Hubert. Or do I call in Harvey and Lester and have them put it away for you? Permanently."

"You think Harvey and Lester are that much sold on you, man?"

"I think so. Now put that thing away."

He takes his face-saving time working the gun back into his belt. It's so easy, I feel a little disappointed. I say, "Now what about those St. Hilary details?"

He looks almost cross-eyed at the muzzle of the gun now centered on the bridge of his nose from a foot away. "I do not function at my best under these conditions, Jimmy."

I put a finger between the hammer and the firing pin and let the hammer ease into the safety position. But I still keep the gun on him. "Better?" I ask.

"Somewhat."

"And those details?"

"But no names."

"Names too. That's so you won't be too indispensable, Hubert." I start to draw back the hammer again, but Coco holds up a hand. "Worthington and Moore," he says. "That's the names."

"Who are they? Our reception committee when we land there?"

"Yes. Worthington is Minister of Justice. Moore is Commissioner of National Police. It will not be just another police case however, because we are coming in as politicals."

"How do we do that?"

"You have the Weatherman record. I was Black Union in London. That will get a heavy play."

"And Harvey and Lester?"

"Victims of the Mafia. They tried to expose the Mafia in Miami and were railroaded into jail for it. So they joined us in our political struggle."

I say, "Do you mean your St. Hilary buddies, this Worthington and Moore, will really buy this crock?"

"Officially and publicly, yes. It's a good deal for them, Jimmy. We land there, the plane is surrounded by security people, Worthington and Moore bravely come aboard—"

"Risking their lives."

"Naturally. They come aboard with all the TV and newspaper people watching, and they palaver with us in private. The whole world holds its breath. Will we kill these brave envoys, will we kill the hostages, will we blow up the plane? Then Worthington and Moore step out of the plane as heroes. They have negotiated the release of the hostages, and they have granted us temporary refuge. We are politicals. A new movement in a wrong-headed but justifiable struggle against the oppressors. We are locked up overnight, sent on our way by chartered plane next day. The hostages are returned safely to the loving arms of their family. Worthington thinks he can make it as next Prime Minister on the basis of this alone."

I say, "But this pair of black angels isn't working for us just so one of them can get to be Prime Minister of that sandpile. Right?"

"Right."

"All right, what's the payoff? How much of the money do they get?"

"Half of it."

I say, "Two million!" and Coco quickly holds up a hand again. He says, "Put away that weapon, man. We can talk like civilized people about this. Do not forget we are civilized people. We are not hoodlums."

I press the gun into his forehead, forcing his head back against the chair. The click, when I cock the hammer, convulses him. He grips the arms of the chair, his fingers spread wide and straining. If his muscles tighten one more notch, he'll disintegrate like shattered glass. I say, "We've got a beautiful partnership going, don't we? The Shanklins get us the guns and the car, I get us the money, and you give half of it away."

He whispers, "Jimmy, that is the price. Man, did you really think it would be some kind of cut-rate deal?"

"You told me in Raiford it could be. But maybe I'll go as high as a million now. Your million, baby. And you'll never miss it."

"Don't talk like that, Jimmy. Man, you wipe me out, you will never see any of that money again. They will ship two million back here and say that's all they found on us. And they will set it up so you and Harvey and

Lester are cut down trying to escape. I'm the only one who can handle it. That is part of my understanding with them."

I think that over, watching the beads of sweat come up on Coco's face. He says, "It doesn't have to come out of your share, Jimmy. Or mine. Take that gun away, and we can talk about it."

I back away from him a little, still holding my sights on his forehead. "Talk," I say.

He sits there drawing in long breaths, getting his wind back. Finally he says, "I believe it when you say Hayworth cannot keep the law out of this. And they will use guns. That means we need Harvey and Lester to make sure there's a stand-off until the police come to terms with us."

"So far, all I hear is a playback. What's new on the tape?"

"This, Jimmy. Once the police come to terms with us, what can Harvey and Lester offer the Company? So let us suppose that once the money is delivered here, and the police agree to cooperate, you tell Harvey and Lester in confidence that it's all right for them to have a little fun with the two girls. Take them upstairs and get some action before the party is over. Then, before any damage can be done, we walk in and wipe out Harvey and Lester. These two lustful animals broke the Company's rules, we saved the women from them, we come on all saintliness. And the women themselves are our witnesses. Do you see how it works out?"

"I do, Hubert baby. Suppose I get together with Harvey and Lester right now and tell them about your little plan for them? Do you see how that would work out?"

"Remember I am phase three, Jimmy. Anyhow, it was wrong from the start for those two to get a million each when they operate together as one member of the

Company. They are taking advantage of us that way."

I say, "Hit me but don't shit me, Coco," but now I really have something to think over, and he has sense enough not to cut into my thoughts. Finally I say, "If we're political, we need a name."

"What do you mean?"

"I mean that when we land in St. Hilary we want a name to hand your friends there. Something the papers and TV will buy. The July Group. How does that sound?"

"The July Group," Coco says. "It has a nice ring to it, man. But what I want your opinion on is, how many of us do you estimate will be landing at St. Hilary?"

He looks at me, the old blacksnake, and I look at him. I say, "The July Group happens to be a very moral organization, Hubert. Those who violate its code by raping helpless females are not entitled to be on that plane, are they?"

Coco gives me his genuine pearly-toothed smile. "No way," he says.

The women are making breakfast for themselves when we get back to the kitchen, Harvey, his chair propped against the wall under the phone, keeping an eye on them. Especially, I take note, on Deborah, who is something to keep an eye on.

I say to Janet, "Dressing-up time, miss," and she hesitates, gauging me. But when I say, "It's up to you. I'm not bringing your medicine down here," she evidently makes up her mind that there are some fates worse than J. Flood.

In her bedroom, she takes a key from a dresser drawer and unlocks the big Chinese-style lacquered box on top of the dresser. There is enough stuff in that box to stock a drugstore.

She spills four meths into her hand, but I pluck two of them out and shove them back into the bottle. "We're not aiming for a real high, doll," I tell her. "Just enough to keep the motor turning over."

She starts to protest, thinks better of it, and pops the pills just like that. One expert gulp and down they go. I lock the bottle away and put the key in my pocket. "If you're a good girl," I say, "there might be more later."

"And what's your idea of a good girl, Flood?" She pulls

open the cord of her robe and drops down resignedly on the edge of the bed. "This?"

"No."

"I see. Only on demand. Whenever the master is ready."

I say, "Those pills couldn't have turned you on yet, so I don't know where the hell you're getting your ideas."

She looks bewildered, then takes on a wise expression. "I gather you and your pretty boys have something going with each other, is that it?"

I control the temptation to let her have one across the face. I say, "If you want to ball right now, bitch, we'll do it. But you'll have to ask for it, just the way you did last time."

"Not me, Flood. Not with you. In fact, the thought of it turns my stomach." She stands up, shrugs off the robe, and gets into panties and jeans, no bra. No bra needed. She takes a shirt from the dresser and puts it on. "All business, aren't you, Flood? But where does the business wind up? I mean, where's the last stop on the plane? Cuba? Somewhere in the Sahara?"

"You'll find out when you get off the plane."

"I'll tell you what you'll find when you get off that plane, Flood. A lot of men in uniforms, and a long-term sublet in a dirty little jail. You're not under the Cuban flag or Arab flag or any other flag some people like to wrap themselves in so they can get away with murder. You're under the skull and crossbones, man, and nobody is buying that wherever you land. So that makes you pretty much a damn fool, doesn't it, when you could have had the money my father offered you and at least a chance to spend some of it before you were put away. Suppose I told you, you had another chance right now to reconsider that offer?"

I say, "Did you ever hear of the July Group?"

157

"No."

"Now you did. That, baby, is what this is all about."

She starts pulling a comb through her hair in front of the dresser mirror, looking at my reflection in the mirror. She says, "Well, this is July, all right, and you and your strong-arm men are a group. I don't see anything more than that."

"Because this is our first big move. With your daddy's assets, we'll be ready to kick the props from under the whole sick, corrupt system. It's coming apart anyhow. All it needs is some people really willing to knock the rest of it down."

"You, *mein Führer?*"

"The July Group, doll. No Cuban flag, no Arab flag, just the American flag upside down."

She looks at me a long time in the mirror. Then she says, "Is it all right, *Führer,* if I wash up and pee?"

"With the door open, *liebchen.* You know the rules."

So she washes up and pees, never seeming to mind in any way that I'm on observation duty at the open door to her bathroom.

Cool. Nobody could play it more cool. And then I realize that this skinny, pill-popping, castrating bitch with the banged-up lip is actually getting to me.

No more of that, Jimmy boy.

158

Marcus
Hayworth

?

When David and I drive up to the Marcy house Uri Shapiro's car is already parked there, and it's Uri who opens the door of the house to let us in. Anna and Elizabeth are in the hallway behind him. Uri looks inquiringly over my shoulder and says, "Where are Emily and the girls? What is this about, Marcus? We're all very worried."

"Emily and the girls are home. They're all right. There's nothing to worry about yet."

"Yet?" Anna says. "And thee looks very worried yourself, Marcus. Thee looks downright sick."

David says, "If we wait to talk about it until the Quimbys are here, we won't have to repeat everything. Meanwhile, if there's coffee—"

There's a strong smell of coffee in the air, and it reminds me that I've had no breakfast and that perhaps some of the sickness I feel is simply hunger. Hunger, at a time like this. But the fact is that when David and I have coffee and toast at the kitchen table, I know that I, at least, feel a little better. Feel a little courage rise in me.

While we are at the last of the coffee, the Quimbys come in and Ethel says to me, "We left the kids with the work crew at the boatyard, so we should have an hour before one of them falls in the water or gets into the machinery or something. What's this all about, Marcus?"

"Not here, Friends," Anna says. "In the parlor."

The parlor has already been set up for a meeting, the precious satinwood desk hauled out before the fireplace, straight-backed chairs arranged in a semicircle before it, although, painfully, three of those chairs must remain empty on this occasion. David, this year's clerk of the meeting, takes his place at the desk. "We will open in silence," he says, and I, wound up so tight, and knowing all the others are too, expect the briefest of silences. Then I become aware that David is deliberately extending it on and on until the spirit of anxiety and impatience in the air is tempered by this calm enforced on us.

At last David says, "This started with a young man, Jimmy Flood, who I believe you all remember," and then he describes events from Flood's arrival yesterday to our reason for gathering the meeting now. All take it wordlessly, but with the shock naked on their faces.

Anna says, "I am not sure thee has found the wisest course, David. I don't see how we can keep this from the town very long. And the more we delay, the worse it will be for Emily and the girls. And surely for Sarah Frisch, who thee says is badly hurt."

David says, "Flood has made it plain that no one but Marcus is to get near the house. That would include doctors. Even if you could persuade any doctor to go walking in there."

Anna says, "James Flood knows me well. He would not be alarmed if I walked in there. If I did that and offered myself in Sarah Frisch's place, she could be taken away and attended to."

Elizabeth says, "Not thee alone, Anna. He knows all of us. He knows of our tenderness to him. We should all go together to the house and hold him in the Light," but Ethel Quimby says tartly, "Elizabeth, I happen to have three kids waiting for me to show up very soon. And I

162

don't think Jimmy Flood will let himself be held up in the Light right now. This is a very sick man."

"Indeed?" says Anna. "Was he that well in the mind, Ethel Quimby, when he was in college and thee upheld his acts of violence there?"

"Please," David says. "Anna. Elizabeth. Please understand that what you're proposing leads nowhere. The one possible way of preventing murder is to isolate Flood and his gang. To put them in a vacuum. To break their nerve this way."

"I'm sorry," Uri says, "but I can't agree. And I know all about our police chief here and how tough he is, but he's the one to handle this, David. He's trained for it. If you and Marcus explain the situation to him, explain our hopes that he could approach the problem without violence—"

"Did you ever hear Duffy on the subject of crime and the only way to handle it?" David demands. "Can you see him waving a white flag and inviting Flood to negotiate with him? And the police in Boston have to be considered too. And the police wherever Flood wants the plane put down."

"I understand all this," Uri says. "But reason can prevail, can't it, with those women's lives at stake?"

"Not enough to make the police put away their guns, Uri. And Flood is just waiting there for the cops to show up so he can blast their heads off. Believe me, I love my wife very much. If I didn't think she'd understand and agree with what I'm trying to do, I wouldn't do it."

"But will she understand?" Uri asks. "Will Emily and Janet? They're depending on Marcus to settle this quickly. All they'll know is that nothing is being settled. And when Flood and his men get angry about it, the women will be the ones to suffer." He turns to me. "Can't you see this, Marcus?"

I say, "I've come to David's point of view. If Flood

can't communicate his threats to anyone outside, he has no reason to carry them out."

Uri says sharply, "These men are criminals. If they get in a bad mood, they're capable of anything, whether you know about it or not."

I shake my head. "I don't accept that."

"Because you don't want to." Uri turns to Kenneth Quimby. "Kenneth, if Flood took over your house like this, put guns to your family's head, what would you do?"

Kenneth sits without speaking a long while. Then he says, "I don't know. I think—I'm not sure—but I think I'd like the courage to do what Marcus and David are doing. To bear witness to what I believe. To what I say I believe."

"But at whose cost?" Uri demands.

"Yes, I know what you mean. But of all the things that led Ethel and me to become Friends, I think it was the peace testimony that meant most to us. 'We utterly deny all outward wars and strife and fighting with outward weapons, for any end, or under any pretense whatever.' I can give you that whole letter word for word, I know it so well. And I've wondered what I would do if I faced a situation where my family was threatened. Whether or not I'd kill for their sake. Whether I'd find myself making exceptions to that testimony. I still don't know. Who can ever tell what he'll do until he's put to the test? All I know now, Uri, is that I agree with Marcus and David."

Uri shakes his head. "You have no right to make them your testing ground."

Ethel says to him, "Uri, you don't have a family. I say that in love, because we know what happened to them in Germany."

"Thanks to Hitler," Uri says. "A Jimmy Flood who really made it big."

"Yes," Ethel says, "but what I'm trying to get across is that ever since you became a member of this meeting,

164

we've all of us tried to be the family you lost. We are your family now. And if we were all locked up in our meeting house by somebody like Flood, and you were put in Marcus' position, I have a feeling we'd all want you to do what he's doing now."

"I approve," says Anna, and then Elizabeth says, "I approve," and when Uri looks from them to me and I nod approval, he slowly shakes his head again in that regretful gesture. "But I won't stand in the way of the meeting," he says.

David says, "Then the sense of the meeting is to support our course of action. I think you all know what that means. Spreading the word about Janet's being under doctors' care in a critical condition. Blocking anyone in town, especially the authorities, from getting the least idea of what's really going on."

"The end justifying the means," Uri says harshly.

It is like hearing an echo of my own reaction to McGrath's compliment, and it stirs a deep discomfort in me. I say, "Uri, that would stand as a condemnation if we were looking for excuses to allow murder. We're only searching for a way to prevent it."

He looks stricken. "Marcus, I didn't mean it to sound like that. My God, I went through it all myself all those years ago. But people like the ones who threw my family into the furnaces—people like Flood—they frighten me. I keep telling myself yes, yes, there is a Light in them as in all humanity, but in my heart I can never really make myself believe it. These are not humanity, Marcus. These are the dregs, the lumpen. Look at all we gave Flood when he was a kid. The kindness, the make-work jobs, the education we almost forced on him. What became of that? He saw the kindness as our weakness, he used the education to sharpen his brain for criminal acts, he made himself a leader of the lumpen, the most dangerous of them. And you think you can prevent him from murdering policemen, and policemen from murdering him? In the end you won't be able to do that, Marcus. All you'll do is prolong the agony."

I say, "Do you want to stand aside from the meeting in this, Uri?"

"Yes. But I know I can't. If I don't tell the same lies, put on the same act as everyone else, this won't hold up at all."

"That's true," David says, and Kenneth says, "You're making it hard for us, Uri."

"Am I supposed to make it easy for you?" Uri demands. "Are those my orders, Ken?"

"No, of course not, but—"

"Then let it go at that. I told you I won't stand in the way of the meeting. I'll do what has to be done, I'll say what has to be said."

Anna says to Elizabeth, "If Herbert Hill at the bank has started to spread the news, we will be getting telephone calls very soon. I will attend to them. I doubt if thee has the mettle to speak falsely, Elizabeth."

"I think I do," Elizabeth says.

"I hope so at this time. And there will be visitors. Thee must follow me in what I say to them."

Ethel says, "Ken and I will spread the word at the boatyard. That's as good as broadcasting it."

There is the sound of cars racketing up to the house. "The commune people," David says, and he and I go to the door and open it as three battered-looking machines pull up on the road and Lou Erlanger steps out of one of them. We walk over to him, and he says, "We've got the old bus blocking the road good our side of your house. Dug it in so it can't be moved. We'll do the same with two of these clunkers here on this side. How far down the road do you want them planted?"

"About at Lookout Point," David says. "That way they can't be seen from here."

166

"No sweat," Erlanger says. "We also had a couple of the women go mushroom-hunting in the woods near your place. They came back right away and said there's a man sitting on your roof with a gun in his hand. It really shook them up. Like, talking about guns is one thing, but having one maybe aimed your way for real is another. They won't go back there now."

"They shouldn't," I say. "David and I will take care of that."

"Yeah, sure," Erlanger says, and gets back into the car. He leans out of the window. "Did you make out all right with the phone company?"

"Hell," David says.

We go back to the house, and I pick up the phone and dial my own home number, my fingers suddenly so thick and clumsy that I have to start twice over before I finally make the connection.

A click, and then a mechanically toneless voice.

"The number you are calling is not in service," says the voice.

Good.

But what happens when Flood discovers this?

Uri and the Quimbys leave, Ethel stopping at the door to suddenly hug me hard. The door closes behind them, their cars move off, leaving the rest of us facing each other in a silence so acute that the ticking of the grandfather clock in the hallway becomes a series of small explosions in my ears.

The phone rings. Anna snatches it up, almost drops it before she gets it to her ear. Then she turns to me. "The commune. Raymond McGrath."

I take the phone. "Ray?"

"Yes. Listen, it's something you forgot—we all forgot. That mailman, Farrow. He's on his way up South Road right now with the delivery. We can see him from the porch. And, man, he is going to drop our stuff here and then head down Ridge Road right into that bus we've got planted there. You know how he is, Marcus. He is sure as hell going to get the law up here as fast as he can."

"Ray, you'll have to stop him. Tell him that story about Janet. Tell him I ordered the road blocked until the doctors give me the word. He can leave our mail and the Marcys' mail with you."

"It won't work, Marcus. Not the way he feels about us here."

True. The mail route is up South Road from town, then

along Ridge Road and down Quaker Lane, and never have I encountered Henry Farrow, the postman, at my box without getting a lecture on my foolishness in renting to a gang of Commie sex maniacs and drug addicts. A meddlesome and angry man, Henry Farrow. Faced with the chance to do damage to the commune, he will work it for all it is worth.

Unless I intervene. I may be a fool to Henry Farrow, a dangerous fool at that, but I am still Marcus Hayworth. "Ray, as soon as he gets there, have him call me here."

"He's outside now."

"I'll wait."

I put a hand over the mouthpiece so that I can tell David what's going on, and he says, "Ah, damn. Damn," so that Anna and Elizabeth glance at him sharply for this language. Then there is a voice over the phone, Henry Farrow in a temper.

I talk to him. Talk to him passionately, lying, indeed, with all the intensity Digby had put into his Pentecostal performance last night, and Farrow's temper slowly dissolves into embarrassment, into sympathy, into a muttered "Yeah, that's too bad" or "Sure, I understand, Mr. Hayworth" any time I draw breath. And in polite language I promise a bribe if Ridge Road is left inviolate for the next day or so. "As soon as this is over, Henry, I'll want to show you my appreciation." The Santa Claus who bribes you just to do your proper job every year, Henry, will show up long before Christmas this year. "No need, Mr. Hayworth. Glad to help out for Janet's sake, even if it means a little trouble," lying his own polite lie, although maybe I'm being unjust in that, maybe some of James Flood has rubbed off on me.

I put down the phone, and David says, "It worked?"

"It worked."

"You're doing fine," David says.

I am doing fine. We are all doing fine.

So far.

169

James Flood

Nine o'clock.

Harvey takes over for Lester on the roof. Lester moves down to the kitchen, plants his transistor on the table and monitors the local station. The first word to the public about the July Group will probably arrive over that station. Meanwhile, Lester leans back in his chair against the wall, keeps one eye on curvy little Deborah, the other eye on the rest of the women.

Coco prowls.

I check out the shuttered windows of the house, then go into the library across the hall from the living room and pipe in on the big radio there. It's part of a stereo set that takes up half of one wall. The color TV in a corner is, from the look of it, the biggest and best. A fair percentage of the books in those shelves from floor to ceiling are, I suspect, collector's items. The oriental carpet on the floor is definitely a collector's item. The pieces of furniture in the room, mahogany, walnut, teak, are definitely collector's items.

Simplicity.

I attended their meetings for worship sometimes. Part of it was the money. If I stayed after coffee hour, washed up the dishes, swept out the building, I could count on a handout. Part of it was a perverse need to luxuriate in the warm, oozy bath of hypocrisy provided by the Friends. They sat in silence, but now and then one of them felt called on to deliver a message to the rest. Always a predictable message, always tepid, always reducing what should be a gale force of emotion to a gentle pitter-patter of lukewarm raindrops on a well-shingled roof. They had it made, the Hayworths especially, so they sat and waited on a Light which let them clearly see how sweet and kind and reasonable they were.

Simplicity. With trimmings.

They warmed up to their business meetings by reading from something called *Advices and Queries*—a copy to little Jimmy for his enlightenment, free of charge—and the query that hit my funny bone hardest was *Do we keep to moderation and simplicity in our standards of living?* I memorized it, knowing that some day I'd work up enough guts to stand in meeting and deliver a message of my own on the question, let some passion heat up that passionless room, send Jeremiah out of his corner to belt their sweet Jesus cold with one swing.

Made gutless by no money, never did it.

But thought about it. In college, every time the monthly check arrived from them. And in Raiford. Again and again in Raiford.

The sun is burning off the Lake George mist. The house, windows shuttered tight, is heating up. But there is central air conditioning in this simple domicile. I go out into the hall to the thermostat, switch it on. A big baby, that conditioner. The house shakes under its thud as it turns over, and a minute later a coolness steals into the hallway.

Oh yeah, man, simplicity can be beautiful.

Ten o'clock.

Coco walks into the library. "I'm taking my turn on the roof now. You will relieve me at eleven o'clock."

"I'll be there."

He nods toward the radio. "Lester says there is no news about us yet."

"Lester is telling it like it is."

"Does that seem natural to you, man? I mean, about the news. Could Hayworth really keep it hushed up so long, once he started to make the arrangements?"

"It looks like he can. Don't worry. Any minute you'll be getting it all over a national hookup."

"You let me know when that happens." Coco looks around the library. He nods approval. "A quality room. Some of the old money in St. Hilary can show the same thing. It takes a long time to put together a room like this."

"And a lot of that old money." I point at the desk. "I used to do homework there sometimes, when I was in high school. Hayworth got in a mood to help now and then. Great on math, cast-iron head for everything else. He read a couple of things I did for the school magazine—good stuff, Hubert, really good—and all he saw was punctuation."

175

"That is what you have on your mind at a time like this, man? Your happy school days?"

"Dear old Golden Rule days, Mr. Digby." I go over to the desk, take the heavy brass stiletto-style letter opener from the leather cup there and gouge a track full length across the slick mahogany surface. "Therapy," I tell Coco.

He is not in a playful mood. "You told Hayworth the deadline is twelve o'clock. What is the chance of some action before then?"

"Depends on how long he can hold back Duffy and the FBI. If it's up to Hayworth alone, he'll deliver the money and try to get it back from the insurance company and the hell with it. That's how his mind works. You have a revolution marching down Front Street in town, you ask how much money it'll take to make everybody break it up and go home happy, and you pay it. Duffy might not buy that. So if there is any action before deadline, it'll be Duffy out there on the road with a bullhorn. What the hell, it's not his family in here with us."

"All right," Coco says, "whoever it is except Hayworth, I'll pin him down. Keep an ear open, man. One short burst, a cop with a bullhorn. Two short bursts, heavy stuff moving in."

"If it's Duffy, save him for me. And you're overdue up there now. You don't want to get Harvey too heated up."

Coco, the old blacksnake, slides out of the room. A few minutes later Harvey, the bull of the Everglades, comes in. He is shirtless, gleaming with sweat. "Man, it is hot up there."

"Better than cold. Or rain."

"That's a fact." He knits his brow. "Suppose it does rain? How do we spot anybody moving in on the house then?"

"Don't worry. I arranged for clear weather right up to St. Hilary."

Harvey hee-haws. Then his brow wrinkles again. "What about nighttime? Suppose we're stuck here in the dark?"

"We'll convert some of those brass lamps into spotlights. With the house blacked out, we can cover the whole perimeter that way. And there's almost a full moon tonight."

"You arrange for that too?"

"That too, Brother Shanklin."

"I'll bet you did." He remembers something. "Oh, Coco wants you up on top."

"Why?"

"You're asking me what's on that crazy nigger's mind? He just said send you up right away."

I am on my way out of the room when Harvey remembers something else. "Oh yeah, he told me about us being the July Group now. I like that."

"I thought you would."

I go up to the roof. The house, with the conditioner blasting away, is almost too cool. When I get my head above roof-level through the trapdoor, it is like being blasted with a heat ray. Coco, Uzi in hand, binoculars slung around his neck, is already dripping sweat. When he unslings the binoculars and hands them to me, they are wet to the touch. He points toward the road. "Take a look at that, man. There could be somebody coming along there very soon who is not either Mr. Hayworth or Mr. Duffy. Right there on the road beyond those yellow flowers."

"What the hell are you talking about?"

"Take a look. Just beyond those flowers."

I focus the glasses on the flower bed and beyond it, and see what he is talking about. The mailbox, its metal flag down, waiting for the morning delivery. The commanding officer must never show that he may have missed a detail. I say, "It's a mailbox. Country style. And odds are nobody's hiding in it with a machine gun."

"Very funny, man. But you did not allow for it. You told Hayworth to keep those crazies down the road away from here, but you said nothing about mail delivery."

"I didn't have to. He'll make sure there's no delivery today."

"If he remembers about it. You did not."

"Hubert, are you calling me a liar?"

"All right, all right, I am not calling you anything. But do you know the man who makes mail deliveries here?"

"Used to be a guy named Farrow. Still might be, the way they operate in these parts."

"I don't think so. I think today it might be the same car, but with a plainclothesman driving it."

"Then just blast anything that shows up. Why make a big deal out of it? Worried about damaging the U.S. mails?"

"No, Mr. Flood. I am worried because from that car to me is exactly the same distance as from me to that car. Meaning that if I do not knock it out first round, and there is a sharpshooter laying low in the back of it—"

"Baby, that is the name of the game."

"Not my game, Jimmy. Not yours either, if there is going to be phase three. So I want one of the women standing right here next to me. And if you want to paint a bull's-eye on her tit for the benefit of anybody coming down that road, you can do it."

"Oh? I thought you were the one who was so much against wasting any of the women."

"None of them will be wasted that way, believe me. And none of us, either."

It is not a bad idea. I go down to the kitchen, and after telling the ladies the whys and wherefores of the matter, I cut Mamma Emily out of the herd, and she follows me up to the roof and goes on duty as docile as a cow being led to pasture.

Eleven o'clock.

Time for my turn on the sun deck.

But I wait until I catch the hourly news roundup—three minutes and six commercials take care of the world—and there is still no flash about the action at Hayworth House.

I go into the kitchen, where the transistor is blasting out the same shortage of news. Harvey and Lester are at the table, Harvey working on a sandwich, Lester lovingly shining up his Colt. The window of Sarah Frisch's room is shuttered like all the others in the house, and through the doorway of the darkened room I can just make out the old lady propped up in bed and Deborah sitting beside her. Janet is standing at the window as if she can see through the closed shutters.

Harvey says to me, "I took all the knives, anything sharp around here, and put them in a box on the top shelf. If they need something for cooking, they can ask for it."

"Good."

"And I caught that Deborah trying to untie the old lady when she thought I wasn't looking. I told her to knock it off or she'd get tied up the same way."

"Only with her legs open," Lester says. He looks happy at the idea.

It turns out Deborah is taking this in. She walks out into the kitchen. "You don't have to be so rotten about it," she says to me furiously. "You can't keep her tied up like that. It's hurting her."

"That's too bad. I told you I don't want her wandering around if things start happening in here."

"How far can she wander?"

She is picking the wrong time for this nonsense, after eleven o'clock and getting near deadline. I slam her across the cheek so hard that it whips her face sideways and sends her staggering back a couple of steps before she can get her balance. "You're lucky," I point out as she stands there, a hand pressed to her cheek, her expression showing she doesn't really believe this can be happening to her. "If Harvey or Lester land on you, your head'll go right through that wall."

Janet comes out of the bedroom. "I told you," she says to Deborah, and there is no sympathy in her voice, only contempt. A hard-nosed piece, all right. She pulls a handful of ice cubes from the refrigerator, slaps them into a kitchen towel, and hands it to Deborah. "Use that. It'll feel better." She turns to me. "Isn't it our turn to go hold hands up on the roof?"

Cool. Even cooler than those ice cubes.

We go up to the attic, and Janet climbs the ladder to the roof effortlessly as a cat going up a tree. Coco gives her a hand up to the sun deck, and when I follow her through the trapdoor, he says to me, "Anything on the radio yet?"

"No."

"There should be."

"Not if Hayworth is getting his way. So far, that's what it looks like."

Mamma Emily is sitting on the planking of the sun

180

deck looking wilted. Janet helps her to her feet and says, "Are you all right?"

"Yes, of course. Perfectly all right. How is Sarah Frisch?"

"The same." Janet gives me a dirty look. "Deborah will tell you how things are going."

Coco passes me the binoculars and then after going through the trapdoor he steers Emily down. Janet stands waiting for instructions. It strikes me that what Coco had up here with him was a pigeon; what I have is more in the falcon class. Comes trouble, she could be more menace than hostage.

I point to the railing. "Over there."

Janet walks to it. When she sees me unbuckle the strap from the binoculars, she catches on fast. She says, "That won't be necessary. I won't try anything stupid."

"Sure you won't." She offers no resistance as I tie her wrists behind her back, then tie the other end of the strap to the railing. I move up against her, put an arm around her waist, studying the terrain beyond the road, trying to get the picture anybody on the ground would have of us. A sure bet, I can see, that while we're as close together as this, nobody, whether from the front of the house or the back, would try to wing me.

I realize that the waist I am gripping is flat and hard, the muscles rigid against my touch. I slide my hand over the sharpness of the hipbone, down and around, and I find that her small tight butt is surprisingly soft. "Jesus," she suddenly says. "Right up here on the roof?"

I pull my hand away, and too late, despise myself for doing it. What I should do is give her a real working-over, both hands, then take her right up here on the roof. But I don't. I say, "Only by invitation, doll."

"That'll be the day."

From the look on her face, if she had a mouthful of bullets she could spit them right through me. I move away from her a little to cool her down. "When does the mail get delivered here?" I ask.

"It's probably in the box now."

"It isn't. Now what does that mean to you?"

"It means my father is following instructions. Seeing to it nobody gets in the way while he's putting your money together. Don't worry. He'll deliver on schedule."

"What makes you so sure?"

"I know my father, Flood. You told him what, when, and how to deliver. As long as he works from the instruction book, he functions beautifully. No imagination, Flood. No doubts. No uncertainties. So you don't have to worry he'll come up with some brainstorm to unsettle your pretty plans. He won't."

"I take it if you were in his spot right now, you would."

"You're goddam right I would. The army, navy, and marines. Tanks, cannons, and bombers. Either you and your freaks would come out on demand with your hands up, Flood, or you wouldn't last very long."

"Neither would your mother and sister, baby."

Janet shakes her head. "No, I don't think so. Crazy as you are, you must know they'll be just what you need, comes the crunch. Because they're even more freaked out than you. They're the ones who'll get up in court and say that none of this is your fault. You came from a broken home, you never got the love you needed, the whole gorgeous bucket of whitewash is all yours when the time comes, Flood. Keep that in mind the next time you get ready to knock Deborah's teeth out or aim that gun at my mother."

"I see." What I see is that she is tough, she is smart, and she is impossible to figure out. I ask, really curious about it, "Did you ever stand up and give them that kind of message in meeting?"

"Don't push, Flood."

"I'm disappointed in you, baby. All this big talk up

here, but the same sanctimonious crap down there where it counts."

"Be grateful for that sanctimonious crap, Flood. It's the only thing that keeps cases like you from being stood up against a wall and shot the minute you get one inch out of line."

Holding the Uzi waist-high, I aim it at her. "But look who's carrying the gun, baby." She stares at it, all the fancy speeches drying up in her mouth. That old black magic. Unpredictability. She doesn't know if I will pull that trigger or not. Hell, how can she if J. Flood himself doesn't know whether or not he'll do it. From a distance, I watch Flood's finger tighten on the trigger. I have a feeling that maybe he is moving things too fast and in the wrong direction, fooling around with The Button this way, but he is on his own now, and there is nothing I can do about it, nothing I want to do about it.

Suddenly Flood and I are together again.

I say to Janet, "One thing you've made clear, baby. If it comes to a showdown—if it turns out one minute after deadline that daddy still needs persuasion—you are the disposable hostage. That doesn't leave mamma and sister off the hook, but you are number one on the list. And do you know what? Watching you and daddy, I get the feeling he wouldn't even mind if I finished you off right in front of him. Anybody else on the list, yes. Not you. What do you think of that?"

She looks sick. She looks as if the dose of pills in her can't carry her any more. She shakes her head. "You're wrong, Flood," she says. "He'd have to mind. That's what the instruction book tells him. I'm the one who wouldn't mind."

Coming on to twelve o'clock, a few big clouds move in from the west, so that there is a constant play of light and shade on the woods around the house. Logic or no logic, it gives the effect of something going on among those trees, so I work the binoculars hard. Nothing shows. Nothing at all. And I can even make out knotholes on the tree trunks. These glasses are the best. German-made, picked up in London by Coco, not so much for practical purposes as to square the count against the shopkeeper who had swindled him on the price of some camera film. Oxford Street, Coco said. Half of London is always out on Oxford Street. Just step out into that crowd, man, and you are lost for good.

I am sighting the glasses on the woods when Coco shows up on the roof. Not looking for a slug through the head, he calls a warning from the trapdoor, then hauls himself up and comes over to me. "You see anything out there?"

"No."

"And not a word about this on the radio yet. It is five minutes to twelve now. Do you think Hayworth is waiting for the exact second before he shows up?"

"He might be."

"I don't think so. Jimmy, are you sure you gave him enough time to get the money together?"

"Yes."

"Then what happens if he does not show up in the next five minutes?"

"I phone the bank. If he's not there, I get hold of Duffy at police headquarters. Any other questions?"

There goes that hand up again in pained protest. "I am not criticizing, Jimmy. I just do not like waiting for things to happen. I am a high-strung sort of fellow."

"Well, don't take it out on me. Go on down and ask Harvey and Lester how to be low-strung."

"No, thank you. That is another thing. It is Lester's turn up here again, but I want to take over for him now that it is getting close to the time. With one of the other women."

"All right," I say, "take over for him. But not with one of the other women. This one will do fine."

He glances at Janet where she is leaning back against the railing, her head down. Then he walks over to get a closer look. He says to me with surprise, "You've got her tied up?"

"Seems so, doesn't it?"

"She looks in bad shape, Jimmy. Take her down with you and bring up that Emily lady. She is a cool one."

"This is a cool one too."

Coco puts his hand under Janet's chin and lifts her face. She is very white, her eyes are closed. He says to her, "Are you all right?"

She doesn't say anything, just makes a motion with her head, yes.

"You see?" I say to Coco. "But if she wants her mamma to stand in for her, all she has to do is ask."

Janet motions with her head, no.

I say to her, "It's time for some happy pills, isn't it? But you'll have to come down with me to get them. In that case, mamma comes up here."

Janet opens her eyes and squints at me. She pulls her chin away from Coco's hand. "Go to hell," she says.

"Tough, stringy meat," I tell Coco. "She'll have to cook some more before she softens up." I hand him the Uzi. "I'm going down to phone now. Something can blow any minute, so keep your eyes open. If Hayworth forgets he's supposed to park the wagon out on the road and not bring it up the driveway, remind him of it with the gun."

"No sweat," Coco says. "But whatever you get on the phone, man, you let me know right away."

When I get down to the kitchen it looks like a family party there, Emily, Deborah, and both Shanklins around the table, and the transistor on it blasting out the end of the midday news. I motion at the transistor, and Harvey says, "Still nothing. Man, it's like they don't want anybody to know what's going on here."

"And it's after deadline," Lester says. The news turns into a commercial, and he tunes down the volume. "You know what I've been thinking?" he says to me seriously. "I've been thinking there's this Hayworth, and they load up his wagon with four million cash, and he says he is fetching it back here, but what the hell, four million cash, so he just takes off some other place. Like Canada. Maybe Mexico."

Emily says, "That's ridiculous."

"You're right," I tell her. "What isn't ridiculous is that it's after deadline. I thought Marcus had more brains than to lay your necks on the block like this."

"Jimmy, it's only a little after twelve. I'm sure there's a reason for his being delayed."

"So am I. But I want to hear it from him personally." I point at the phone. "Now you'll call the bank. If it's him, hand me the phone. If it's anybody else and they say he's out, just hang up."

187

Emily is not as much in control of herself as she's putting on. She fumbles with the receiver, her hands shaking. She holds the receiver to her ear, but doesn't dial, just stands there listening. To what?

I say, "What the hell are you waiting for?" and she says, "There's no dial tone. No sound at all."

I put the receiver to my ear. She's right.

I ask, "You have any trouble with these phones lately?" and she shakes her head. I shove her out into the hallway where there's a phone on the small table next to the coatrack. "Go on," I tell her, "try that one."

Same thing again. Dead phone. Room by room, we check out every phone in the house. No question, the service is completely out for the whole place. Why? Hayworth is smart to block off mail delivery here, but what oddball reason could he find to cut off phone service? One possible. With the phones working, reporters, neighbors, busybodies would be free to keep calling the house and maybe make waves.

No waves. This has to be the answer.

Which means that Hayworth is somehow keeping Duffy under tight control every which way.

And should be pulling up here any minute now with the Company funds.

I shove Emily back into the kitchen and give Harvey and Lester the news. Harvey doesn't like it. He says to me, "What makes you so sure it was Hayworth cut off the phone? Suppose it was that police chief?"

"Why would he?"

"Because you told us he'd most likely try to do things his way and come charging right up that hill. He cuts off the phone, it means we can't scare him out of that."

"Shit."

Harvey gets red in the face. "Well, that's what you were trying to do just now, wasn't it? Scare Hayworth into getting a move-on."

"He's already been scared into it. He's only fifteen minutes overdue anyhow. And if Duffy has his way and comes charging up that hill, he'll find out fast enough we're not playing games. Either way"—I motion at the two women—"we hold all the aces. Right?"

"Right," says Lester, but Harvey shakes his head. "I think—"

"Don't," I tell him. "You think too hard, Mr. Shanklin, you are likely to get a hernia in those brain muscles."

I cut it short at that and head up to the roof, surprised that Coco hasn't already deserted his post to come down and get the word. Another couple of minutes, I know, and he'll do it.

First thing I see is that Janet is untied and is standing in the middle of the sun deck beside Coco. All right, that's why she's up here, to serve as cover for anybody on duty, but we can't have two captains on the ship, can we? "Who the hell told you to cut her loose?" I say to Coco, and the next thing I see is the muzzle of the Uzi swinging my way, getting a bead on my chest.

So our last confrontation has taught Blackie nothing, or the one before that, or any of the others along the way. He is not a slow learner, he is just a quick forgetter. I put my hand against the butt of the Colt in my belt, and Coco says, "No, man. That would be a mistake."

He has said it before under the same conditions, but his tone is different now. Smooth and easy. Mellow. I hesitate, and that is the mistake. Coco says, "You are always making big things out of little things at the wrong time, Jimmy. Now take the hand away."

I am not always making big things out of little things at the wrong time. But right now, I realize, I am winding up tight when I should be staying loose. At least, loose enough to take a good, hard look at my partner. This is the one who came up with the idea of cutting Harvey and Lester out of the picture. Now if I were Hubert, the old blacksnake, who would I really want for company after phase two is all cleared up: very sharp James Flood or a pair of very dull rednecks? When the plane lands in St. Hilary, where I am boss man of phase three, who would I rather have to boss around than the brothers Shanklin? All right, somebody will be needed to ride shotgun on that plane, but why stay with troublesome J. Flood when the Shanklins are such untroublesome naturals for the job?

So all that talk about scratching Harvey and Lester off the books was candy-coated crap, a way of smoothing out any prickly suspicions of Hubert, the wily one. A good mind at work there in Hubert, but it has made one fatal mistake. It has underestimated the sharp, precise, analytical intelligence of the would-be victim.

Coco says again, "Man, take that hand away," and now with a sharp, precise view of the situation—he will waste me here and now if I try for a showdown, and Janet Hayworth will swear he did it to protect her—I take my hand away from the gun butt.

"What about that phone call?" Coco says. "Did you talk to the man?"

"No. All the phones are out."

"Out?"

"Out. Dead."

"That does not make sense."

"It does, if Hayworth wants to keep everybody out of the way while he's setting up delivery."

Coco jerks his head toward the road. "What delivery?"

He is sweating hard as it is. It is a pleasure watching him sweat even harder, faced with one of those unpredictables he hates. I say, "What do you want to do about it? Drive into town and ask why the delay?"

"Do not talk foolishness, man. Talk business."

"All right, if Hayworth has his way, he'll be here any time now with the money. If Duffy or the FBI have their way, they'll be here any time now with guns. Either way, we're ready."

Like it or not, Hubert has nothing better to offer. He chews on this fact awhile until he gets it down. Then he says to me, "Meanwhile, I do not want this woman up here with me ready to pass out. Bring up one of the others."

I bring him up Mamma Emily for company. Then, on the way down with Janet, we detour into her room, where I allow her a bare pick-me-up of meth. A nice compromise. The large jolt she measures out at first

191

would charge her up too much. Cutting it out altogether, if she's really gone on the stuff, could mean withdrawal convulsions, and this is no time for convulsions.

Later, maybe.

Marcus Hayworth

The letter kills, but the spirit gives life.

Not always.

Not now.

Anna Marcy is abiding by the letter. Late in the morning phone calls start coming in from town. By one o'clock they are coming from Lake George Village, from Glens Falls, from Bolton Landing. It seems as if the whole length of Lake George is churning with the news that Janet Hayworth had a serious accident, that the Hayworth house is locked against the world during the crisis, and that the Marcy sisters can provide information.

Anna answers each call with patience, holding scrupulously to the letter. "Yes, I have been told Janet had a bad fall. No, I cannot tell thee more than that." Literally true, she has been told Janet had a bad fall. Literally true, she does not feel free to tell any outsider more than that. So here is the letter giving life. This is how long-ago Friends manning stations along the Underground Railroad learned to answer the slave-hunters who broke down their doors to demand the whereabouts of fugitive Negroes. The letter can give life.

But is it giving life in this case, or is it threatening life? More than an hour has gone by since I was supposed to deliver Flood's plunder to him. By now his nerves must

195

be as raw as mine, but while I sit here in my self-imposed helplessness, he may be raging through my house, taking out his fury on my family and housekeeper. Has already given Sarah Frisch and me a dose of his medicine. I try to close my mind to what he might do to his hostages, and the trying only makes the sickening images before me that much more vivid.

And yet.

And yet if our inaction leads Flood to torment his hostages, what would the sight of guns aimed at him do? Very young I learned that you never, never drive a barn rat into a corner. Learned it the hard way by having the cowering, twitching, beady-eyed lump I was jabbing at with a rake handle suddenly become a vengeful fury, streaking up the handle, the needle-sharp teeth sinking into my thumb, and sinking even deeper as I screaming tried to shake loose that horrible grip. I did, and then it was I who ran from the rat, not the rat from me.

Corner James Flood, jab the handle at him, and if distance happens to protect you, he may sink those teeth into anyone else closer at hand. Meanwhile, he must know—he is not totally mad, there must be some logic working in him—that the safety of the hostages is, in the end, the surest guarantee of his own safety.

The phone rings again. Anna goes out to the hall to answer it; Elizabeth, in a straight-backed chair across the room, continues her knitting. A mindless activity, knitting. At monthly meetings for business, all the women knit steadily, but whenever one of them enters the discussion it's plain that only the fingers are engaged with those needles, the mind is closely following the proceedings.

No, not all the women. Janet, on those rare occasions when she chooses to attend meetings for business, does not knit. She sits, hands idle, eyes veiled, almost as if she is judging the meeting rather than taking part in it. She speaks seldom, and when she does, the comment she offers is always a bitter one, as if it is drawn not from the Light in her, but from a darkness.

A darkness.

What is frightening about that now is that while I believe Emily and Deborah can maintain a peaceable front before Flood, I am not sure Janet will stand up under the test. That darkness in her makes her too self-willed, too ready to show her dislikes. If she fails to realize the extent of Flood's madness, she can bring disaster down on everyone around her.

Might, at this moment, have already brought down that disaster.

But even David, on the prowl in the woods behind my house, will not be able to find that out. He wouldn't let me go along on this scouting mission. Someone must remain here to deal with the outside world if it becomes necessary, and I am the one for that.

So here I am.

Elizabeth knits.

And then Anna comes in from the hallway, her face worried. She says to me tensely, "The doctor. Orin Jeffries. You must speak with him."

"You let him know I was here?"

"Do not make hasty judgments, Marcus. If I did not let him know it, there would be even more trouble with him than there is now."

Orin Jeffries, for all the differences between his outlook and ours, likes to think of himself as a friend of the family. A narrow-minded, loudly opinionated man, he is one of the last people I want involved in this crisis.

I no more than pick up the phone and say "Orin?" when he bursts out with "Is that you, Marcus? What are you doing there? What the hell is going on, anyhow? Do you know the story I've heard about Janet?"

"About the accident?"

"About a fall she took last night and an operation being set up in your house by some neurosurgeon brought in from out of town. Now let's get it straight. Was there an accident? Was there an operation?"

"Yes."

"And who did you get in when it first happened, may I ask? I was home all night. And my girl's been checking out every local man, and none of them was called in. So who was it? It damn well had to be somebody, Marcus, because you can't get a surgeon to come out here on your own say-so. Not that I believe for a minute that any responsible surgeon would operate under those conditions."

"Orin, I don't want to talk about it now. I'll explain later. When it's all over."

"You won't have to wait that long. Because I've been doing some pretty hard thinking about what could have happened to Janet. And what you're really up to."

"Orin—"

"Just you hear me out, Marcus. I have a hunch that girl overdosed last night, didn't she? Maybe came close to killing herself. And somehow she was pulled out of it—I suppose your son-in-law's had plenty of experience with that kind of thing—but now you are so totally goddam terrified of a scandal, you'll do anything to prevent it. If I'm wrong about any of this, you just tell me."

I don't know what to say. If I say he's wrong, I'm back to a story he's already torn to shreds. If I say he's right—but I don't have to say anything. He says it for me. "No, don't bother to cook up some more fantasies, Marcus. She did overdose, didn't she?"

"Yes."

"Deliberately?"

"I don't know."

"Or you're not saying. Well, I warned Emily to let you in on it when she came to me in a panic about the girl's condition, but oh no, she had to protect you from the nasty facts of life. She never did tell you, did she?"

"No."

"All right, then let it be on my head, I'm telling it to you. Your daughter's been saturating herself with barbiturates and amphetamines and whatever the hell other high-potency stuff she can lay her hands on for months now. But get one thing straight, Marcus. I never prescribed more than a minimum dosage for her. The absolute minimum. From what Emily said, I knew the girl was loading up on it, but obviously she's been getting it through other sources. That's what you have to do now. Not lock her up in the house to protect her reputation or any such damn nonsense, but find out who's supplying her and take action against it. Now is the time, Marcus. Not tomorrow."

I don't have to lie further. I can only say, "Orin, if I had known—"

"Blame Emily for that. She never told you I recommended Janet for psychiatric treatment, either, did she?"

"No."

"Well, I did. Referred her to a couple of excellent men. One in New York, one in Philadelphia. She took one look at them and ran. And this is a serious business, Marcus. Considering that girl's depressive state, it could be close to life and death. That's why you have to move fast. For starters, have a heart-to-heart talk with your son-in-law about it. And take a good close look at that collection of freaks you rented to down the road. By the way, Janet isn't comatose, is she? She did come out of it all right?"

"Yes."

"Well, you're a damn fool not calling me in at once, but I'll drive over now and take a look for myself. And maybe do some plain talking to all of you."

"Orin, you can't come to the house now. It's out of the question."

"Damn it, are you still on that track, Marcus? Take my word for it, there won't be any police report, any scandal."

"I appreciate that, Orin, but you can't come to the house now. I absolutely forbid it."

"Sure, sure, we'll talk about it there."

"For God's sake, you can't get to the house. The road is blocked."

"Ridge Road? Blocked?"

"Yes. From both sides."

"How? Why? Marcus, you sound demented. What the hell is this? The phone out, the road blocked, you're giving me all kinds of wild ideas. Listen to me. Is there something going on out there you can't handle?"

"No. You have to believe that, Orin."

"Jesus Christ, what you're saying, the way you say it, all I can believe is that you're being mysterious about some mess Janet is in. You've lectured me more than once on the beauties of being open with people. All right, how about trying that out on me right now?"

"I'm sorry, Orin."

His phone is slammed down. It takes me a moment to realize what that explosive sound means, and even then I stand there numbly, the receiver still held to my ear.

I can cope with my enemies, a wise man once said, but God protect me from my friends.

I go into the parlor. Anna says to me, "Orin Jeffries is a meddlesome man."

"Very meddlesome," Elizabeth says. Her knitting needles click away without a stop.

"He means well," I say, and then to Anna from the bottom of my heart, "I'm only sorry you let him know I was here."

"It could not be helped. He said if I knew so little of what happened to Janet, he would drive out to your house. The only thing to do was call thee to the phone."

"What will he do now?" Elizabeth asks me. "Will he come up here, does thee think?"

"I don't know. He doesn't believe that story about Janet we made up, but he does suspect we're mixed up in something serious. I don't know what he has in mind to do about it."

"He is meddlesome because it fattens his pride," Elizabeth says. "If he had a true concern, he would do only what thee asks him to."

"Well," Anna says, "all we can do is wait and see."

We wait.

It is after two when David returns. His shirt is plastered wetly to him, his arms are scratched, his pants dotted with burs. The virgin woodland along the ridge makes rough going.

He walks directly into the kitchen, gulps down a glass of water, then another. Then he sits down on the edge of a chair and starts to pick the burs from his jeans. Anna puts a paper towel on the table for him to lay them on.

He says, "They're keeping watch from the widow's walk with binoculars. Taking turns up there. And with one of the women alongside whoever's turn it is. Emily was there with Digby, and then it was Deborah and one of the muscle men. Smart. Not even Duffy would get too reckless, the way they have it set up."

"You didn't see Janet?" I ask.

"No, Deborah was still up there when I pulled out. Anything happen here?"

"Yes," I say. "Orin Jeffries phoned. I handled it badly."

"I suppose the word got to him about Janet's accident. And he's sore because you didn't call him in on it."

"No, he doesn't buy that story. He's convinced that Janet took an overdose of pills and we're trying to cover it up. When he insisted on driving up here, I had to tell him the road was blocked. That really set him off."

David considers the bur he is holding. Finally he says, "Maybe it's all for the best. The accident story is too thin anyhow. This way Jeffries is making a real case for us."

"At least in his own mind. I doubt if he'll tell anyone else about it."

"I'd gladly forgive him a breach of ethics right now," David says. "The more people he tells, the better for us."

Anna says reprovingly to him, "Orin Jeffries is our doctor too. I prefer he does not go around telling tales about his patients."

"Well, it's not likely he does," I say.

There is much more I want to say, but I have to wait until I get David out of the house where it can be said privately. I lead him toward the road, and when we are out of earshot of the house I put it to him straight out. "David, the reason Jeffries suspects Janet overdosed is because she's been taking dangerous amounts of those pills for a long time now. Emily knew that. Did you?"

"Yes."

"And Deborah?"

"Yes."

"Then why wasn't I told?"

"I felt you should have been. Emily and Deborah disagreed."

"They were wrong," I say. "Terribly wrong. David, what is this all about? Jeffries even suggested you might be responsible for Janet's loading up on that stuff. And that you and the commune people might be supplying her with it. And I know, from what's been let slip now and then in talk among us, that you and Deborah do smoke marijuana, don't you?"

"Marcus, marijuana and pills have nothing to do with each other. As for supplying Janet with pills, hell, man, I've been battling with her for months to give them up."

"You mean she's an addict?"

"Whatever you want to call it, she's completely dependent on those things. Twenty-four hours a day. I don't even know how she can function as well as she does, the amount she's taking."

"But why? Am I supposed to believe that with everything Janet has, she still finds her life so unbearable that she can't face it without drugs?"

"Oh God, the way you put that. Marcus, that is right out of the textbook. You have no idea how it sounds."

"I asked you a question, David."

"I suppose you did. All right then, I managed to get her talking about it a couple of times. It wasn't too coherent either time, but from what I could make of it, you're the problem."

"I?"

"Yes, you. The heroic image she worships. The godlike male. Capable, confident, perfect in all his works. A hard marker, too. No matter how desperately she tries to pass the test, she knows she never can. That's a hell of a thing to live with, Marcus."

"No. You've seen me with her. Seen the way I try to get along with her. If you can believe for one moment—"

"Marcus, I'm not saying this is the reality. I'm saying it's her view of it."

Her view of it. But that doesn't make it any the less real to her. All that painful distortion. Has to drug herself into abiding with this monstrously self-sufficient, flawless, unfeeling image of me she's conjured up. If she only knew me. If, for that matter, I only knew her.

I say in bewilderment, as much to myself as to David, "But if I'm the problem, why didn't she just pack up and leave? She's good at her work. She could have gotten a job in New York. Settled down there."

"I don't know. Maybe she's afraid to. But if you go to her yourself, ask her that—"

Abruptly it reminds us both of something we have been close to forgetting for this moment.

I can't go to her. Not now.

James Flood

In this merry get-together of the Company—of the July Group—on the sun deck, Coco gobbling away like a turkey watching someone sharpening up an ax, Harvey chewing over everything like a cow working on its cud, Deborah taking it all in with those cute little ears, I get the feeling of compromise in the wind. No question, says Coco, that Hayworth is stalling so that he can soften us up for a cut-rate deal. No question that he has enough control over the police, the troopers, the FBI up to now so that he can keep them ringed around us in the woods until dark, when they will be able to make their strongest move. Now suppose when Hayworth shows up, he offers us the million he talked about, instead of four million? Two hundred and fifty thousand dollars a man, is that bad?

"Well now," says Harvey, kind of liking the sound of it.

"Very bad," I say. "Forget it."

Sunset is around eight o'clock, gobbles Hubert. The night. Bad things happen in the night.

"Forget it."

What the crafty son of a bitch doesn't say is that if after collection time we wipe out Harvey and Lester according to plan, and then he wipes me out, he—Hubert Digby, all by his lonesome—will wind up with all of that million he's getting ready to settle for. His St. Hilary boys are on a percentage, so he can live with them. The unmourned dead will be one Flood and two Shanklins.

Forget it, Hubert.

Because when that plane lands at St. Hilary, the only passengers aboard will be J. Flood and three hostages.

"Eight o'clock," says Coco, the old compromiser. "That leaves us only six hours before dark, man. How long do we wait for Hayworth to show up?"

"That's a good question," says Harvey. Harvey is getting real talky lately. Obviously he is feeling his oats after the way he handled phase one. Getting right up there in the Napoleon class.

I say to Coco, "What's your proposal? That we pack it in now? Thank the ladies for a good time and haul ass down to Albany for a big night on the town?"

"Very funny," Coco says. "But what I am proposing is that you read what your options are. The way I read them, man, is that if Hayworth does not very soon contact us, we have to very soon contact him."

"How?" Harvey says. This is too much even for Napoleon. "Phone's out."

I say, "That's all right, Harve. There's a couple of dozen lawmen out in those woods and at least one pair of field glasses. All we do is print up a sign that says *Hayworth, please contact us* and hold it up nice and high."

Coco says, "God damn it, do you think I am making a joke? Yes, there are possibly more than a couple of dozen men out there and for sure a pair of field glasses." He motions at Deborah. "Now what if we scare them into showing themselves?"

Harvey says, "You mean a put-on? Make like we'll waste her?"

"Yes."

Harvey sizes up Deborah. "I could hold her over the

edge there. Could do it for five minutes easy. They ought to be all shook up before then."

It's an idea. The bad part is that it's Coco's idea, which makes it a chip knocked off my image as boss of phase two. But it's an idea. Coco will be attended to in good time.

I say to Harvey, "Hold her by the ankles. Tight. You let her go, and with the three of us up here together, you'll draw enough fire to blast this roof off."

Coco says, "No. I don't like it this way. Perhaps there are not only field glasses out there. Perhaps there are cameras too. What kind of picture will that make?"

"It's your idea to start with," I point out. "What the hell kind of picture do you expect to make?"

"A little psychodrama. We tie her to that rail, we put the gun on her, we look like business. Like a firing squad."

Harvey shakes his head. "I like it my way better." This boy is hungering to show his muscles to everybody out there, whoever they are. And, for that matter, to Deborah.

She is working herself into a panic. "Jimmy, please. This is crazy. This is so far out it doesn't make sense. My father'll be here as soon as he can. You know he will."

Harvey slaps the Uzi into Coco's hands and then grips the back of Deborah's neck between two of those oversized fingers. He wrenches her head around and aims it at the road. "Will he? All right, you show him to me. Just show him to me." But he doesn't give her a chance to show him anything right side up. He doubles her across the railing on her belly, so that she is tilted head-down over it screaming, and then with no effort at all he grabs an ankle in each hand and holds her suspended like that away from the railing. She twists and turns, clutching for the railing and manages to get a grip on one of the posts. She hangs on like a leech. It is something to see the way

Harvey, belly jammed up against the railing, arms straight out, manages to drag her loose. He holds her far enough out over the slope of the mansard roof below so that there's no chance of her now gripping anything. Too bad, at least from his angle, that she's wearing those tight jeans. Otherwise he'd have the view of a lifetime.

Coco is standing there, hypnotized by all this, not even realizing he's holding the Uzi, until I say to him, "God damn it, we're wide open from the other side. Cover the back of the house," and he heads fast across the sun deck to keep an eye on the woods of the back slope.

I move in close to Harvey in case some sniper out there is itching to take his chances on an easy target. I look at my watch. "You said five minutes?" I ask Harvey.

"Five minutes. That ought to be more than enough for them."

It might be. I slowly make a sweep of the whole perimeter with the binoculars. I am pulled up short now and then by the sense of a bush stirring unnaturally, of something glinting on the side of a tree trunk. I fix hard on them, feeling the binoculars getting more and more slippery with the sweat on my hands. A drop of sweat suddenly stains a lens. I polish the lens carefully before resighting. A couple of dozen men out there? There could be a hundred. Two hundred. By now they could have called up the whole goddam National Guard and have it planted out there. I concentrate on each of the biggest trees along the road. If that isn't an elbow sticking out there, a knee, the edge of a helmet, what is it?

Deborah's upside-down body writhes in Harvey's grip. He says between his teeth, "You fool around like that, bitch, you are going to get hurt real bad," and she stops writhing. I look at him. His arms are not as rigid as they were. He is starting to breathe hard.

I look at my watch. Still two minutes to go, still no sign of life out there. Nobody flapping a white flag. What makes them so sure they won't see that curvy little body slide head-down along the steep pitch of the roof and over its edge? Or is Duffy asking for that so that he can take the three of us out together? Give up Deborah in return for the three of us, and then try rushing the house against the one who is left?

Harvey says to me, "How much to go?" His arms are trembling now, his face is twisted, he is sucking in each breath loudly. I look at my watch and see time is up. He said five minutes, and he's already done better than that.

I keep my eyes on the watch. "Almost a minute yet."

"Are you sure?"

"I'm sure." Anyone else would give up now, would say what the hell, another few seconds isn't worth it, and lay down the barbell. Not Harvey Shanklin. Harvey knows that somebody out there is also timing him, and that when five minutes shows on the Olympic electronic timer, he wins the gold medal. "You're getting soft," I tell him.

He could drop her at that. It's what Hayworth deserves. First Deborah. Then Mamma Emily. That should really convince Marcus. Then, the best joke of all on him, he'd be stuck with Janet. Have to pay out four million for Janet, who he'd probably hate to pay a dime for.

"Ah, man," Harvey wheezes, "it has got to be time now," and he hauls up Deborah, puts her on her feet, keeping an arm locked around her. Smart enough, at least, to use her for cover until he gets his wind back. She sags there in his grip, her face bright red, her eyes closed. She looks ready to pass out. Harvey says to me, "Are you real sure somebody is out there?"

"Yes."

Coco slides across to us, moving fast, keeping low, the Uzi ready to sight on the white flag which, as it happens, is not showing in the woods. If he turns on that Eye-lond whine about unpredictables, if he even uses the word unpredictable, I will finish him off here and now. But all he says is, "Nobody showing?"

"Nobody," Harvey says. He grabs a handful of Deborah's hair and pulls her head back. "What the hell is your daddy trying to do?"

The savage grip on her hair distorts her face. "I don't know," she says. "He'll be here. Please. He'll be here."

"God damn, you better make him know that." Harvey yanks hard, and Deborah yelps. He yanks again. "You better sing out so he can hear that."

"Let her be," Coco says. He sounds disgusted. "This is not getting us anywhere."

A challenge. J. Flood is not getting us anywhere?

Harvey lets her be. We stand there. We wait. Not a sound. Nothing. Not even a bird, and this is bird country. If there are men in that cover, wouldn't the birds sound off? Or would they take off?

Quiet.

All I hear is a pulse banging in my head, fast and loud.

Coco says, "There is something very peculiar going on."

Another challenge?

"You know what?" Harvey says. "I don't think there is anybody out there. At least, nobody that gives a good goddam."

And now this?

First the old blacksnake, now the new Napoleon? Next thing, Lester will be heading a committee to investigate phase two.

"Downstairs," I say. "We'll have a little meeting and settle with Mr. Hayworth fast."

"How?" Harvey says.

"I told you we're having a meeting. You be there and you'll find out. Meanwhile, get Lester up here to take over. You can do the voting for both of you at the meeting."

Lester reports for duty on the sun deck with instructions from Harvey. The women downstairs heard Deborah howling, they are all freaked out about it, we better bring Deborah down there and show her to them so that they can see she's still all in one pretty piece.

"Take her down," I tell Lester, "but bring her right back."

When they're back, Lester says to me, "Nothing on the radio. You know, I was wondering. Suppose the man didn't make it to town? Suppose he cracked the car up along the way, so nobody even knows about this?"

"He made it," Coco says. "So you just stick to business up here. And hands off the girl."

Watch it, Hubert, you are thinking out loud again. The headline when all the smoke clears away: DIGBY SAVES WOMEN FROM SEX-CRAZED GANG. At St. Hilary, the microphone shoved into Deborah's face. "Oh, yes, if it wasn't for Mr. Digby, who knows what those monsters would have done to us? Besides, he comes from an oppressed minority. And probably from a broken home."

Saint Hubert the Rip-off.

Lester says to Saint Hubert, "Yeah, sure, stick to business," because while Lester might be smarter than one of those alligators in his back yard at home which can just about tell wet from dry, he is not that much smarter. A willing worker, not a student of the classical rip-off.

We sit around the table in the kitchen for the meeting, Mamma Emily still a little shook up from Deborah's howling, Janet on a bummer, overdue for her next dose of jet fuel, Harvey and Coco itching for the shuffle and deal, J. Flood presiding. The transistor makes background music and sells soap powder. The next regular news report is due at four o'clock, but there could be a news special cutting in any time.

I say to Emily, "I don't have to tell you Marcus is a damn fool stalling like this, because sooner or later he is going to deliver. But what I want to know is this. Before he got out of here, did he tip you off to this double-cross? Did he say anything about making a move after it gets dark?"

"Jimmy, you were here. You know he didn't say anything to me."

"I wasn't watching that close. Nobody was."

"He didn't, Jimmy. I give you my word."

It makes sense. From Hayworth's angle, the less she knows, the less we can get out of her, no matter what pressure we put on. He has simple values, Friend Hayworth. His money first, his women afterward. Ship him a set of ears and fingers as a warning, he'd hold on to his money that much tighter. Who needs a wife without ears and fingers?

Coco, the old blacksnake, is no Lester. He moves in fast. He says to Emily, "Do you understand what your husband is doing, lady? He is risking your lives with his nonsense. Now why would he do that?"

"I don't think that's what he is doing," Emily says. She looks frightened at letting that much out, then clamps her mouth shut.

"Go on, tell them," Janet says.

216

Coco looks from one to the other of them. "Tell us what? What the devil are you talking about?"

"A thought I had," Emily says. "An idea. I don't know if you'll understand."

"We will make a large effort to understand, lady," Coco says.

"All right, it's the idea that nothing will happen tonight. Nothing at all. I think my husband is trying to see that nothing happens to any of us. You men as well as the girls and Sarah Frisch and myself. Then after a while you'll understand nothing will happen, and you'll go away."

"Go away?" Coco says. He leans toward her, his face screwed into one big black question mark. "Just go away? Like that?"

"Yes."

This is too much for Coco. He sits back, slowly shaking his head. "Lady, do you know you are crazy?"

Janet says, "The phone's been cut off. There's no news about this on the radio. Nobody has showed up. Not my father, not the police, not anybody else. Nobody. Do you really believe it's because they're waiting for the dark to do something? Why? What difference does it make what time of day or night it is, as long as you've got us locked up in here with you?"

I can see the wheels in Coco's head spinning hard. Whatever else Janet is, she is no simple soul like her mamma. He says to her, "Are you serious?"

"Why not?" Harvey cuts in. "I told you up on the roof I don't think anybody's out there, didn't I?"

"You did," I say. "So how would you like to take a walk out there and make sure of it? If you're right, you can bring us back some flowers."

"How about you doing it?" Harvey says. "You're running phase two, aren't you? Not that I can figure where the hell you're running it to right now."

217

Napoleon.

Is he asking for Waterloo right here in front of the ladies?

I slide the gun out of my belt under the table, but he catches sight of the motion and grabs my wrist. His grip is paralyzing. He lifts my arm above the table and pulls the gun out of my hand. There is no use trying to hang on to it, I just let him have it. But I look at him. He understands that look. He says uneasily, "You rile too easy, you know that?"

I say, "Give me the gun."

Everybody is watching. Everybody knows he doesn't want to give me the gun. They see him fight this out with himself and lose. He shoves the gun in front of me on the table. I don't reach for it, and that makes him happy. "You know how you are, Jimmy," he says. "You let every little thing rile you up."

"You damn fool," Janet says to him. "He knows what I'm saying makes sense. He knows my father. And you just blew a chance to walk out of here and take him along with you."

Coco says to her, "What does he know about your father? What are you getting at, woman?"

I say, "What she's getting at is that she thinks her daddy is a true believer in non-violence. Hallelujah, man. He went to jail as a C.O. in the World War. He doesn't swat flies or bad guys. He even takes in dangerous charity cases to reform them."

That hits Mamma Emily where it hurts. "Jimmy, you weren't taken in here as a charity case. You were never treated like one. You know you weren't."

"Emily baby, my old man sweated his whole miserable life away in that bank on Front Street, and for how much? So when he hit bottom, what could be sweeter for the boss than to take in the kid, have him do the dirty work around the place to keep him out of trouble. Don't give the old man what's coming to him, just give the kid a handout. Get the whole meeting in on it too. Then Sunday morning they can all sit there and think how fucking noble they are."

Emily can't believe her ears. "Jimmy, we never thought anything like that!"

Coco slaps his hand on the table. "What difference does any of this make? What does it have to do with getting some action going here?"

"The action is starting now," I tell him. "This is a big news story. The biggest. If it got out, you'd hear it on that radio every five minutes. That means it didn't get out. I don't know how Hayworth is working it, but so far he's keeping Duffy bottled up. Now we pull the cork."

"How?" Coco says.

"You answered that upstairs. Hayworth won't come to us? All right, we go to him. Take one of the women in the car and drive right down to the bank. Let him know fun time is over. It is now showdown time."

"Man, if the law is all around us out there, how do we get through them even with the woman in the car? You think they will let us go cruising around for the fun of it? Even if they do, that leaves the house to them while we are out in the open like pigeons."

I say, "We don't leave the house to them. We only need two in the car, one to drive, one to hold a gun on the woman. The other two stay here."

Coco reaches forward and slides my gun to the middle of the table. Not exactly in the middle, but a couple of inches closer to him than to me. He says, "If you are signing up volunteers, get this straight. I am volunteering for the home guard."

"It was your idea to start with, you chicken bastard."

"I will tell you my idea. Send one of these women to town alone. Give her instructions for Hayworth. She already knows what happened to that Deborah. She will know that if Hayworth does not deliver fast, it will really happen next time."

I say, "You mean, hand over one of these women to Hayworth for no return? Then what? Another one to-morrow and another the day after?"

"Shit," Harvey says to me. "What are you talking about tomorrow and the day after for? What about right now?"

"Fine. So how about right now you and I pile into daddy's car and take ourselves a ride into town?"

"No," Harvey says. "Not me. Not Lester either."

Emily says to me, "Jimmy, I can drive into town and tell them whatever you want me to. I give you my word I'll be back."

"And who'll let you come back once you're there? Forget it."

"You are just being stubborn, man," Coco says.

"Because I'm thinking ahead. Get it into that goddam thick skull that the way you want to do it is the way Hayworth wants us to do it. And we hand over one of the women now, he'll know he's playing his cards right."

Harvey says, "Emily here says she'll come back. You want to make sure of that?" He gets up, hauls Janet out of her chair and twists her arm behind her. She groans and arches back against the pain. Emily yells "Oh, please!" and is up and grabbing at him, but he simply slings her halfway across the room. He shoves Janet's arm up a little more, and now her face is turned toward the ceiling, her lips drawn back with pain, her teeth clenched. Harvey says to me, "You think Emily won't come back as long as this is happening?"

I am one tick of a second faster than Coco in getting to my gun, even though I have to sprawl halfway across the table to grab it. He does not argue the case when he sees it in my hand. Stretched like that across the table, I sight the gun on Harvey. "Let her go."

Janet is partially shielding him, but he's so bulky that there's still plenty of him left for a big fat target from one foot away, and he knows it. "What the hell," he says, "I'm showing you how to handle it."

"Let her go."

I am going to squeeze the trigger, and he can feel it coming. What he isn't sure of—what I'm not sure of myself—is whether I'll squeeze it if he does let her go. So he doesn't. He says, wheedling, "Come on, Jimmy. You're making like she's your private property or something."

"She is. Let her go."

I am suddenly shaking with a chill. I could be in a deep freeze the way it grabs me. A head-to-foot, teeth-chattering iciness, even my eyes blurred by it so that I have to squint to make out Harvey. What I make out is that he's getting a good look at the gun shivering in my hand. He lets go.

"Get away from her," I order, and he backs away from Janet, holding up his hands to show what a friendly little old redneck he is. He says, "It makes no difference, Jimmy. Not me, not Les, that's how it is. You don't want any of these women to go deal with Hayworth on her own, you go with her."

As suddenly as that chill hit me, it is fading away. The shakes are going too. Everything is coming back into focus. I motion with the gun. "The car keys," I tell Harvey.

Moving very carefully, watching the gun all the while, he digs the keys out of his pocket and drops them into my hand.

"All right," I tell Janet, "we're going for a ride to your daddy."

Up in her room I allow her another charge of meth—I am not all that sure she can operate without it—and before she puts the bottle away I am tempted to pop a couple of pills myself. I have malfunctioned. There is no other word for it. Malfunctioned. Outside is Duffy's turf, FBI turf, and somehow I have been jacked into doing what no smart general ever does, move into enemy territory without supporting troops. That's the guerrilla style, Che's style. Stupid, visionary bastard didn't last long that way. I consider the pills in my hand, then drop them back into the bottle. The one trouble with joy-popping is that when you think you are moving smart, you can angle off stupid and never know it.

Downstairs again, I have Emily find me a length of clothesline, and I hack off a length of it and run a slipknot into it, a handy little noose. At the front door Harvey and Coco are standing by, Harvey holding the other Uzi. He says, "I told Les to cover you from the roof. I'll take care from here."

Nice of him. From the sour look on his face and Coco's, when I walk through that door I have almost as good a chance of getting it in the back as from the front. Coco doesn't keep me wondering about why the sour looks. He says, "You be back, man, and with everything set up. You make a private deal with Hayworth and then take off on your own, you will not get that far from us."

"You can make sure of it yourself," I tell him. "There's plenty of room in the car for one more."

He isn't buying that. He opens the front door a crack, looks through it, opens it wide. All anybody can see out there is Adam and Eve country before the apple. Peace, man, at least up to those trees across the road. I slip the noose over Janet's head and around her neck, winding a couple of turns of slack around my left hand to make sure there's no sudden getaway, and she just stands and takes this like nice doggie ready to go for a walk with the master. I press the muzzle of the gun to the side of her head so that it will be conspicuous from a distance. "Slow and easy," I tell her as I push her out onto the porch, staying close behind her, my chest up against those bony shoulder blades.

We cross the porch, go down the steps, and move in a sort of sideways shuffle along the front of the house. Clear of the house, I hear Lester call from the sun deck, "Nothing showing, Jimmy," so I steer Janet at a fast clip across the open ground to the garage. I settle her behind the wheel of the LeSabre, and after reaching over to turn the key in the ignition, I get down low in the back seat behind her, my knees on the floor. I rest the gun barrel along her cheek and tug on the noose to show her it's there. She makes no move to loosen the grip on her throat, but just says, "The seat's too far back."

"Then fix it."

She rolls the seat forward. "Which way do we go?"

A sound question. South Lane is the shorter way down the ridge, and turning into Front Street from it brings us right up to the bank entrance. But Hayworth has rented the Oates' house to the counterculture, and there is no sense steering through any tripped-out pack of monkeys if I don't have to. I say, "Past Lookout down Quaker Lane. And move it."

She handles the car like a racing driver. We come down the driveway already picking up speed and hit the road like a rocket. Thrown off balance as we swing north, I accidentally grab the noose tight. Janet yells, "Christ, you're strangling me!" the car slewing this way and that until I give her slack, and she leans forward gasping, pouring on the speed again. Just beyond the bend of Lookout Point, we see it together. A barricade. Two cars angled across the road, their wheels sunk into the dirt. A bunker planted there, and who knows what kind of heavy fire waiting behind it. As Janet comes down on the brake, I sink my fingers into her shoulder. "Don't slow down, you hear? Get around to South Lane. Fast!" and she swings the car right up on the sharp slope bordering the road, slamming through fence posts and wire, then makes a wide turn, the car almost heeling over, then back through fence posts and wire to the road heading the other way. I don't hear shots from behind us, which means they spotted Janet at the wheel and aren't taking any chances on blowing a hole in her. You don't take any chances, baby, you don't score any points.

We're getting close to the house again when I realize that if Lester doesn't recognize the car first look, we can be hemstitched stem to stern by Uzi slugs, so I order, "Hit the horn! Keep hitting it!" and we go past the house this way, the horn blasting away, Lester probably wondering what the hell it's all about. Then we are into the woods the other side of the house. "Watch it," I warn. "Maybe another roadblock."

There is an S curve midway between the house and the Oates' place, and sure enough, when we are in the middle of the curve I see it planted there across the whole road like a goddam fortress, an old bus sunk down in the dirt the way the cars were, but this one with enough room in it for a battalion, and I say, "Back to the house!" and Janet tries the same trick she used before, full speed up and around on that slope, ripping through the fences, then we sideswipe a tree with a rattle and bang, and the car goes out of control, bouncing across the road and on down the slope of the Lake George side, caroming off one tree then another like a pinball, until what's left of it pulls up short in a clump of bushes. There's a stink of gasoline all around, and Janet quick cuts the ignition. The good news is that we're alive. The bad news is that now I'm on the wrong side of the road and have to cross it on foot to get back to the house.

The doors of the car are twisted out of shape, but I manage to force one open partway and get us both through it. I drag Janet down to the ground next to me while I sight the gun up the slope, waiting for somebody to show on the roadside.

I wait.

Nobody shows.

They had to see the car go off the road. Are they ordering up the whole battalion to check it out?

Still nobody shows.

Janet is on her belly next to me, watching the road too. I keep my shoulder against hers so I can grab her if she makes a sudden move. She makes the move, but it is only to turn over on her back and start to pull the clothesline leash up over her head. I knock her hands away from it. "Let it be."

She lets it be. Just lies there, eyes closed. But I remember how she went up that ladder to the sun deck, so I know she can move quick as a cat when she has the impulse. Just to keep her from having the impulse, I rest my leg between hers, the weight of my hip bearing down

225

on her hip, and Christ, cut off from the house, pinned down like this, waiting for the first of Duffy's heroes to show up, I find I am getting horny this way.

She must know it too. I take a look at her face but nothing shows on it. She could be asleep, from what I see. She isn't. She says, "My mother is right, Flood. It's empty out there. All empty."

"Then who the hell set up those roadblocks, baby?"

"It had to be my father. And David. That bus belongs to the commune, Flood. And those two cars aren't police cars. Use your brains. First no news on the radio, now this. I'm telling you nobody knows about all this except my father and David. And they're giving you a message loud and clear."

"Like what?"

"Like go away, that's all. You and your gang just go away. Listen to me, Flood. You can cut right across here into South Lane and walk into town, and I'm telling you nobody will even look at you. Or you can take that back trail from the house down to the highway. Either way, I can have a car ready for you right there."

"With my money? And my plane arrangements?"

She opens her eyes now, looking at me. She shakes her head. "No. If my father knew you wouldn't keep us as hostages even after he paid you off, he would have done it himself by now. This way you don't lose but you don't win. You come out even. That's not bad, considering what you've gotten yourself into."

"It's not good either. Not by a million dollars and a trip out of the country."

"Look—"

"No, you look. You're trying to peddle the idea that daddy could cut off phone service to the house and stop mail delivery along that road and set up roadblocks on it, all without the cops knowing. Without anybody in the whole goddam town knowing. All right, baby, now you tell me how he did it?"

"I can't. He did it, that's all."

"That's what you'd like me to believe. And then he turns over his house and his family to me until I'm tired of them. That also makes sense to you?"

"Yes."

"Like hell. You already gave me the lecture on how daddy goes by the book, daddy doesn't have brainstorms. You mean you changed your mind about that all of a sudden?"

"No. I just think he's not using my book." Suddenly she has my thigh locked tight between hers. "Flood, let me arrange for a car so you can get away without any trouble, and I'll go along with you. You'd like that, wouldn't you?"

It turns me off like a cold shower. "Quit talking like an old movie, baby. Because you are a beat-up dyke and you are strung out on crystals and downers and they never made that movie." I pull free of her and stand up, keeping low. I yank her leash. "Now we're going up this hill and across that road fast. Then we hit the dirt on the other side and see what happens."

I don't like the idea of dragging her behind me on a run like this, but it would be foolish to put her in front of me where she can suddenly stop me short in the middle of no man's land. She gets to her feet, a little wobbly, but when I say "Now!" and take off, she is right at my heels at the other end of the leash. The car has plowed a track down the slope, and we follow this up, stumbling and tripping over chopped-off tree roots and shredded twigs and underbrush.

I waste no time checking out the road. It is all-or-nothing time, so we sprint across it full speed, then make it up the slope on the other side, floundering through the underbrush among the trees, Janet holding the leash with both hands to keep it from slicing through her neck as I hustle her along, until we hit a monster tree with a trunk thick enough to offer complete concealment from the road. I pull us up behind it to get my wind back. Janet sits down on the ground and leans forward, her shoulders heaving as she sucks in air.

Finally she says, "Oliver Twist. Jesus, what a story you do have to tell, don't you, Flood?"

"Shut up." That voice is a magnet for any patrol scouting through these trees, now that they know I'm back on this side of the road.

She doesn't shut up. "Your father used to get boozed up and belt you around for kicks. You mean you really liked that better than what those terrible people up on the ridge were handing you?"

Kicks is the word. I drive my shoe into her ribs hard enough to knock her sideways, and as she lies sprawled out there I boot her in the flank to make sure she finally understands who's boss here and what he can do about it.

I say, "We're heading back to the house now. If you don't want to be dragged there by that rope, get on your feet."

She doesn't move, just lies there on her back, arms out, jaw slack, eyes slitted open so I can barely make out a glimmer of light in them. Faking it? I prod a shoe into her side. "Up, baby."

A cat. The next thing I know, she grabs my legs out from under me, and down I go, the gun flying out of my hand. She throws herself right over me to get to it before I can, her knee slamming me in the jaw on the way. She twists free as I get a hand on her ankle, then we are on our feet facing each other. She is looking at me, I am looking at that gun. She has it clutched in both hands, a finger on the trigger, aiming it at my face, and Christ, somehow she knows enough to cock it. The motion of the barrel as it weaves unsteadily but always in my direction almost hypnotizes me. I raise my hand cautiously. Janet looks completely out of her skull, her face twisted, tear tracks showing through the dirt on it.

"Easy," I say. "Easy, baby," reaching for the barrel very slowly, half inch by half inch, and suddenly she cries out, "Oh, God damn you, Flood," and wildly flings the gun away.

My mistake. I start to go for the gun instead of her, and next instant she darts away, heading through the trees in the direction of the Oates' house. The hell with the gun. I go after her, twenty yards behind, slipping my knife from my pocket as I go, springing open the blade.

Nobody shows among the trees yet. Duffy must have set up his cops along the property line from the bus to the top of the ridge, getting them ready to move after dark. And here is this skinny bitch heading right for that line like an Olympic runner, steering through and around stands of trees so that sometimes I lose sight of her. Twenty yards away is too much. Close together, the knife at her throat is what I need for protection from the enemy.

Her mistake. She comes up to underbrush thick as a wall and hesitates, looking uphill and downhill, then starts uphill. That hesitation is all I need to cut the distance between us in half. Then she is gone. Completely gone. No sight of her anywhere. No sound of her.

Somewhere behind a tree. Maybe down on the ground huddled in a clump of bushes. I wait, my back to that wall of underbrush, sighting uphill, checking out each tree, each clump of bushes. Dead quiet now. But sooner or later she'll have to make a move. The sound will zero me in on her.

The one advantage she has is that she's probably watching every move I make. That means that if I start searching in the wrong direction or get myself tangled in

229

these bushes, she'll be off in the opposite direction before I can corner her.

The sound comes. A rattle and thump, not uphill among those bushes and trees, but behind me among that underbrush. It could be her, somehow trying to worm her way through what looks like impenetrable brush. It could be Duffy's men, seeing me alone and with only a knife in my hand, finally getting up courage to take me out. I wheel around, and a sound behind me tells me I have been suckered into it. From where she was hiding out, Janet had lobbed a stick into the brush, and as soon as I tumbled for this stupidest trick of all, she took off. There she is, scrambling up the ridge, glancing back at me now and then as I go after her.

It is the looking back that undoes her. Too late she sees the fallen tree up ahead, a tangle of limbs and the trunk angling right into that wall of underbrush, making a pocket she can't get out of. But she tries. She clears those limbs, vaults the trunk, and then goes down full-length across branches on the other side.

I move in on her. She is on her back, her ankle caught in a fork of the branches. A runaway doggie never properly trained to heel, the clothesline leash still around her neck.

She glares up at me as I bend over her, the point of the knife at her throat. There is no sign of fear in her. She looks as if, given another chance with that gun, this time she would pull the trigger.

"You're giving me a lot of trouble, baby," I tell her. "Too much trouble."

She whispers, "The deal still stands, Flood. Take your gang and go away. I'll help you every way I can."

Help me every way she can. And while she's saying it she is working her ankle loose from the branches. A little turn here, a little pull there, smooth and subtle, trying not to shake the branches. But I see them shake, and I jam

230

my heel down on her knee hard. She screams, and I drop down and clamp a hand over her mouth to muffle any other screams. But there is no more noise from her. She's out cold. Slack all over, the leg I tramped on twisted at an odd angle. Broken.

I unhook the ankle from the branches, run a hand over the leg. I can feel the fracture just below the knee, but there's no bleeding showing through the tight jeans, so it's a simple fracture. Move her carelessly, the bone can go right through the flesh and she can bleed to death. The temptation to have it this way, the even hotter temptation to simply shove the knife into her belly, slice her open and let her guts spill out, no. To wind up minus one hostage, this hostage especially, and with nothing to show for it, no.

The way she is, showing the hurt marks but able to sound off, makes her the handiest line of communication I can ask for.

Live bait.

Working fast, I find two branches that can serve as splints. I fit them on each side of the broken leg, then pull the leash from her neck to tie them tight with. No, I'll need that length of rope. So I pull her shirt off, rip the sleeves away and use them to strap the branches to her leg. She groans when I do it, her head moves from side to side, but she remains out cold. I turn her over on her belly, slice the clothesline in halves and bind her wrists behind her. Roping her ankles together probably isn't necessary, the shape she's in, but I'm taking no more chances with this one. I tie her ankles together anyhow, then gag her with the remnant of the shirt. It isn't time yet for her to do her broadcasting.

She comes to when I get her over my shoulder, eyes opening, incoherent sounds coming from behind the gag. There's no weight to her at all, but those bound legs thrust out ahead of me make an awkward package as I move downhill toward the road, always close to ramming them into a tree or some of the heavy growth I have to steer around. If that happens, I can be knocked right off balance, let go of her, set myself up as a beautiful target for a sniper. With her draped over me like this, I'm safe until we reach cover near the road.

The cover is there, a good-sized tree about fifteen or twenty feet above the road, the rest of the way down to the road just high grass, perfect for the operation. I slide Janet to the ground and squat down, my back against the tree. Her eyes look glazed. "Can you hear what I'm saying?" I whisper, and when there's no response I run a hand over one of those undersized breasts, then grip a nipple between my fingers and squeeze it hard. She makes strangling noises in her throat, shakes her head wildly from side to side, and I release her. "Can you understand what I'm saying?" and this time she nods yes.

"Good. You're going for a trip by yourself down to that road, baby. They'll see you from that bus, and they'll sure as hell hear you when I get that thing off your mouth. When they come to haul you away, you tell them that one hour from now—no more than that—if somebody doesn't show up right in front of the house to talk business, they'll be getting another bundle like this delivered to them. And it won't be with just a broken leg. It'll be in pieces, like something you have to fit together before you even know what it is. One hour, that's the time limit. Do you have that straight?"

She nods.

"You understand this is the real thing? No more fun time?"

She tries to say something through the gag, but when I reach for her breast again she cuts it short.

"You're learning," I tell her, then pull the gag off and give her a hard shove to start her down the slope. She rolls over and over, screaming all the way down until she winds up on the edge of the road and the screaming suddenly stops. From the look of her, out cold again.

If I had a gun, I can lay low here and parley with whoever comes to get her. Without a gun, I'm a rabbit in a trap if they move in around me. But no rush. Time to take off when I see the first one show down the road.

I get down behind the tree, my eyes on that bus a hundred yards away, and wait.

What gives me the feeling that I have gone through exactly this kind of watching and waiting before?

The waterfall.

That toy waterfall on the back slope of the ridge. Janet, naked on a blanket, that tight little ass getting the sunshine. J. Flood, demon cameraman, getting ready to snap the picture of a lifetime.

So here we are again, baby, and how do you like it this time?

I wait.

Then I hear it. A grinding of gravel under slow-moving wheels. And see it. First a flicker of sunlight on metal, then the car itself. Green body, white trim. Police.

The bend of the road, the overhang of the trees allow me only glimpses of it as it crawls up to the bus, stops there. A courier. Or maybe General Duffy himself. Somebody in the bus has seen that half-naked, trussed-up body on the road, has called back to headquarters about it, and now it's decision-making time for the general.

Janet doesn't move. I scoop up some pebbles, toss them at her, and now she moves, her head jerking from side to side.

"They're here, baby," I call to her. "When they get to you, talk fast," and then I belly-crawl up the slope and get to my feet and head in the direction of the house.

Marcus
Hayworth

Four o'clock.

David leaves to once more scout the house from the edge of the woods.

Four-fifteen.

Uri Shapiro phones. He and Ethel Quimby have been phoning regularly. His voice is low, hard to make out. Someone must be there with him in his office. "Has anything happened yet?"

"No."

"Marcus, is it all right if I come up there now? I'm no use here in the store. I can't think straight."

"Yes, come right up."

Painful to hear him sound like this. A philosophical sort of man, almost pontifical in manner no matter the provocation, he now sounds terrified.

But he is no different from the rest of us. We are all terrified, though it shows in different ways. I go back into the parlor and see Anna Marcy in her rocking chair, Elizabeth at her knitting, and I see how old they have suddenly become. Both have been defying all their years until now, and now all those years show.

And David. Before he departed on the second mission, he was not quite the same David any more. Cracks showed in the self-assurance. His speech, his motions became more and more abrupt. The eyes were abstracted. At one point he said uncertainly to me, "I wonder if—" and after I waited for the rest of it and finally asked, "Wonder what?" he only looked at me blankly as if he couldn't comprehend the reason for my question.

And I am terrified too, but strangely, it seems to be lodged only in the pit of the stomach. Somehow, in my mind I am able to stay sufficiently remote from events to evaluate, calculate, plan moves in this deadly game, so that the mind miraculously grows more and more precise in its functioning while that one spot in the stomach absorbs all the punishment.

I force myself to face one agonizing question squarely. If I had been bolder with Flood, if I had agreed to meet his every demand only on his assurance that the women would not be taken away as hostages after delivery was made—

No.

No chance of that. He would never yield up the hostages until he was safely out of the country. Safely settled elsewhere. And even then—

Am I sure of that?

Yes.

In that case, everything must be done as we are now doing it.

I try to put myself in Flood's place. Surely he knows by now that he can't communicate with the outside world. Possibly he's had one of his men scout far enough away from the house to learn that the road is blocked in both directions. So I am Flood, watching the time crawl by, driven wild by frustration. What do I do? What is there to do?

A fire. The garage would go up like kindling. And that kind of fire would be observed miles away. An alarm would go out, the fire department and the police would race for the scene, would somehow get past those roadblocks to the house itself. That's all Flood can want. Somebody, anybody, to hear his ultimatum.

Fire.

I go outside, half expecting to see smoke roiling up from among those treetops on the crown of the ridge, but there is no smoke. Not yet. I am standing there watchfully when Uri Shapiro drives up. He gets out of the car, trots over to me anxiously. "What is it? What do you see?"

I explain to him, and he nods. "Yes, fire. It's a possibility. Ah, God, that madman. That madman. Marcus, what's going to come of this? How will it end? How will you even know it's ended, the way you're doing it?"

"I've been thinking about that. Ken's truck—the one he uses for outside boat-repair jobs—that truck has a phone in it, doesn't it?"

"I think so. Yes."

"That's what we need. There's no way out for Flood now but that back trail down to the highway. With Ken in the truck on the highway keeping watch there, he can stay in touch with us here by phone."

"Would Flood risk the highway? Out there in the open, no car of his own—"

"With the road here blocked, what other way out does he have? And if he takes any of the women with him, he can decoy some car on the highway into stopping. Ken can let us know before anything like that happens."

"But if he takes any of the women with him—"

I cut him off with the familiar old phrase, "We must move as the way becomes clear, Uri, one step at a time. I'll phone Ken now."

The boatyard's workday ends at four, but Ken is always there for a while after that. He is not there now. Nobody is there, says the watchman who answers my call, except himself. Mrs. Quimby came by in the car a little before quitting time and picked up Mr. Quimby and they just took off.

"Where?" I ask. "Do you know where they went?"

"No, sir, Mr. Hayworth. Most likely back to the house."

"Thanks." I'm about to put down the phone when the man says, "Oh yeah, Mr. Hayworth. I'm sorry about your daughter. I hope everything comes out all right."

"What?" Then I realize he is talking about the accident we fabricated for Janet. "Oh yes. Well, thank you."

"You know, Mr. Hayworth—"

The impatience raging in me is too much to control. "Damn it, I can't talk now!" I say and hang up abruptly. Let him charge me with bad manners. Better than being able to charge me later with failure to prevent murder.

I dial the Quimbys' number. Ken answers. "Marcus, we were just on our way up there. What's going on? Has anything happened?"

"No. Ken, you have that phone in your truck, don't you?"

"Yes."

"Then don't come up here in the car. Use the truck."

"You need the phone? Why?"

"I'll tell you when you get here." A worrisome thought strikes me. "Ken, about the children. You're not—"

"No, no, we've got a sitter for them."

"All right, I'll be waiting for you."

I go into the parlor and see Anna holding a warning finger to her lips. Elizabeth, her head against the back of the chair, her knitting in her lap, is sound asleep.

Anna whispers to me, "What did thee want of Kenneth?" and when I tell her, she nods. "A good idea."

"I hope so."

"We live in hopes, Marcus." She starts up as the phone rings, deafeningly loud it seems to me in my state of nerves, and she goes to the phone, casting an anxious eye at Elizabeth, who never stirs from her sleep. I follow and am at her shoulder when she answers. "Yes," she says. "Yes."

Bad news. I can tell from her voice it's bad news.

She holds the phone out to me. "The police," she says. "John Duffy. He must speak with you."

The police. John Duffy.

I don't want to answer that call.

The police know. John Duffy knows.

And this is how it will end. With the armed assault on the house Flood wants, with gunfire.

At best, my relationship with Duffy is strained. As Banker Hayworth, I have his grudging respect. As Friend Hayworth, I bewilder him, sometimes anger him. To him I am the dangerous eccentric who signed peace petitions during the worst of the Vietnam war, who protested his always heavy-handed treatment of the long-haired young-sters flocking into town during summer seasons, who appeared with an outraged delegation at the town hall after those notorious Labor Day raids against nude swimmers and marijuana smokers when our detention cells—built fifty years ago to hold half a dozen occupants at most—were packed like the Black Hole of Calcutta for that weekend by forty young people, almost all of whom were found not guilty at their trials. Worst of all, John Duffy feels that my leasing the Oates' house to McGrath and Erlanger and their tatterdemalion commune is a slap in the face deliberately aimed at him, which it is not, nor was ever intended to be.

John Duffy and James Flood.

Ten years ago it was Duffy who made the arrest when Jimmy Flood accidentally fired a bullet through the arm of a trash collector in front of his home. It was Duffy who tried his hardest to get the boy put away. It was the lawyer hired by me, after Flood senior came drunkenly blubbering to me for help, who managed to get the child placed in my probation. It was Duffy's triumph when Jimmy, in college, made headlines by becoming the most violent of student activists.

It must be an even greater triumph for Duffy now that Jimmy Flood has made me and my family his victims. And that I myself connived to cover up the crime. In fact, made myself an accessory to it by not reporting it to the police.

Duffy and Flood.

Flood wants a confrontation between them, a deadly showdown, and now Duffy will be glad to provide it. Like a pair of gunslingers in a western movie, they will have it out on the public road, only in this case they will have it out with my family between them. And surely, neither John Duffy nor James Flood will be the first victim or the only victim when the assault is made.

A showdown. A lunatic showdown and then official regrets to all the bereaved at all the burials.

"Marcus"—Anna is thrusting the phone at me, a hand over the mouthpiece—"thee cannot just stand there. Whatever there is to say to John Duffy, thee must say it."

I take the phone, braced for the angry outburst to come. "Yes?"

There is no outburst. Duffy's tone is almost apologetic. "Mr. Hayworth? I've got a couple of alleged perpetrators here—"

"What?"

"A couple of alleged perpetrators. Name of Raymond McGrath and Louis Erlanger. You know who I'm talking about all right, Mr. Hayworth. Now look, I got a pretty good idea what you folks up there are getting handed to you by these characters. So all you do is come right down to headquarters, and we'll straighten it out one, two, three. Or if you want me to bring them up there—"

"No." So he doesn't know yet! But McGrath and Erlanger? Of course, those roadblocks. "No," I repeat sharply. "No need to come up here. I'll be there right away."

"Yeah. You do that, Mr. Hayworth."

I put down the phone. I must be there right away. If I'm not— Meanwhile David is out of reach and the Quimbys are going to show up soon. So it is poor Anna who will have to shoulder the load. She seems more steady of nerve than Uri Shapiro. I tell her, "Duffy's arrested Ray McGrath and Lou Erlanger. I think he's found out about the roadblocks."

"Does he know yet about James Flood?"

"I don't know for a certainty. I'm going there now. Meanwhile, tell Uri about this, and David when he gets back. And tell them not to leave here, not to do anything until they hear from me. When Kenneth gets here in the truck, he's to drive around to the highway and park where he can keep an eye on that trail from my house. He'll know where the best place is. Make sure to get the number of the phone in the truck, ask him how we call him on it."

"And he is just to remain there?"

"Until he hears from me. I'll make it as quick as I can. If I have to, I'll call you from town."

"I will take care of it."

She says she will, and she will.

Uri is pacing the roadside. Getting into the station wagon, I call to him, "I have to go to town. Anna will explain," and as I turn down the road I see him in the mirror, standing there, gaping after me.

Headquarters. As far back as anyone's memory goes,

it had been called the station house. Then Duffy was appointed police chief, and now it is headquarters. The blue uniforms of our old force have become a military-gray, the sidearms and belt of cartridges conspicuous. The easygoing, neighborly manner of the men in the old uniforms has become the sharply aggressive style of the men in the new uniforms.

Duffy's style.

But, I ask myself, does he have any choice of styles? The older generation of Scammons Landing wants law and order at any cost, the younger generation wants anarchy, and it is the older generation who pays the bills. And John Duffy is the man in the middle. An angry and blundering man trying to handle an impossible job.

I pass the meeting house, make the turn down Quaker Lane, driving recklessly fast. If Duffy knows about the roadblocks—indeed, knows enough to phone me at the Marcy house—how much more does he know? Have McGrath and Erlanger told him about Flood's invasion of my home? They have every right to under these conditions. Going to jail on my behalf was never part of our bargain. Or are they only waiting for me to be the one to tell him?

And if I do, how do I persuade him to give me time, precious time, knowing in my heart that he is beyond such persuasion?

There is no place to park in front of the station house, so I drive around behind the building and park in the area reserved for official use. The young policeman having a cigarette inside the back door recognizes me, although I don't recognize him. I know all the old hands here, very few of the younger ones. He says, "Chief Duffy? Sure, I'll take you up there, Mr. Hayworth."

"That's all right. I know where the office is."

One flight up, down the long corridor, last door to the left. I knock on the door, and Duffy's voice is brusque. "Yeah, yeah, come on in."

I force myself to push open the door, my heart pounding as if I have just run up a dozen flights of stairs. "Oh, it's you, Mr. Hayworth," Duffy says. He gets up from his desk, looks me over curiously. "Say, you have been going through something, haven't you?" He pulls a chair into position for me across the desk. "Drink?"

"No. No, thank you."

"Yeah. Well—"

He seats himself facing me, rests his arms on the desk, hands clasped. He leans forward, studying me again. A wiry man, hard-featured, thin-lipped, all spit-and-polish in that starched gray shirt and black tie. And continuing to study me until at last he shakes his head in a bemused gesture. "It beats me," he says. "It just beats me that people like you—"

"Yes?"

"Look, you don't mind if I come right out with it, Mr. Hayworth, no holds barred?"

"No."

"All right then. People like you mean well—I'll buy that—you mean well. But you sure can make a mess that way for yourselves and everybody else around."

He does know about Flood! But why is he taking this long way around to him?

"This morning," Duffy says, "I heard talk that something serious happened to your daughter. To Janet. Some big doctors were up there, you had the phone cut out, you didn't want anybody near the place until it was all over. You even had the route man hold up the mail delivery. Right?"

"Yes."

"Mr. Hayworth, can you look me in the eye and tell me it's all true about Janet and the doctors' being there and that whole line?"

"John, if I knew what you were getting at—"

"I am getting right to the bottom of this mess. Because Doc Jeffries called me this afternoon worried sick, and he had some pretty strong opinions about what's going on up there. And they made sense. For one thing, he's your doctor and you never even called him in on the case. For another thing, you told him Ridge Road was blocked, he couldn't even drive up to your place if he wanted to."

"That's true. The road is blocked."

"Oh, you don't have to tell me that. Because when I sent a man up there a little while ago to check it out, he found it sure as hell is. And by what? That old bus licensed to those sons of bitches—you'll excuse the language, Mr. Hayworth, but that's what they are—those sons of bitches you leased that property to up there. That

247

commune. And when my man laid it to McGrath, who runs the works there, McGrath let the cat right out of the bag. That gang of hopped-up hoodlums is running a cold war against you, Mr. Hayworth, and you're taking it laying down, because you think that's the way to handle them. Which it isn't."

"A cold war?"

"You want to argue about just what words to use, don't bother." He switches on his intercom. "McGrath and Erlanger," he addresses it. "Up here. On the double."

They are brought up in handcuffs by a uniformed man. Shaggy-haired, bearded, dressed in what more than ever looks like a ragman's discards in these official surroundings, they stand there silent and expressionless. And I am the one responsible for those handcuffs. I open my mouth to protest them, but a warning motion of McGrath's head closes it for me.

Duffy says to them, "You two made a statement to the arresting officer, you made a statement to me. Now I want Mr. Hayworth here to listen to it so he knows you weren't blackjacked into it."

"Sure," McGrath says. "The baron here—"

Duffy bangs his fist on the desk. "The name is Hayworth. *Mister* Hayworth."

"Is it now?" McGrath says in an exaggerated brogue. "Well, Mr. Hayworth here gave our kids orders yesterday not to use the road in front of his castle. Except he missed one detail. It happens to be a public road. So we figured that if we can't use it, it's only fair that he can't use it."

"And," Erlanger puts in, "in case he didn't know how we felt about him, we called him up every now and then to let him know. Too bad he put the phone out of action. It looks like tomorrow we'll have to start writing him letters."

Duffy says between his teeth, "Where you'll be tomorrow, prick, the only writing you'll be able to do is

on a brick wall with a tin spoon," and I think incredulously, My God, he believes them. He believes them
because he is hearing what he wants to hear. He turns to
me. "So there isn't anything wrong with your daughter, is
there, Mr. Hayworth?"

I hesitate. From his expression, that split second of
hesitation has given him his answer. "No," I say.

"No." He leans back, relishing this. "And all that
malarkey about doctors up there, that was just to cover
up a whole different mess, wasn't it?"

"Yes. But it—"

He holds up a hand. "You don't have to apologize. Like
I said, you mean well, Mr. Hayworth. I know how it is.
You painted yourself right into a corner when you rented
to these animals, but you got your pride, you hated to
admit it. Anyhow, now it's out in the open, so there's no
need to be so sweet and tender about it. Know what I
mean?"

"Yes."

"Good. Now I've got this team nailed for blocking that
road and for harassment. It adds up to about ten different
charges. So all you do is sign the complaint and agree that
when the trial comes up—"

"No."

Duffy's face reddens. He stares at me, plainly hating
me. "We went through this once before, Mr. Hayworth.
Remember a kid name of Jimmy Flood?"

"Yes."

"You got him off the hook when he should have been
locked up and the key thrown away. You remember how
he paid off for that?"

"Yes," I say. "I remember. But this isn't the same
thing, John. This was a misunderstanding. I'm sure it's all
cleared up now."

He compresses his lips, chews them, sits there slowly
shaking his head from side to side, a man marveling at the

incomprehensible. "All cleared up. Meaning, whatever these animals want to do to you is all right. You'll take it and like it."

"It was a misunderstanding." I can't think what else to say. And I can't take my eyes off those handcuffs.

Duffy's eyes narrow speculatively. "Tell me something, Mr. Hayworth. Are you scared of them? Is that what it is? You think that if they get what's coming to them, they'll land on you for it?"

"No. I shouldn't have tried to keep the children from using the road." I nod at McGrath, trusting him to pick up his cue. I say to him, "If you're willing to let bygones be bygones—" and he blandly responds, "Well, sure, man. Like, maybe we did push a little too hard."

"So there it is," I tell Duffy. "It's all over. All settled."

"All settled?" He looks at me with contempt, then at McGrath and Erlanger, then back at me. I have a feeling he is barely controlling the impulse to pull out his pistol and put a bullet into each of us. "There's those road-blocks," he says to me. "And that phone you had to take out of service. Is that how you figure it's settled? With Ridge Road closed up and your phone dead from now on?"

"No. Of course not."

Duffy aims a finger at McGrath. "You hear that? The first thing you do is clear away the junk you planted on that road. And fast. I'll have a man up there before dark to see it was done. If not, so help me God I'll make a felony out of it. I'll really ream you with it." He aims the finger at me. "As for your phone, Mr. Hayworth, you can get it ready for action right now. There's a lot of people you owe calls to, starting with Doc Jeffries. Maybe they'll sleep easier knowing there's not a bunch of doctors operating on Janet up there. Only a gang of junkie hoodlums operating on you."

He picks up his phone. He dials with a flick of the

finger. "Operator? Emergency phone service." And I can only watch him helplessly. The phone service will be restored. Someone, anyone, even by accident, will call the house, and the instant that ring sounds there, James Flood will know he is in contact with the outside world again.

A line of communication. That is his real weapon.

And all I can do is take the phone from Duffy, and like a man weaving his own noose, tell the girl in charge that I want my service reopened and give her my number and listen as she brightly says, "Yes, sir. It's after hours, so it won't be right away. But it shouldn't take long."

"How long?" I ask.

"Oh, an hour maybe."

"No rush," I say.

She laughs. "Well, it's nice to hear somebody say that, sir."

That's it.

An hour. And then Flood will be handed his deadliest weapon again.

Duffy nods at the officer with McGrath and Erlanger. "Let them go," he says, and the handcuffs are removed. Then he says to me, "People like you make this a rough job for me, Mr. Hayworth. Too rough sometimes."

"I'm sorry."

"Yeah, sure you are."

I follow McGrath and Erlanger downstairs and wait while their wallets are restored to them. When they start toward the front door I motion them the other way and lead them out to the official parking area, out of anyone's earshot.

I say, "I don't think I have to tell you how grateful I am to you for everything. But you know what it might mean if you take away those roadblocks. Can't you delay on it?"

Erlanger shakes his head. "I don't see how. A lot of our

251

people are getting uptight about this whole thing anyhow. They're thinking about what happens when it gets dark, and there's that gang right down the road looking to make some kind of move."

"It's not five-thirty yet," I point out. "That still leaves us almost three hours until dark."

"I know. But that bus and those cars are planted there solid. It'll take a lot of work to get them away. If we don't start on it right now—well, you heard the man. He's sending somebody to check us out on it, and I say he means business."

"And there's the phone," McGrath says. "Once it's working again—"

"It won't be," I say. "I'm canceling that order."

"Even so," Erlanger says. "Look, Marcus, our people went along with this up to where Duffy busted us, but that really turned them off. That makes it Duffy's play now. Maybe the best thing for you to do is just go back in there and tell it to him like it is."

I turn in appeal to McGrath, but before he can say anything, Erlanger says, "No, Ray. This is how it is. This is how it has to be."

This is how it is. This is how it has to be.

"All right," I say, "I'm still grateful to you for everything. All of you there. I'd give you a lift back, but since I can't get across to the Marcy place from yours—"

"No, that's all right," Erlanger says. He seems anxious to be done with all this. "A couple of our women followed along in a car. They're waiting for us around in front."

"And Marcus," McGrath says, "it looks like sooner or later Duffy has to take over. Maybe Lou is right. Maybe this is the time."

They move off, Erlanger briskly, McGrath with dragging feet.

Sooner or later.

No. Not yet.

I use the public phone in the station house. With people walking close by, I keep my voice low, so it is hard to make myself understood at first. Finally I do. The same voice at the other end of the line, but now irritable. "Weren't you the one who just—"

"Yes, but that was a mistake. I definitely want that order canceled."

"You really ought to make up your mind, mister. That order already went in. But I'll see what I can do."

"It's very important. Please do your best."

I can't tell you why it's important, girl, but for God's sake, do your best.

Six o'clock.

Before I even pull off the road at the Marcy house, they are all gathering outside the door, and now Ethel is here and David is back again. Before I answer their questions, I have my own to ask. First David. He shakes his head. "The same. One of the men up on the widow's walk and one of the women. They switched around while I was watching. Brought up Emily and brought down Deborah. I didn't stay long."

Then Ethel. "I spoke to Ken a couple of minutes ago. He says he's parked off the highway near the trail, but he isn't sure what you want him to do."

"I'll speak to him now. How do you call him?"

"You have to use the operator. I'll do it for you."

She does it for me. An endless list of code numbers and letters. Then Kenneth's voice, "Marcus?"

"Yes. Ken, exactly where are you?"

"Right near that culvert that runs under the highway here. I can see anybody coming down the trail as soon as they reach the road."

"It's too close, Ken. They'll be looking to flag down a car, and if they see the truck parked there, they'll probably head right for it. It's too dangerous for you that way. Give them more room."

"And then what?"

"If they show up without any of the women, call the state troopers at once. Tell them to come fast and to move in from both directions."

"Suppose Flood has any of the women with him?"

"Then call me here."

"But, Marcus—"

"No. Just call me. Meanwhile, don't take any chances."

"I won't. And tell Ethel not to worry."

I put down the phone and tell this to Ethel. She says, "I don't understand. If the police already know what's going on—"

"They don't know." There is bewilderment on the faces around me. "John Duffy called me in to press charges against the commune. He thinks they're responsible for whatever's going on up here."

"He would," David says.

"Anyhow, he let them off. But they're removing the roadblocks now."

Uri says, "So how much longer can we—" and I shake my head. "Not much. An hour. Two hours."

"Meanwhile?" Uri says.

We stand there. I have no answer to this. No one has. Then Anna motions toward the parlor. "Meanwhile," she says firmly, "we will draw strength from a prayerful silence."

A prayerful silence?

A tearful silence for Elizabeth and Ethel. Elizabeth, her knitting put aside, sits with clasped hands, eyes fixed on the open window, the tear stains shiny on those dried-out old cheeks. Ethel, head bowed, now and then sniffles audibly. Only Anna, among the women, remains dry-eyed, looking straight at me but not seeing me. Of our meeting, she has always been the one who can most quickly center down, can most readily yield to the comfort and strengthening of the communal silence.

The clock in the hallway chimes the quarter-hour.

Six-fifteen.

Pray? Each time I try, I find I am making bargains with the Creator. Each prayer starts: "If you will only—" and then I stop short. Who am I to ask the Creator to initial a contract which starts: *In return for good and sufficient payment* . . . ?

When the phone rings, it sounds to me like an exploding bomb. To everyone else as well, from the way they are out of their chairs at the first note.

Nearest to the hallway, I am already at the phone when I remember that Anna must be the one to take all calls here. I wait, twitching with impatience, as she makes her way to the phone. Just enough time for me to wildly conjecture that it is Kenneth calling from the highway, no, it is Flood himself. Having found the phone working again, he is now making that contact with the outside world he so desperately needs to make. But why to this house? No, it must be John Duffy. He's hit on the truth—

"Yes?" Anna says to the caller, then hands me the phone. "Raymond McGrath."

McGrath?

"What is it, Ray?"

"It's good, Marcus. Now don't get all shook up. We've got Janet here."

"Janet? My God, how is she? What happened to her?"

"Man, I told you not to get shook up. She's all right. Beat up some and it looks like her leg is broken, so it's hurting bad, but no big damage done. Flood dumped her on the road all tied up about fifty yards your side of the bus, and when we went out there we saw her and brought her back here. But, Marcus, we ought to get her down to the hospital, and she won't let us. Here she is. Try to talk some sense into her."

Everyone is around me now at the phone. All I have time to tell them is, "Janet's at the commune. She's all right," and then Janet is saying to me, "Please listen. It's hard for me to talk, so just please listen."

"Yes. I will. But what about Mother and Deborah? How are they?"

"All right when I left the house."

"And Sarah?"

"Dead."

"Dead!" I shouldn't have blurted out the word like that. Everyone around me seems stricken into shock. David reaches for the phone, but I thrust his arm away. Janet's voice continues in my ear, sharp and demanding. "Are you listening to me? Will you please just listen to me?"

257

"Yes. Yes. Go ahead."

"All right then. Flood and the others still don't know she's dead. We didn't want them to know it. If they did, it wouldn't matter to them any more if they killed somebody else. Do you understand?"

"But what happened to you? Why were you—"

"No. I'm getting to that. Ray told me what you're all trying to do. We already thought that might be it, Mother especially. And it's working. It has to work. Because I don't think Flood will hesitate to kill Mother or Deborah if the police show up there now and try to get at him. Maybe not the others, but Flood is really insane, he is really out of his mind.

"But what's happened because neither you nor the police showed up is that Digby is against Flood now, and even the other two aren't so sure. It got to where Flood had to do something to cool them down, so he was having me drive him into town to make contact with you, except that we found the road was blocked. He was in a panic then. He thought the police were all around us. I didn't know what he would do when he got back to the house. So I crashed the car. But I didn't have the nerve to do it right, and he wasn't killed. He wasn't even hurt. I didn't have the nerve, do you understand?" Her tone is becoming so intense that while she hasn't raised her voice at all, I feel as if she is furiously shouting the words at me. I say, "Janet, please. You shouldn't—"

"No. I didn't have the guts to do what I had to do. And I had another chance. Out in the woods I had his gun in my hand, I pointed it right at him, and I couldn't pull the trigger. And you don't know how much of this is all my fault. Everything Flood is doing to us is my fault!"

"Janet, you must know that's not true. Now let me talk to McGrath."

"No. He's already told me everything. About what happened with Duffy, too. But if Flood finds those

258

roadblocks gone, he'll just take off in a car with Mother and Deborah. So Ray agreed to leave the roadblocks there. And you can't call in the police. That's what Flood is waiting for so he can really cut loose. And you can't let it happen. You mustn't let it happen."

"We're doing all we can. But what about you? McGrath says you're badly hurt, you ought to be in the hospital—"

"I'm not going down there! Can't you see the questions that'll be asked, the way all this will be stirred up?"

"Janet, let me talk to McGrath! Right now. Do you hear me?" Then, mercifully, there is McGrath saying, "It's no use, Marcus. She's really freaked out about the hospital. We'll do what we can for her here. We've got some stuff, you know, so we can sort of sedate her. She can hold out for a while that way."

Sedate her. Pills. "Ray, she might have a lot more tolerance for anything you give her than you—"

"I know all about it. Leave it to me. Meanwhile, you heard what she said. We'll take our chances here and leave the roadblocks. But you'll have to give Duffy some kind of excuse for us. Otherwise, his Boy Scouts will be up here in a little while checking us out."

"I'll take care of it. Ray, what about your people there? Lou and the others. Are they going along with this?"

"Lou for sure. Some of the others too, now that Janet had it out with us. The rest are piling the kids into the cars now, they'll camp overnight down by the lake. Make it like a party for the kids. You know, Marcus, this Janet—she's quite a woman."

"I know. Tell her I know it. Make sure she understands that, Ray."

"I will. Hang tight, Marcus. It could be a long night coming up."

I put down the phone, and David demands, "What did they say? What's it all about?"

I explain it to him, explain it to them all in as few words as I can, and Elizabeth says, "Sarah Frisch has family. They must be told about her."

"Not yet," Anna says. "There is no help for her now. It is Emily and Deborah who must be our concern."

"All night," Ethel says to me. "Do you really think this will go on all night?"

"It may."

"But there's Ken. He's put in a brutal day at the yard. I don't see how he can keep awake out there all night."

"He won't have to," David says. "I'll drive down and take over for him."

I suddenly remember something it needed only a minute to forget. "Duffy. I have to call him before it's too late."

Too late, sorry, says the man who answers the call at the station house, the chief already closed up shop for the day. Left about ten minutes ago, Mr. Hayworth. Yeah, maybe he can be reached at home.

But I cannot reach him at home. The phone rings and rings on emptiness. And again I undergo that strange duality in me. All my fear is churning through my guts, centering in a sharp pain in the pit of my stomach, but the mind is functioning coolly and precisely.

I phone the station house again, get the same man. I ask, "Do you know if the chief left orders for anyone to check out Ridge Road in a little while?"

"Maybe he did. I can look it up."

"All right then. If he did, you can cancel those orders on my say-so."

"Hey, now look, Mr. Hayworth—"

"On my say-so. Just make a note that we can't get equipment out here tonight to remove those roadblocks I talked to him about. Everything will be taken care of tomorrow."

"Oh. Well, I guess if you already talked to him about it—"

"Right. I'll call him about it first thing in the morning. And you can save your man a trip up here."

"I'll see what I can do, Mr. Hayworth."

I put down the phone.

A long night coming up, McGrath said. And still two hours before it starts.

James Flood

The gun.

One Colt Police Positive.

Heavy.

Now how the hell far could she have heaved it?

Think, Jimmy boy. We were standing in the middle of this clearing, she facing the direction of the house, I with my back to it. So she was facing north, I was facing south. She flung the gun away with a backhanded motion, to her right. To the east. So why am I on my belly, scrabbling through these thickets on the west side of the clearing, ripping my arms apart on these barbed-wire briers?

Because, Jimmy-O, you have already combed through all that brush and grass on the east side of this clearing. No dice.

What makes you think this is where it happened? Consider that one grassy opening among these fucking trees looks like every other grassy opening among these fucking trees.

I work my way back out of the thicket, blind with sweat, my arms bloody from brier slashes. I am winded. For all the muscle-building Cap'n Sharpless provided me aboard his handsome fishing craft down Miami way, I am really winded.

Take five, Flood. You've earned it.

I lie spread-eagled on my back, eyes closed, head pounding, and take five. I also take stock. I left her there on the road. Check. I saw the police car pull up and make contact with the bus. Check. I crawled and scurried—stop and start, crawl and scurry, better safe than sorry—up the ridge in a line for the house, then, out of range of the road, I looped down and around to where the gun should be. Check.

But isn't.

Check.

Come back with your shield, baby, said the mamma Spartan, or on it.

Four handguns. One for each of us. Exactly one. Now why the hell did Harvey order just four handguns from Santiago and company? For what it was going to cost us, he could have ordered six, or ten, or fifty.

Come back with your gun, Flood, because there could be trouble up there in Fort Hayworth. Get that sour smell there when you left? Gangrene of the morale. Coco already has it bad. It is showing on Harvey. Lester? If Harvey has it, Lester will catch it.

No gun, Flood? Nothing for the doctor to hype the patients with when he walks in on them? Make a note. Once in the house, pick up one of those Uzi's fast.

Otherwise.

Janet the cat. Scrawny, treacherous, joyless, joy-popping bitch. The mistake was in not gang-banging her right at the start to show everyone the score, then a repeat every hour on the hour until she yelled for daddy. Would go crawling to him naked through these briers, begging him to pay his dues.

The company you keep. The Company you made. Two Shanklins, one Digby. Two half-wits, one wit-and-a-half. Heads together, they are talking now. Get Flood. Wrap him up and sell him. That's right, Jimmy boy, get those hands behind the back, feet together, and don't fiddle with these knots. When the police move in, run up a white flag. A deal. What are we offered for two hostages—no, three, figuring in the old lady—and J. Flood? And how would you like him delivered, Mr. Duffy, sir, dead or alive?

That was the real mistake, the lion inviting three hyenas to dinner.

Up yours, hyenas.

You've already taken five, Flood. You've already taken more than ten.

Slowly, carefully I get to my feet, straining to sound out any popping of a twig, any hissing of knee-high grass as someone works his way toward me. Nothing. Obviously, if any of General Duffy's troops had me in his sights, he would have put me away by now like Peter Rabbit. Obviously, I am well within my own perimeter, well outside Duffy's. It's been a while since I was upright on my legs, they feel rubbery.

I move toward the house, not directly but paralleling the road and out of sight of it. Ten yards, and here is another opening among the trees. A granddaddy tree over there. A monster. Wasn't that the one right behind her when she was holding the gun on me? This is the place.

It isn't. I thrash back and forth through the grass with a stick. I get down on my belly again and poke into the underbrush. No gun.

Take another ten, Flood.

That's right. Stretch out face-down this time, get a good whiff of this mulch, and consider the facts. Fact: the hyenas are more dangerous to you now than the police dogs.

Is it a fact? Consider, Flood, that after one short week in Raiford, they took off their hats to you. And you had no gun there, no pig-poker, nothing. But they stayed clear of you. Why? Because you had something in the eye that told them to stay clear. Don't tread on me. Coco could be the old blacksnake. I was the copperhead.

I still am.

I come to the edge of the woods at a point where I can't get a view of the sun deck, so I work my way downhill until I come to a place where the angle is right. Coco is on duty up there now, and with Mamma Emily for company. Even from this distance, it's easy to see the old blacksnake is twitchy. Gun at the ready, he stands close beside mamma, who is sitting on the flooring there, only her head showing above the rail, then he disappears to the back side of the sun deck, then comes to the front again.

Back and forth.

I let him repeat this a few times, then gauging it so he can recognize me first look at this distance, I step out into the open, waving both arms, calling, "The door! Open up!"

Next thing the barrel of that gun swings right my way, and I twist aside, hit the ground hard, flattening myself as I wait for the blast. One. Two. Three. Four. Five. No blast. I raise my head and squint at the sun deck. Now he recognizes me, the jumpy son of a bitch. He waves me in.

I come in, moving fast across this open space, zigzagging to throw off any snipers beyond the road. The door swings open as I come up on the porch. It is slammed shut behind me.

Trouble.

Harvey and Lester are here in the hallway. Sleepy-eyed and empty-faced most of the time, they are now wide awake, mean-looking. "What happened?" Harvey says. "Where's the car? Where's the girl?"

"Man, you head off one way," Lester says, "next thing that old car comes zooming back the other way. What was that all about?"

He has a brain that can handle one thought at a time. This must have been the thought since he saw it happen. Methodical. He has laid out the inventory in the hallway near the stairs. A nice neat row. One submachine gun, two rifles, eight G.I. cartridge boxes, six grenades. And four gas masks.

I drift toward the inventory, holding up a hand to show I am having trouble getting my wind back. The hand is quicker than the eye. They watch the hand and the hard breathing, not the direction of the feet.

Coco comes oozing down the stairs. Submachine gun in hand, pistol in belt, knife up the sleeve. The one-man gang. He is watching the feet. He watches me pick up that unloaded Uzi, but when I move toward the cartridge cases he is already there, blocking the way. "Where is your weapon, man?" No heat in the way he puts it. Just a question. Passing the time of day. And gently rubbing the business end of his very much loaded Uzi back and forth against my belt, where there is no weapon. Brave, because there is no weapon.

I say, "There's roadblocks both ways. And cops. The girl cracked up the car when we were getting away from them. I suppose the gun is there with what's left of it."

"And the girl?"

"No damage. I gave her a message for the cops. They want to move in here, we're ready for them. They want to make sure nobody gets hurt, Hayworth goes through with delivery right away."

"I see." Coco shows me his teeth. It could be a smile. "The girl wrecks the car, and you pat her on the head and give her a message for the police. Are you sure that is how it went, Mr. Flood?"

"The idea was to get word out there, baby. Now it's out."

"Perhaps." The Uzi's muzzle gently nudging my belt buckle. Coco, the old blacksnake, trying to hypnotize the snake charmer. But Harvey is having none of this game. "For chrissake," he says to Coco, "go on and tell him." Then without waiting for Coco to tell me, he does it himself. "That old Sarah is dead, you hear? You know what that means?"

Cool, Jimmy boy. Calm, cool, and collected. "Sarah? How did that happen? She was all right when I left."

Lester can't believe his ears. "All right? Man, you pistol-whip an old lady like that, and you think she was all right?"

Harvey says to me, "Goddam, you know what it means with her dead?" He points at Coco. "He told us plenty about what it means."

Coco digs the Uzi hard into my belt buckle. No more teeth showing. No more smile. "I told them what I was told in St. Hilary, Mr. Flood. What I already told you right in your ear. If any of these women are killed, we are not welcome there. Do you hear me now, Mr. Flood? Do you understand exactly what you have done? When you wiped out that old woman, you wiped out phase three. Wiped out one whole week I put in negotiating with those Island bastards, bargaining with them—" He is starting to gobble now, he is so wound up. His spit is flying in my face, his eyes showing red. I have the empty Uzi loose in my hand, the hand is starting to twitch. Twitch convulsively on its own. If I move fast enough, swing that barrel into his gun— But with his finger tight on the trigger, even jarring it might get me blown apart.

"Oh yes, man," he says, drawing it out, stretching it out into a long hiss, a long moan, shaking his head over it. "Oh yes, man. You have that old black magic, man, that old juju. But it is all backward, man, because everything you touch turns to shit!"

"You hear him?" Harvey says. "And what about that private deal you wanted to make with him? You get the money and then you knock me and Les off. What about that, Jimmy boy?"

"You mean he told you I came up with something that wild? And you believed him?"

"Who am I supposed to believe? The way you made it out, right now we're walking out of a plane on the Islands with four million cash in our bags. All right, you show me some palm trees outside, and I'll believe you."

Cool, Jimmy boy. Calm. And collected.

I say, "This is getting like a bunch of acidheads on a bad trip. If we sit down around the table right now, and you let me—"

"No," Harvey says. "Whatever you want to tell us, you tell us standing right there. And without throwing a fit. You throw one of those fits, you just might not come out of it."

"All right," I say, "you want it boiled down so even Lester can understand it, nothing's been changed for us except the time limit. Either Hayworth pays up right away, or the police move in. It didn't happen yet, but it will. Either way they want it, we're ready for them."

Coco's lip curls. "Police?" he says. "What police, Mr. Flood? The ones in your brain?"

Harvey says, "That Emily keeps telling us there are no cops out there. She keeps saying that's the way Hayworth would handle it, so nobody gets hurt. She don't look like any liar to me, that woman. She means it."

"Then why don't you try it on for size?" I ask. "There's cars in the garage. Go on, take your pick and try it. But if you hit a roadblock backed up by a couple of dozen cops, don't lay it on me."

"You saw them out there?" Lester says.

"I saw them. And their fucking roadblocks."

"Hayworth could put up a roadblock," Harvey says. "Anybody could. What the hell is there to a roadblock?"

I look from one to the other of them.

The lunatics are really in charge of the asylum now.

I say, "You can see the shape I'm in. Look at me. If you think—" and then Coco is jamming that gun hard into my gut again.

He says, "Man, we have been listening to the radio, you hear me? The news, man! The news! And there is still nothing on it about us. If anybody out there knew about us, you could not keep the news people from making a big thing of it. This is headlines, man. This is television stuff."

"There's ways of keeping big news quiet," I say.

"Like hell. And that Janet girl. You have been looking to rip off that girl. You take her away, you come back without her. How much of a rip-off was it, Mr. Flood? How dead is she?"

Lester says, "You really think he laid her out same as the old lady?"

"She was under his skin like a bloody tick," Coco says. "She gave him the itch."

"Never mind her," Harvey says. "I want to know about us. Where do we stand now? What's our move? That's what I want to hear."

No answer.

What's the matter, Coco baby, cat got your Eye-lond tongue?

Night is coming.

Panic time for the hyenas.

In Raiford, I told them it depended on Hayworth. Could take three hours or three days. Could mean cold

274

war or hot war. That's all right, Jimmy. We're with you, Jimmy. Shee-it, let it take four days, if it pays off a million dollars a day.

And now night is coming.

Panic time.

Did they really think there were days without nights to them?

I'm holding an empty gun, you're holding a loaded one, Coco baby, so phase two is now yours. What do you want to do about it?

Coco doesn't know what. Gun jammed into me, he can only shake his head slowly back and forth considering his troubles.

Coco the blacksnake.

Flood the copperhead.

I say, "What do we do, stand here like this until the cops knock on the door?"

"Cops," says Coco, the unbeliever, but Harvey and Lester look uneasy. They glance up the stairway. They can count well enough on their fingers to know that nobody is up there on the sun deck keeping watch.

Now.

It must be said in the right tone. A shade of impatience, a touch of concern.

I say, "If nobody wants to stand lookout all alone, we can finish this meeting up there. All of us. Where's the girl? Deborah?"

"Locked up in the cellar," Harvey says. "Once we found out the old lady is dead, no need for anybody to watch after her."

So far, so good.

I say, "All right, Deborah can stay down there. Mamma'll be enough company up on top anyhow."

Now to ease the pressure of that gun barrel in my belly. Not too fast so that there will be abrupt consequences, not too slow so that Coco will suspect I am worried about consequences. Imperceptibly I lean back a little, and the pressure is gone. I move, not too fast, not too slow, toward the stairway. I am alone on it the first three steps, then Coco is right there behind me, then Harvey and Lester.

Flood the Pied Piper.

Up one flight. Up another flight to the attic. Up the ladder. The trapdoor is bolted. I shove the bolt clear, push up the hatch. Face to face with Emily. Wild-eyed. "Jimmy, where's Janet? You didn't bring her back with you. What happened to her?"

"Nothing." I am on the sun deck now, the pack taking their places around me. "I left her on the road. Right now she's telling the police that fun time is over."

Emily grabs my arm. "She's all right? You're sure?"

"Yes, God damn it." The woman is right in the middle of the stage, fouling up the scene. I have to shove her away.

"Jimmy—"

"Knock it off!"

Good. I am doing the talking, I am giving the commands, the current of leadership is passing from Coco back to me.

The binoculars are on the floor near the railing. I pick them up, and down low behind the railing I sight into the distance beyond the road. Trees, the bark clearly defined. Emptiness between the trees. General Duffy is not ready to make himself a target yet.

Downstairs, Coco knew there was no enemy out there. Now he is not so sure. Not so quick to stand up at this railing with a bull's-eye painted on his forehead. He crouches behind me, the Uzi leveled at my back. "You want cops?" I say. I thrust the glasses at him. "Take a look, baby." And there are Harvey and Lester, wondering about it, getting into a crouch too, just to make sure. "The back," I order them. "Cover the back!"

276

Commands. Sharp, decisive commands. Order out of confusion. They move to the back railing fast, get down there on guard.

Coco is sighting through the binoculars. "Where, man? Where do you see anybody?"

"Look. There. Straight ahead." I stand, and he is instantly up behind me. Mistrustful. I aim my Uzi at the distance and pull the trigger on nothing. Click.

Now.

If Coco's finger is too tight on his trigger—

But now. It must be now.

I fling my gun aside. "Damn!" I turn halfway around. "No load. Give me that thing."

I reach for it. He lets it go.

I swing around all the way to face him, and he knows what's coming before it comes. He grabs at the barrel, but before he can deflect it, the burst hits him in the chest like a pile driver, knocks him back on his heels, arms thrown wide reaching for nothing. Another burst, chest to crotch, and he goes down on his back in that position. He was probably dead before that second load, but you never know.

And Harvey and Lester facing me from across the sun deck, guns on me, brains scrambled. And not a sound from Mamma Emily. Hands over her ears, she is backed off to the side staring at me. Not at little Jimmy Flood, cut-rate hired hand, but at James Flood, the doomsday man.

I wait. Harvey and Lester wait. The O.K. Corral.

But I will need them.

When Duffy comes to finish what he started ten years ago, I will need them.

Not too fast, not too slow, I lower my gun. I point it at what's left of Hubert Digby. My turn to slowly shake my head. I say to my partners reproachfully, "You believed him. That's what I can't understand. You believed the lying son of a bitch."

"Man—" Harvey says. His gun droops. Lester's gun droops. "He told us—"

"You believed him. You didn't have the brains to see that once we got the money, he's the only one who could go the rest of the way himself. They're waiting for him at St. Hilary, not us."

"But he made sense," Lester protests. "Like about that old Sarah. Man, when it comes down to wasting old ladies—"

"And the radio news," Harvey says. "That still makes sense."

"Not much," I say. "What makes sense is getting ready for the cops, if it's them instead of Hayworth. The guns and ammo, some extension lines and lamps—"

"Old ladies," Lester says. Another idea has taken root in that skull. Three in fifteen minutes. A record for Lester.

"—and Deborah," I say. "Bring her up here. We'll all stay right up here until things take shape. This is control center."

"Control center," Lester says, testing the sound of it. "Control center."

He likes it.

Marcus
Hayworth

There is no end to it.

We go through the motions. One must go through the motions.

David leaves in the station wagon to relieve Kenneth—a roundabout trip to town, then north along Front Street to the juncture with the highway, then back along the highway—and at last the wagon reappears, now with Kenneth at the wheel.

David phones from the truck. "Anything happening?"

"No. I told you I'd call you if there was anything to report." I say it too sharply, nerves rubbed raw by the obscene ticking of that ancient clock near the phone stand, the deadly motion of its pendulum. The pit and the pendulum. But I am here among company at least, and he is sitting there alone in the truck, the end-of-day shadows growing long across the highway. "I'm sorry," I say. "I didn't mean it to sound like that."

"Sure. I understand."

"David, how long will you stay there?"

"Till it's really dark. Eight-thirty, nine o'clock. No use staying after that. They'll never be able to make it down the trail once it's dark."

"Meanwhile, you won't take any chances, will you? If you see them coming?"

"Trust me. Only chance I've taken so far is with the state troopers. They pulled up a few minutes ago, wanted to know why the truck is parked here. I told them motor trouble, and they let it go at that. Now I've got the hood up and I make like I'm working on the motor now and then."

"Good."

"Yes, well—"

There seems nothing more to say. Rather, there is too much to say which best remains unsaid. But we remain on the phone as if we are clutching at each other in our silence. At last I can't hold it back. "Those men must know Flood has let them down. If only Digby takes over for him—"

"It could happen, Marcus. It might have happened already."

I'm grateful to him for that. It's what I wanted from him.

The motions.

Suddenly Anna remembers we have not eaten. She and Elizabeth prepare sandwiches, coffee, a fruit drink. The thought of eating makes my gorge rise, but Anna, ever the tyrant, insists I do. One mouthful does it. I leave the room, vomit up what little there is in me down to the last drop of bile.

It is hard to get rid of that taste.

John Duffy.

What if I were to go to him right now, say, "John, is there any way that without passion, without guns, without killing—"

No.

If I were in his place, and he came to me with that plea, would I comprehend him? Would anyone? Duffy and Flood, Flood and Duffy. Both blindfolded and locked in a cage where the only way out is over each other's dead body.

Madness. There is a madness in the world around me. And what of you, Friend Marcus?

There must be no killing.

My father, at meeting for worship that First Day morning after I told him I had chosen prison rather than service in the army. Gray-faced, shaky-voiced, announcing this to the meeting, then the voice growing stronger, delivering his message: *Every man has the right to die for his beliefs. No man has the right to kill for them.*

Look deep into your heart, Friend Marcus. At this moment, if you faced Flood with a gun in your hand as Janet did, would you kill him?

I don't know. I'm not sure. Besides, what good would it do? There are others with him.

We are talking only about James Flood, Friend Marcus. A cold-blooded murderer who threatens the lives of your wife and daughter.

How can I know? Kenneth said it for me: How can any of us know until we face the moment?

The truth, Friend Marcus. The truth.

Yes, I think I would kill him.

The madness is in me too.

The motions.

The women clean dishes in the kitchen. I go outside, Kenneth and Uri following, and we make a meaningless patrol up and down, up and down, on the road in front of the house. I am grateful that neither of them feels compelled to say anything.

That sound.

It comes from far away, the quick rapping of a woodpecker's beak on metal. It freezes us all in our tracks. And there it is again. The breeze carrying it is blowing northward, coming from the direction of my home. I know what it is even before Kenneth says it. "Guns!"

"The police?" Uri says.

The police? How could they even drive past the commune without McGrath letting me know?

I sprint for the house, fling open the door hard enough to take it off its hinges. Now I can't remember the phone number. That number has been the same for twenty years—thirty years—and now I can't remember it. Then I do.

An unfamiliar voice answers. "Marcus Hayworth," I say. "I have to speak to Ray McGrath right now. Fast," and then, not all that fast, McGrath is saying to me, "Yes? What is it, Marcus?"

"Ray, the police. Were they around there? Did they go by on the road a little while ago?"

"The police? No. No sign of them. Why?"

"We heard what sounded like gunfire here. Coming from that direction."

"Gunfire," McGrath says. "Ah, damn. Damn."

He is thinking what I am thinking. Not the police. A firing squad. Or can this be the means that Flood has struck on to establish communication with me?

"Ray, don't tell Janet. How is she?"

"We've got her halfway under, but she's still hurting bad. Flood rigged up a splint on that leg, but it's got to be set right. And if you just say the word hospital to her, she starts climbing the wall."

"What about a hospital out of town?"

"No way, man. We try to get her there without her okay, we'll have a real mental case on our hands. She says she'll stay with it this way as long as she has to. But it can't be too long, Marcus. You hear me?"

"Yes. I understand."

I put down the phone. Flood rigged up a splint on that leg. An act of kindness? A touch of humanity? And the gunfire. A signal to me? After all, what sense could there be in executing one of those hostages? What sense? Flood needs only one hostage, so there is one to spare. And he must be wild with frustration by now. And who else to vent it on?

And here I am, keeping myself at a distance, with no way of getting answers to any of this.

The clock sounds seven. Seven chimes spaced so that the tone of one must fade away completely before the next is heard. More than enough time for me to make up my mind about what must finally be done.

The Friends are gathered around me, waiting on me. I say to them, "I'm going to the house now."

"I have been thinking of that," Anna says. "I am going too."

I am caught completely off balance by this. I hold on to my temper with an effort. "No, Anna. That's impossible. I'm going alone."

I can tell from their faces what is coming. I move toward the door before they can muster their objections. Kenneth plants his back against it. "Hold on, Marcus. What do you expect to gain by this?"

"Flood might be ready to compromise. If not, his men might be. There's no way of finding out unless I talk to them."

"Why would he compromise?" Uri says. "He still has Emily and Deborah there with him."

"He'll have to release them. I'll make that plain to him. After that, he can have whatever he wants."

"But he won't release them, Marcus. He won't trust you enough for that."

"No," Anna says. "Marcus is right. He will go to them, and I will go too. How can someone be held up to the Light, if thee does not speak with him?"

I recognize that look in her eye, that set of her jaw. Damned maddening stubborn old woman. Temper gets the best of me now. "I must go alone, don't you understand? If anyone comes with me, it only means another hostage for them."

"I am not afraid, Marcus. And it will be a comfort to Emily and Deborah if I am there."

"That is true," Elizabeth puts in. "I will go too."

Kenneth remains with his back to the door. "Look," he says, "nobody is going. Nobody at all." And to me, "All right, you can't take any more of what you're going through. I understand that. That means it's time to go to the police, Marcus. It's their job now."

"Ken's right," Ethel says to me. "If there was any sense to meeting with Flood—" And it is Anna who abruptly cuts her short. "Ethel Quimby," she says in a hard voice, "I did not stand in the way when thee and Kenneth went to demonstrations in Washington and twice spent nights in the jailhouse there. Thee may not stand in my way now."

"Oh? Well, if you think there's any resemblance between those demonstrations and this kind of reckless, useless gesture, Anna, you don't know what it's all about."

"But she may," Uri says. He struggles to find the words. "I think—I feel—how can I put it?—that to try now to seek the Light in James Flood may be part of the great design. And how often that message has come to us in meeting. 'Ours not to complete the task, but neither may we lay it down.' "

Oh God, I think, another recruit in the making. Uri, of all people.

I say to him caustically, "The Light in James Flood? Uri, be sensible. You might as well talk about the Light in the devil."

"But thee will join with us?" Anna asks him.

"If you go, I must. I have no choice."

"Anna," I say, "get it into your head that these men are dangerous criminals. Murderers. And this is not the same Jimmy Flood you knew as a child. Maybe you see yourself tenderly counseling with him, but believe me, it won't be like that."

"How does thee know that for a certainty, Marcus?"

"All right, all right, that settles it. If you make it impossible for me to go alone, then I won't go at all. Nobody will."

"Whether thee does or not," Anna says, "there are three of us who will. But not Ethel and Kenneth."

"Look," Ethel says, "if you're trying to bug us into agreeing with you about this—"

"Ethel, I am only saying that thee and Kenneth have small children. Thee should remain here to attend to calls on the telephone."

"Oh." Ethel looks almost contrite. "But then you admit that what you want to do is foolish and dangerous."

Before Anna can answer, I say, "For the rest of you, yes. Absolutely. Not for me. Try to understand that it's the only thing left for me to do now, if I don't want to call in the police. Me alone."

Anna shakes her head slowly. "Marcus Hayworth, if thee wished to be alone in this concern, thee should not have brought it to meeting. Thee should not have laid the weight of it on us."

"Please," Uri says. "We are facing a terrible question that cannot be answered by sharp tongues and angry voices. Our Friendly heritage tells us to move only as the way becomes clear. So I say, let us share a silence now and wait upon the Light for that clearness."

James Flood

Get ready.

What's left of Coco is carted downstairs, stashed in a bedroom. Mop up the blood. The hell with mopping up the blood, I say, but Lester says no, it's making Emily sick to the stomach, so he mops it up. Methodically. When he's done and there are still stains showing on the planking, I expect him to sandpaper down the wood, but this far he doesn't go.

Methodical.

Five mattresses are brought up from the bedrooms, doubled up, squeezed through the trapdoor. No one else could have done it, my troops make it look easy. A mattress is propped lengthwise against the railing on each side of the sun deck, north, south, east, and west, hopeful barricades, and the remaining mattress is laid out in the middle of the plank flooring for the off-duty man during the siege. Two on duty every minute, one catching up on his sleep.

A bonus package. A chair for mamma. The troops have developed a soft spot for Emily along with their hard-on for Deborah. Lester calls her mamma. *Take it easy, mamma.* Harvey respectfully calls her lady. *No sweat, lady.* I think they're apologizing to her this way for what happened to the old crone Sarah who used to do her dirty undies for her. They are establishing a nice distance from nasty old J. Flood this way. Harvey and Lester, the white-hats. Flood, the black-hat. I don't make an issue of this. The relationship between the general and the troops is not all that warm right now. It will warm up when the action starts.

But these are good troops, none better. The immovable objects. And J. Flood is the irresistible force. Up to now, the question has always been what happens when the irresistible force bangs into the immovable object. No one has considered the interesting possibilities if they sign up for the same project.

Methodical.

Four standing lamps are brought up from the library, lashed to the corners of the sun deck. Brass reflectors, the reading lights replaced by high-powered two-hundred-watt bulbs, they will really light up the perimeter. What looks like a mile of extension wiring pulled out of sockets in the bedrooms, plugged into the attic outlet. Switched on, everything works.

Harvey cleans out the refrigerator, brings up a carton of food and bottled water. There isn't too much food left. The Shanklins, super-locusts, have been into it all day. But there is, Harvey reports, some odds and ends in the pantry. Good. No danger of starvation for the locusts.

Now Deborah up from the cellar. Scared but in fair control. She and Emily have a touching reunion. I watch the troops as they watch Deborah comfort mamma, push her down into her chair again, bend over her with that butt waving at them in those tight jeans. Food, drink, and that beautiful butt—what more could any troops under siege ask for?

Finally, the rest of the weapons and ammo brought up. Lester brings them to me at the foot of the ladder in the attic, I pass them through the hatch to Harvey. His last trip up, Lester also brings some oversized pots from the kitchen.

"What the hell are these for?" I ask. I take one to hand up to Harvey, but Lester pulls it away from me and sets it down on the attic floor.

He says, "Man, things get moving up there and you have to take a piss, you just going to wave it in front of that old lady?"

Wave it in front of Deborah? Gladly. But in front of mamma?

A real gentleman, this pile of muscle.

An authentic mamma freak.

Cute.

But not so cute when the seven o'clock news comes on. He—our sharpshooter—is on duty at the front railing with the binoculars and an M-14, I'm at the back railing, when Harvey on the mattress brings up the volume on the transistor, and we wait on the word from Out There. Lester comes over and squats beside Harvey. A lot of words come out of the transistor, but not the right ones. When it's over they both turn and look at me. Harvey hasn't been talking to me, and he isn't opening up now. He just gives me an accusing shake of the head. Grim.

Lester isn't settling for that. "They don't know yet," he says to me. He sounds mean and he looks mean, our mamma freak. "Nobody out there knows yet."

"They know," I tell him. "Maybe you won't get it over the transistor, but don't you worry your curly head about that, boy. You'll be getting it over a great big bullhorn any time now, loud and clear."

Score three million for Hayworth.

The four million is put together only on Mondays, and the next Monday is a long way off. Too long.

Will you settle for the one million on hand, Mr. Flood?

Yes.

No.

One million plus one hundred thousand. One million for J. Flood, one hundred thousand for the St. Hilary reception committee. Worthington and Moore. If they don't like it, too fucking bad. They will have the gun on me, but I will have the gun on the ladies. Or lady. And a pocketful of grenades. Take what you're offered, gents, and take the ladies. Now Flood is in the cabin. What's left? Pilot, co-pilot, flight engineer, and J. Flood. And a grenade ready. Where to, sir? Mideast. Burnooseville. Sheik country.

The last of this July Group. Sign on a couple of eager-beaver Arab shitheads, the beginning of the next.

I am facing due west, the slope down to Highway 9, the sun just over the tops of the trees blinding me. Harvey is stretched out on the mattress, soothed by the Memphis country-and-western coming over the Adirondack network. I push a shoe into his ribs, shove the

Uzi into his hands. "Take over for a minute. I have to go down and get my shades."

The room where Coco and I waited out the night. Coco, the old blacksnake, tried to get the troops to mutiny, but he couldn't quite make it. You win some, Hubert, you lose all the rest. And look who's wearing your gun in his belt.

The shades are on the dresser. Flood's reflection is in the mirror. The winner.

Down the hall the open door to Janet's room, the drug department. Shuttered dark. I go in, switch on the light. The magic lacquered box. It's been a hard day, it could be an even harder night. I unlock the box, pop two meths. Underdosed. Pop another pair.

Her bed, no mattress on it now. The same bed as ten years ago. Now on top of her, now under her, doing my panicky futile best. She handling the little troublemaker, angrily rubbing it. *Jesus, kid, what's the matter with you?*

The mistake now. As soon as I smelled daddy's double-cross, a gang-bang. That's the treatment, baby. Harvey and Lester holding those skinny legs apart while J. Flood climbs aboard for the first ride. Different from ten years ago, isn't it, baby?

Or is it?

It would have to be. No question about it. Right now I'm ready, just getting the smell of her in the room.

But she's not here, Jimmy boy, only the smell.

All right, I could have done the counting, the other three could have done the work. Until *Daddy, daddy, help me!*

And where is daddy?

Shipping those bagfuls of money to New York, baby. Three million saved is three million earned.

Tricky daddy, keeping Duffy under control this long, knocking out that phone there.

Probably had the service stopped. If he cut the line, he'd knock out every phone along the ridge, and the company would have to get on it sooner or later.

Did it?

The phone is on the night table. I walk over to it, pick it up.

And slam it down again.

A yell from above. "Yo, Jimmy!"

One yell is worth a thousand words.

Up the stairs to the attic, jet-propelled.

Duffy.

Ah, Lester baby, save him for me. Maybe I don't have your touch with the rifle, but give me that first shot at him anyhow, right through the bullhorn. No. Lower. Right through the belly so he can feel it and know it.

Up the ladder to the sun deck. Grab up an M-14 and then—

And then?

They are all lined up at the front railing, troops dead center, hostages off to the side, everything—instructions, orders, warnings—everything gone out of those Dade County Shanklin heads. Perfect targets. Passengers at the rail of the good ship *Lollipop*, Harvey working the binoculars, watching the flyingfish.

"Down!" I shout. "Get down, goddam it!"

"Fuck that," Harvey says. "Come on over here."

Not General Duffy on the march?

Then it has to be Hayworth.

I get to the railing, and Harvey shoves the glasses into my hand. He points. "Up the road there. What the hell is that all about?"

I focus the glasses. Hayworth. Easy to make out even without the glasses. And with him, others. Four others drag-assing along the road. Anna Marcy, the queen bee, all piss and vinegar. Elizabeth Marcy, out-of-this-world daffy. A bald, big-beaked, skinny little man—Uri Shapiro, their Jewboy Quaker. And that last one with the baseball cap shading his face. Baseball cap. Same cap as ten years ago. Quincy. Quimby. Ken Quimby. The one with the big-mouth, big-ass wife.

The righteousness committee.

Scammons Landing Monthly Meeting.

I don't believe it. I am looking at it and I don't believe it.

Hayworth stops. They all stop. Hayworth and Anna Marcy are doing some hard talking. Suddenly Anna cuts loose from them, starts up the road by herself. Jesus, the cranky old bitch must date back to the French and Indian War. Throw a slug into her now, she'd just go up in a cloud of dust. Now the others are tagging after her.

Emily says to Harvey, "I told you who they are." She moves over to me and pulls at my arm. "Jimmy, you know them. Tell him who they are. You mustn't hurt them."

I shove her away. I say to Harvey, "You can see it's Hayworth. What's the difference if he's carting some freaks along with him? The thing is that we're back in business."

"How? I don't see them carrying any bags of money. You show me those big bags of money, and then I'll say we're back in business."

"Man," Lester bleats, "all we are is right back where we started."

One ape echoing the other ape. Brother apes. Cool it, Jimmy boy. What can you expect when you deal with animals? But I don't like the feeling in me. Too cool. Icy cold. A chill in the gut, a roaring in the ears, the hands shaking. The Button. Keep away from The Button, Flood, because there are two Shanklins against one of you. And from the look of them, they are ready for the showdown.

Easy, baby.

I say to them, "Use your brains. We've got Hayworth back, and we've got four more hostages to work him over with. All we have to do now—"

"You said there was cops out there," Lester cuts in. "Man, you think if that was so, they'd let anybody like that come walking down the road?"

"And what did he bring them here for?" Harvey demands. "What the hell is he up to?"

Easy, baby. Easy does it.

I say, "How do I know? Maybe a prayer meeting. That's their business, prayer meetings. And Hayworth conned them into this because he wants to keep stalling. But the stalling is over now. The man is going to see close up what happens when you push it too far in. He is going to smarten up real fast."

Now Emily is all over Harvey, pulling at him. "Please, please, don't listen to him. They can't hurt you. Nobody wants to hurt you. You must know that by now. All they want you to do is go away."

"Yeah, yeah," Harvey says. She is working her way up to a crying fit, and instead of bringing her out of it with a hand across the face, he is trying to untangle himself from her without doing necessary damage. The silly redneck son of a bitch actually looks embarrassed about it. "Yeah, yeah. It's all right, lady."

The parade is up to the driveway now. Next thing they'll be on the porch ringing the doorbell. *Subscribe to* Friends Journal, *sir? Contribute to the Friends Service Committee? Share a prayer for a deserving fat cat?*

Who's in charge here anyhow, Flood?

Since when do the birds hypnotize the snakes?

Move.

I say, "I'm going out to settle with Hayworth. You keep an eye on those woods and cover me from here."

"Cover you?" Lester says. "From what? You still making out like there's cops out there?"

"Don't you bet my life against it, Lester baby. Just watch those woods while the talking goes on. You can count your money meanwhile. Four million dollars and only three of us customers."

Harvey smells something wrong. A sharp nose, Harvey. "Why go out there?" he says. "Why not bring them all in here?"

How to tell him that what I have to do out there I might not be able to do up here with a couple of Shanklins so close. One Shanklin especially. Lester, our musclebound mamma freak.

I don't tell. I say, "I don't want them in here. When I'm done with them they'll be heading right for town to spread the word. That's the name of the game right now."

Harvey shakes his head. "Man—" but before he can get any more out, I say, "You're in such a goddam sweat about not getting this over the radio. Can you think of a better way of doing it?"

No answer.

"All right," I say. "The one thing you don't do if there's any action is waste Hayworth. No mistakes. Remember, he's the meal ticket."

No argument.

They are coming up the driveway now.

Bring on the clowns.

Marcus Hayworth

Out of shadowy woods, into a dazzle of sunlight.

The house.

All shuttered, the windows like blind eyes.

Up there, the widow's walk.

Hard to see against the glare. I shade my eyes. A bulky figure at the railing. Then another. And there, off to the side, two slighter ones. The women. Alive.

So there had been no firing squad. I am dizzy with relief. "Up there!" I say, pointing. "Emily and Deborah!" and Kenneth says, "Yes, I can make them out," so I know it is no mirage.

Dizzy with relief while everything in me is a jelly of fear. If I were alone on this mission, it would take every drop of courage in me to carry it out. I am not brave. I conceal this from the world, but it is the truth. When I see danger ahead I cannot stride toward it but must drive myself toward it. Now, fear for these people beside me is demanding too much courage from me.

There is another figure at the railing now. A smaller one than the pair bulking beside it. Flood. Just the sight of him pulls me up short. If it were only Digby. But Digby is not showing himself yet.

I stand staring at the remote silhouette of Flood, my eyes watering in the sunset glare, but what I am seeing is

Ethel's face when Kenneth said to her, "I'm going too. But you stay here. Anna's right. Somebody has to tend that phone."

She knew what he meant: If anything happens to me, somebody has to tend the kids.

Her face.

No. I can make the rest of the distance by myself, but not in this company. They have come far enough. Incredible that they should have come this far. But here is the end of the line for them.

I tell this to them, and they hear me out. Then Anna says, "Thee knows the sense of the meeting, Marcus. Are we to have meetings on this every step of the way?"

"They can see you from there, Anna. That's all that's needed."

"If they can see us, they must know we come in peace. So they will not harm us."

We come in peace.

Dear God, we have been coming in peace for more than three hundred years now, and where are we?

Ours not to complete the task. Neither may we lay it down.

She believes that, this tight-lipped, shriveled old woman. She and Elizabeth have lived their lives by it, but always apart from the world, shielded by it. What do they know of the real world today and its savagery? Have they seen Sarah Frisch on her bed, beaten, dazed, tied hand and foot? Have they already forgotten her murder?

Angrily I remind them of it, but Anna only shakes her head. "Marcus, thee knows I am not here to see Emily and Deborah from the road. I am here to share with them."

The last Hayworth to use the plain talk, the old talk, was my grandfather. Awesome to a child when the old man was in one of his rare bad tempers. And now—am I possessed by him or am I only trying to communicate with Anna in her own kind of language?—I find myself saying in scathing tones, "Thee is a fool, Anna Marcy. My wife and daughter do not want anyone locked up with them to share their troubles. They want James Flood to be given his money and sent away. And thee stands in the way of that."

She squints at me, studying my face as if I am someone she might know but can't quite recognize. Then she reaches out a foot and marks a line close to my feet in the dirt of the road. "What is it, Marcus?" she asks. "Does your faith extend only this far and no further?"

"Anna—" I start to say, but she wheels around, and on her own she is moving down the road toward the house. Elizabeth instantly trots after her. Kenneth and Uri follow, Uri helplessly calling, "Anna!" but she is as deaf to him as she has chosen to be to me.

Faith plunging into the fire.

I cannot call them back, I cannot drag them back, there is nothing to do but move quickly and get in front of them.

Lead them into the fire.

From the head of the driveway, I can clearly make out everyone on the widow's walk. All of them are fixed on us as we approach, Emily and Deborah gripping the railing, the man called Harve with binoculars to his eyes, the other one—Les—standing with a gun to his shoulder, the gun aiming in our direction.

But Flood is no longer there. He could be on his way down to the door. Still in charge. Not Digby, the more rational one, as I have been desperately hoping. Still Flood.

The door is suddenly pulled open. Someone shadowy stands inside, back to the door. "Hold it."

Flood.

I stop. All of us stand as we are. I could not stop Anna Marcy, but James Flood can.

He sidles out on the porch, back still pressed to the open door, the pistol in his hand menacing us. He scans the distance over our heads. With all the evidence offered him, does he really believe that there's anyone out there who might be a danger to him?

Yes. I think he's mad enough to believe it.

He looks it. Filthied from head to foot, shirt torn to shreds, hair and beard unkempt. And his expression as he stands there regarding us. The spider regarding all these luscious flies drawn to his web. Turning a smile on and off. No, a grimace. On and off like a nervous tic, the clenched teeth suddenly showing, then an instant later not showing, the face becoming rigid.

I say, "Flood, you can see for yourself—"

"Shut up!"

Drunk? The words come out slurred, as if he has trouble mouthing them. When he walks down the steps his legs do not seem all that steady. He approaches to within a few feet of us and makes a sweeping gesture back and forth with the gun. "Line up, motherfuckers."

The same thick voice. That gun in our faces, his finger on the trigger. We are standing in a cluster. I move back a step so that I am side by side with Anna and Elizabeth. Uri and Kenneth move up so that we make a ragged line. Game-playing. The obscenity and the threatening gun are his idea of game-playing. Sooner or later he'll be ready to talk business. Meanwhile, we must bear with the game patiently.

He looks along the line and focuses unsteadily on Anna. "Scared, Anna?"

"Yes. But I am not afraid of thee, James Flood. I am afraid for thee."

"Oh? Anna baby, did anyone in this bunch ever tell you what a miserable old bitch you are? They didn't, did they? Well, now you know."

Game-playing. Thank God, Anna is wise enough not to rise to this provocation.

Flood turns to me. "The money, Marcus? Where are you keeping it? In your pocket?"

"That's why I'm here, Flood. To settle with you about the money."

He makes that sweeping motion with the gun again, back and forth. "And what are they here for?"

"They only want to show you no harm is intended. You know them, Flood. You know that's the truth."

307

"No harm? You son of a bitch, what do you call your kind of double-cross? Stall that stupid little Jimmy Flood. Screw around until the cops are lined up, ready to go."

"No. Listen to me, Flood. There are no police around here. They don't even know about all this."

"And those roadblocks? And that patrol car checking them out?"

"I don't know about any patrol car. I put those roadblocks there."

"You're a liar, Marcus. A fucking greedy liar." Drunk, no question about it. The words are garbled. The bearded lips writhe in the effort to get them out. "So what about the money? What's there to settle? You pay, I collect. That's how we settle, right?"

"Yes. But there are some conditions—"

"Conditions? Who the hell are you to set conditions?"

"Flood, be reasonable. Let the women go, and keep me here. They can arrange everything."

"Yeah?" At least he is thinking it over. Bloodshot eyes slitted, at least he is thinking it over. "Arrange everything," he finally says. "How long is that supposed to take?"

"The vault is set for eight tomorrow morning. If you allow a couple of hours after that—"

"No. Tonight."

"But the vault is set automatically. It's impossible to—"

"That's your problem. Blast the goddam thing open if you have to. Because this is the real thing, baby. So far, it looks like you don't believe a word I say to you, but I am going to make you a believer, baby. Because these are the conditions. You are going, and everybody else stays right here. And you've got three hours to get to town and clean out that bank for me. And take care of those flight arrangements too."

"Flood, it can't be done that way!"

"You mean Duffy won't let you do it that way, now it's getting on night? Because that's when he takes over?"

"No. I give you my word he doesn't know anything about this!"

I seem to be getting drunk myself on the bursting tension in me. The words pouring out of me sound in my ears as hoarse and slurred as Flood's. It doesn't matter. They mean nothing to him anyhow.

"I am going to make you a believer, Marcus," he says. "Here and now." Again that sweeping motion with the gun. "Turn around. Not you, Marcus. Everybody else."

I stand rigidly in position. Hesitating, moving uncertainly, the others, one by one, turn and face the road.

"A believer," Flood says thickly. "Right here and now." He moves toward Anna, stops a few paces behind her. He motions at her. "Nobody'll miss this one, Marcus. She's overdue. So she gets it now. And every three hours from now until you get back with the goods, another one of these clowns gets it. No more talk, Marcus. Action." He aims the gun at the back of Anna's head. "Watch it happen, Marcus."

"Flood!"

He won't really do it. He can't do it. But that is the click of the pistol being cocked. And that grimace. Sheer pleasure in what is coming. He will do it.

My eyes are fixed on that widening grimace as I set myself to spring at him, and suddenly there is no grimace. An explosion above my head, a look of agony—staring eyes, gaping mouth—where there had been a grimace, and now Flood is toppling forward, going down on his hands and knees, releasing the gun as he strains to force himself upright again. No use. Arms and legs give way, and he goes down flat on his face. There is a small red stain on his shirt at the shoulder. It steadily grows larger, strings of it worming their way outward.

Women screaming. I look up at the widow's walk.

Emily and Deborah. Les, the rifle still at his shoulder. Harve.

Harve is aiming a finger at me. "Don't move!" he shouts. "Nobody move!"

There is still no escape.

It is Emily who provides the materials, it is Harve who applies the first aid, stripping away the bloody shirt, pouring raw alcohol into the small hole in back of the shoulder, the larger wound above the nipple where the bullet had made its exit, packing bits of cloth into the wounds, padding them over, binding the pads with adhesive tape. It is a crude and painful treatment, and unconscious though he seems to be, Flood, his face ashen, writhes and moans under it, his eyelids fluttering now and then, his lips curling back spasmodically to show clenched teeth.

Les is stricken by this. He leans over Flood. "I didn't mean it, Jimmy. I swear to God I went for the gun. That's all I was aiming at. You know that, don't you?"

Harve, hard at work, says sharply, "He's out cold, so how can he know anything right now? Stop talking foolish, and just get these people locked up in that cellar." He nods toward me. "Except him."

Les is glad to be of service. He has exchanged the rifle for a submachine gun. He motions with it. "All right, everybody, you heard the man. Let's move."

Except me.

I am left here on my driveway with Harve and James Flood. So poisonous is Flood's effect that while Harve is buttoning him into one of my shirts which Emily was ordered to fetch for the purpose, and moves Flood's arm so that it almost brushes my shoe, I involuntarily step back from it as if it would sting me.

Harve gets to his feet. He looks down at Flood reflectively, then says to me, "Crazy bastard was all of a sudden strung out on knocking off old ladies. Like that Sarah. He gave it to her for good, you know that? Wiped out the nigger too. All of a sudden kill-crazy, you know what I mean?"

"Yes." So Digby is dead. It hadn't been imagination when we thought we heard gunfire from here.

"Your fault," Harve says.

"Mine?"

"Sure. The way you screwed up everything was what got to working on him. Now you're going to unscrew them."

"Whatever I can do to keep anyone else from being hurt—"

"Fuck the speeches. Just you answer what I ask. Got that?"

"Yes."

"All right, now why'd you bring those people up here?"

"They wanted to come. They wanted to show you that you weren't being threatened in any way. All of you."

"Yeah, that's what your wife said. And you know what? You're all a gang of freaks. How'd you keep the cops away?"

"I didn't let them know about this. That's the truth. You have to believe it."

"Shit, you don't have to sell me. If there was cops in on this, you think they'd let you and those loonies come waltzing up here like you did? But with those roadblocks and the phone out and all, they'll catch on sooner or later, won't they?"

"Yes."

"So the jackpot question is when. Tonight maybe?"

"I don't know. It could be tonight."

"And how about your friends down in the cellar? Sure as hell, somebody'll start wondering about them pretty soon, right?"

"Yes."

"Now listen close." The face is no longer so vacuous. There is a sharpness in the eyes. "When you told Flood that bank vault was set for eight o'clock, was that on the level?"

"Yes. Set automatically."

"So we pull out of here right now. You, me, Les, and Jimmy. We hit the road in a car and just kill time out there until eight o'clock. Then you get us the money, and that's all there is to it. No fuss, nobody gets hurt. You stay with us until we have the money and some kind of head start."

"But you can't get past those roadblocks in a car." His face turns sullen. I must talk fast, talk with conviction. "Anyhow, there's a way down to the highway from the back of the house, and a car waiting there. A pickup truck."

"Waiting there? For what?"

"My son-in-law—you saw him this morning—well, he and I thought Flood might move out that way. We wanted to know about it, if he did."

Harve ponders this, gnawing at a fingernail. "How much of a trip down to that truck?"

"Fifteen or twenty minutes, if we move fast. But we'll have to start now while there's still some light."

Anything to get them away from here. And no matter how much I want to, I can't do it alone. David must be part of it.

It is our turn to be the hostages.

Harve worries the fingernail with his teeth. His eyes

are remote, his brow furrowed in heavy thought. "All right," he says. "That's how we do it. I guess I don't have to tell you what happens if there's any kind of double-cross."

"No," I say. "You don't."

Inside the house, we must wait for Les, who seems to be making a project of locking up his captives in the cellar.

Maddening.

Flood, laid out on a couch, stirs fitfully now and then. The color is returning to his face. And I must get them away from here, I am in a fever to get them away from here, before Flood is himself again. Comatose as he is, his presence is unnerving. The image of him fully conscious again is terrifying.

Finally Les appears in the doorway, and Harve says, "Took you long enough."

"Yeah. There's stairs out to the yard from that cellar, and drop doors. Wired them up good just to make sure."

"All right then, let's roll."

Thank God.

We leave by way of the kitchen. I lead the way, Harve close behind me, the submachine gun nudging my spine. Les brings up the rear, the inert Flood over his shoulder. Passing Sarah Frisch's room, I see the door is closed. She was too old for her duties, poor soul, but I could never bring myself to pension her off. It would have been better if I had.

The slant of the outside cellar doors under the kitchen

window, fresh wire showing through their hasps. The cellar is windowless, but sooner or later Kenneth will work either these doors or the hallway doors open. Then they will come out to the dead, Sarah Frisch and Digby.

And to the missing.

Myself. And David. If he is there in the truck. If he is not, what happens? That way, at least, it will come down to me alone, the intended victim, the proper victim.

Even if I survive whatever is coming, this house will never again be the same for me.

No more sun, but a crimson glare along the far hills as if the woodland on them were aflame just below the horizon. We cross the lawn, enter the trail single file, Harve poking me with the gun every few steps. He is not urging me to move faster, because we are moving at a good pace as it is; he is simply reminding me that the gun is there. Always there.

The going is not hard at first. But after we pass the small waterfall marking where the trail becomes the dry bed of a rivulet winding down to a culvert under the highway, it becomes much harder. There is water in the rivulet during spring thaws; it has shaped the channel into a narrow V, washed jagged rocks into every twist and turn, exposed tree roots at the base of the V. It is a test of good sight and good balance to move quickly along this obstacle course, and the failing light makes it a more and more impossible test. I skid, slide, trip over shadowy obstacles, but never slacken my pace. Behind me, Harve and Les, grumbling and cursing, somehow keep the pace.

Point of no return.

We must get so far from the house before complete darkness that there will be no return to it for them. Never any return.

Then, at a sharp bend, lights show below. Headlights moving in both directions along the highway. "Hold it,"

316

Les says behind us, and Harve catches my arm in a paralyzing grip, pulling me to a standstill. We turn. Flood is on his feet, swaying a little, clutching at his shoulder. Les reaches out a hand to steady him, and Flood angrily thrusts away the hand.

The silence around us is so deep that I can hear the breath rasping in Flood's throat as he looks from one to the other of us. He fixes on Harve. "No cops," he says scathingly. "That's all you've got in that thick head is there's no cops. Then you go to sleep and let them take us right out."

"Jimmy, it wasn't cops," Les says. "It was me. But I swear I was going for your gun. I didn't figure to hit you. I don't know how it happened. I swear to God."

"You?" Flood says.

"Him," Harve says. "You were out of your skull, man, looking to knock off that old lady. And where the hell would it get us?"

Flood tries to digest this. He points at Les and says to Harve, "You let him blast me?"

"Man, you think if we wanted to really blast you, you'd be here right now? And it's working fine this way. We got the man here, there's a car waiting down there, tomorrow we collect all the money he's got to give. And we keep him along with us as long as we have to."

"Where'd you get that brainstorm?" Flood says. Now he points at me. "From him?"

"It's a good deal, Jimmy. Man, you don't like it, you can just park your ass on that rock there and say goodbye right now."

Les says pleadingly, "I near broke my back getting you down here this far, Jimmy. Now what kind of way is that to be going on?"

"It's still phase two, remember?"

"More like two and a half," Harve says.

Flood's breathing rasps in his throat. He puts his hand to his shirt at the waist, leaves it poised there. "I don't have a gun."

Harve says, "You can't handle one anyhow, what with that hole in you. That's another thing. We're stuck in that house, we can't get you any doctoring. Out on the road we can."

"I can do fine without any doctor. But not without a gun." Flood plucks at his shirt front as if to demonstrate the emptiness behind it. "Not like any fucking pigeon."

"Look—" Harve says.

"A gun," Flood says. "Or do you figure on cashing me in if somebody moves in on us?"

"God damn, you know better than that."

"Then show me."

Harve hesitates, then draws the pistol from his belt and holds it out butt-first. I observe that as he does this, the barrel of the submachine gun under his arm swings away from me and is leveled at Flood. Flood observes it too. He takes the pistol awkwardly in his left hand and shoves aside the menacing barrel with it. "Don't be stupid," he says coldly to Harve. "We started this together, we finish it together."

"That is the truth," Les says eagerly.

James Flood is in command again.

He says to me, "Where's that car?"

"On the highway near the trail. It's a pickup truck. My son-in-law is with it."

"All right, let's see. And keep it slowed down. We don't walk out there wide open, understand?"

I keep it slowed down. Another sharp bend, and another, the last one. The channel of the dried-up rivulet becomes deeper and narrower approaching the mouth of the culvert, so we must leave it and walk its narrow margin. The embankment is not steep, but it is a trial for Flood. He strains and struggles, alternately planting one foot, dragging the other, but when Les again offers a helping hand, it is thrust away once more. On the embankment he lurches along half doubled over, making it, I think, on animal courage alone, one arm dangling uselessly, the other hand with a death grip on that gun.

The highway. The northbound lane. Scattered traffic, the headlights flashing in our faces as cars move north to Ticonderoga, Lake Champlain, Canada.

Flood motions with the gun. "Is that the truck?"

It is conspicuous in its cream-colored body, its hood yawning open, its dimmers aimed at us. It is twenty or thirty yards away, parked on the shoulder of the road. Someone squatting there beside the open hood suddenly stands. David. "Yes," I say. "That's it."

Now David takes notice of us, but in this gloom can he recognize me as one of the party? There are four of us here, but there should be four without me. He slams down the truck's hood, starts moving toward the driver's seat.

"Yell," Flood says to me. "Yell your fucking head off. Otherwise, he's the one who gets it right now."

As loud as I can, I yell, "David!" I wave my arms wildly and call the name again. He stops in his tracks, stands staring in my direction.

"Move," Flood says to me.

I move. We come up to the truck, and David says to me in bewilderment, "What happened? What's going on? Where's Digby?"

"Dead," I answer, and Flood says angrily, "Shut up, both of you, and just listen . . ."

He is going to say more, but he doesn't. He is looking—we are all looking—at the car slowing down beside the truck, a flasher blinking on its roof.

The highway patrol.

Dear God, now of all times.

The car stops. The trooper beside the driver thrusts a

sharp-featured face out of the window. "What is this?" he demands of David. "Couple of hours ago you told me it was just a quickie repair job. You figure on putting up here for the night?"

"No. It's okay now. It's all fixed."

"Is it?" Sharp features and sharp eyes. They examine us one by one. Flood has moved up close behind me; his gun is concealed between us. Harve holds the submachine gun behind him. The trooper turns to David again. "Where'd these people come from? They weren't around last time."

Silence. Too long a silence. Then Flood's gun is prodded demandingly into my back. I point at the ridge towering above us. "I live up there, Officer. We came down here when we saw the truck was in trouble."

"Yeah? Well, you all just hold on right where you are."

The car creeps past the truck. It pulls over in front of it. It stops.

"The truck!" Harve says. "Come on!"

Les is already behind the wheel, Harve is scrambling aboard as the two troopers emerge from their car. "Hold it!" the sharp-featured man orders, and then as Flood wheels on him, the pistol aimed at him, the man shouts to his companion, "Watch it, Bobby!" and both of them, guns now in hand, are sprinting, crouching, moving at an angle toward the slope of the road as if to get the cab of the truck in a direct line of fire.

The truck's motor is racing. Above the racket of it, Harve calls, "Jimmy, I've got them covered! For chrissake, come on, get in here!"

"No! We can take them, God damn it!"

"Jimmy!"

"Use that fucking gun! Use it!"

"Down," David shouts at me. "Marcus, get down!"

I throw myself down. Flood's gun is being fired—once, twice—and so close to me that the blast of each shot bangs my eardrums like a blow from a hammer. I recognize the sound of Harve's submachine gun, the quick, violent chattering of it in a short burst. Then guns answer from the slope of the roadside, and again and again.

Silence.

Flood is doubled over, his head hanging almost to his knees. The gun drops from his hand. He moves forward blindly, staggering, not toward the truck, but toward the troopers watchfully crouched at the road's edge. He sprawls forward, hands scrabbling at the ground as if even in his death throes he is going to drag himself as close as he can to the enemy. Then he stops moving.

He is not the only one.

Harve is leaning far out of the door of the truck. His head is drooping lower and lower, the huge bulk of him seeming to sag under its weight. He comes out of the truck shoulder-first and lies there on the roadside.

"Harve?" calls Les. "Harve?"

The troopers move warily on him from both sides when he comes out of the cab, but there is no weapon in his hand. I don't think he knows these men are here, that anyone is here. He bends over the body, not believing what he sees. Puzzled by it. "Harve?"

They wrench his arms behind him, handcuff him, remove the gun from his belt, and he offers no resistance. Still questioning the dead. "Harve?"

Then the realization dawns. The reality. It is no longer a question. It is a wild, despairing bellow, a demand that the dead return to life. "Harve! Harve!"

Somehow I stagger to my feet. David studies my face. "Marcus, are you all right?"

"Yes."

I am all right, but I cannot move. I am paralyzed by the sound of that howling in my ears. I watch the sharp-featured trooper run to the patrol car. Standing beside it, he puts its phone to his ear, at the same time waving traffic on. Cars slow down to see what is happening here. Phone to his ear, he furiously waves them on. "Keep moving! Keep moving, goddam it!"

Keep moving.

I am all right, but I cannot move.

I must stand here and listen to that agonized voice bellowing "Harve!" over and over, the sound of it echoing off the surrounding hills—*Ahrrr—Ahrrr—Ahrrr* —the sound of an animal in pain.

I am rooted to this spot, seeing more clearly than I want to see into the endless future.

Ours not to complete the task. Neither may we lay it down.

The task will never be completed.

As long as mankind inhabits this earth, it will never be completed.

Never.

About the Author

STANLEY ELLIN has been called "a master storyteller." His novels have been translated into twenty languages and have won him an international reputation. He has been honored by seven Edgar Allan Poe awards; and his works have been made into movies by such directors as Joseph Losey, Clive Donner and Claude Chabrol, and into numerous television plays, most notably by Alfred Hitchcock. Mr. Ellin is married, and his year is divided between his homes in New York and Miami Beach.